# Something to Crow About: New Perspectives in Literature for Young People

**Edited by Susan Clancy**
**with**
**David Gilbey**

A collection of refereed papers from the 1998 ACLAR Conference, held at Charles Sturt University, Wagga Wagga, NSW, Australia.

# The Centre for Information Studies

The Centre for Information Studies at Charles Sturt University supports and commissions research and publications in library and information science and related areas. It also provides seed grants to assist in the preparation of titles and undertakes cooperative publishing ventures where appropriate. Centre publications include the following:

*Literature circles: Reading in action*
Darelyn Dawson and Lee FitzGerald  (Occasional Monographs: 20)

*In the picture: Perspectives on picture book art and artists*
Kerry Mallan  (Literature and Literacy for Young People: An Australian Series: 3)

*The other 51 weeks: A marketing handbook for librarians*
Lee Welch  (Topics in Australasian Library and Information Studies: 14)

*The information literate school community: Best practice*
Edited by James Henri and Karen Bonanno (Topics in Australian Teacher Librarianship: 3)

*Providing more with less: Collection management for Australian school libraries*
Edited by Ken Dillon and James Henri  (Topics in Australian Teacher Librarianship: 2)

*Computers for librarians: An introduction to systems and applications* 2nd edn.
Stuart Ferguson with Rodney Hebels  (Occasional Monographs: 19)

*DDC13 workbook: A practical introduction to the abridged Dewey Decimal Classification* Sydney W. Davis, with Gregory R. New  (Occasional Monographs: 18)

*A most delicate monster: The one-professional special library*
Jean Dartnell  (Topics in Australasian Library and Information Studies: 13)

*The adolescent novel: Australian perspectives*
Maureen Nimon and John Foster  (Literature and Literacy for Young People: An Australian Series: 2)

*Disaster recovery for archives, libraries and records management systems in Australia and New Zealand*
Judith Doig  (Topics in Australasian Library and Information Studies: 12)

*Australian children's literature: An exploration of genre and theme*
John Foster, Maureen Nimon and Ern Finnis (Literature and Literacy for Young People: An Australian Series: 1)

# Something to Crow About: New Perspectives in Literature for Young People

**Edited by Susan Clancy with David Gilbey**

**Literature and Literacy for Young People: An Australian Series, No.4**

Centre for Information Studies
Charles Sturt University
Wagga Wagga, New South Wales, Australia
In association with the
Australasian Children's Literature Association for Research

Series Editor: Ken Dillon

ISBN: 0-949060-94-1
ISSN: 1325-4219

**National Library of Australia cataloguing-in-publication data**

---

Something to crow about : new perspectives in literature for young people.

Bibliography.
ISBN 0 949060 94 1.

1. Children's literature, Australian – History and criticism. 2. Children's literature, Australian – Congresses. 3. Young adult literature, Australian – History and criticism. 4. Young adult literature, Australian – Congresses. I. Clancy, Sue. II. Gilbey, David. III. Charles Sturt University-Riverina. Centre for Information Studies. IV. Australasian Children's Literature Association for Research. (2nd : 1998 : Wagga Wagga). (Series: Literature and literacy for young people : an Australian series ; 4).

809.89282

---

Centre for Information Studies
Locked Bag 660
Wagga Wagga NSW 2678, Australia
Phone: (02) 6933 2325
Fax: (02) 6933 2733
Email: cis@csu.edu.au
http://www.csu.edu.au/faculty/sciagr/sis/CIS/cis.html

Cover design by Boyd Bicket

Typeset by Jennifer Sims
Technical editing by Anne McDonald

Printed by Quick Print, Wagga Wagga, NSW, Australia

# Contents

# Preface

The second annual conference for the Australasian Children's Literature Association for Research (ACLAR) was held in Wagga Wagga, Australia, 27-29 September 1998. The conference attracted researchers from across Australia and New Zealand. Contributions from a range of research methodologies and theoretical perspectives were used by established researchers as well as a number of postgraduate researchers and associated professionals. In accepting papers for the conference, every effort was made to be as inclusive as possible of the research needs and interests of members of the children's literature research community.

All papers selected for publication have been through a process of refereeing which was overseen by the Editorial Committee. This process ensured that each paper was reviewed by at least two peer referees. If both made the same recommendation then this decision was upheld. Where the decision was split, the paper was reviewed by a third referee. The majority decision was upheld. Where referees made their acceptance of the paper conditional on certain revisions to the paper, the Editorial Committee used its discretion to ensure that these tasks were completed appropriately.

Referees were asked to consider the papers in relation to the guidelines set out in the call for papers i.e. that there be a strong focus on Australasian Children's Literature through new scholarship/research, reinterpretation of traditional texts and/or contemporary theoretical approaches to children's literature and to provide written comments. The aim of this process was to facilitate feedback to the authors and to achieve consensus that the proceedings adhered to standards appropriate for professional academic endeavour.

The Committee thanks those who so generously agreed to act as referees. It is a demanding and time consuming task but one which is necessary if we are to grow professionally. With the support of such people our children's literature community can only become stronger.

Lastly, at a personal level, I would like to thank my colleagues David Gilbey and John Cohen for all the help and support they have provided both in the organisation of the conference and in the production of these papers.


Susan Clancy
Conference Convenor

# Introduction

## Susan Clancy

*Something to Crow About*, the title for this collection of papers came about because the word 'crow' has a particular aptitude for children's literature, the city of Wagga Wagga and a sense of celebration.

Anyone who has read the original *Peter Pan* will be familiar with this exchange between the adult Wendy and her daughter Jane.

> 'What was the last thing Peter Pan said to you?' Jane asked, one evening.
> 'He said, "You be always waiting for me, and then some night you will hear me crowing."'
> 'What was his crow like?'
> 'Like this' – and Wendy tried to imitate it.
> But Jane replied gravely, 'No, it wasn't. It was like this.' And she did a much more life-like crow.
> 'My darling child, how in the world do you know?'
> 'Oh I often hear it when I am asleep.' (Barrie 1912)

Just as Peter Pan's crow resonates for Wendy and her daughter Jane, so the story of *Peter Pan* echoes through the world of children's literature, whether it be in the original ambiguous form by J. M. Barrie, the Disney film or marketing versions or the critical writings of Jacqueline Rose (1984) in her book *The case of Peter Pan; or the impossibility of children's fiction*. These have become powerful cultural representations and made indelible imprints on those who research and study children's literature.

Perhaps it is serendipity that the city of Wagga Wagga, in which the 1998 ACLAR conference was held, has close affiliations with the crow. It is an integral component of the city's coat of arms and often used in different ways to represent the city. There are many who believe that the name Wagga Wagga means place of many crows and although in more recent times this has been contested, there is no doubt that that the symbol of the crow holds an important place in the culture of the city.

A 'crow' has been defined, amongst other things as 'a child's inarticulate cry of joy' and 'a defiant or triumphant cry', each of which adds to the sense of celebrating what children's literature has to offer. While admitting that when used as a verb 'crow' could suggest the idea of boasting, we can live with this, because like Peter

Pan we are happy to crow about the development of ACLAR as an exciting forum for children's literature.

The emergence of children's literature as an academic discipline has seen struggles and triumphs in the process of establishing itself as a legitimate field of academic endeavour by challenging boundaries, setting itself up oppositionally, and seeking its own parameters to find homes within the more traditional tertiary structures. 'Homes' have been found within cultural and literary studies, education, library science, and each of these has in its own way contextualised the stances taken by critics and academics in their analysis of children's literature. And this very diversity of 'homes' provides the study of children's literature with a richness and depth of colour that enables the development of scholarly tapestries illustrating dynamic and powerful components of our cultural heritage. The papers in this collection are reflective of these different disciplines, theoretical approaches and research practices. They have been arranged into five parts which reflect both the confluence and diversity of interests at work in the academic study of children's literature.

The two papers in Part I provide frameworks to consider critical aspects relating to theory and publishing in children's literature. John Stephens, in 'Children's literature, text and theory: What are we interested in now?' uses a sample of twenty-four recent journal articles to argue that predominant interest is in fiction and literary history and not so much in poetry, film, drama and theory. His main focus however, is on the way in which these articles play out the notion of intertexuality. Through the use of picture books, in particular the work of Anthony Browne and Colin McNaughton, he establishes the case for intertexuality to be treated not as a fashionable new word to be used without understanding but as a thought-provoking concept that can provide 'a stepping stone to other ways of thinking about children's texts'. Robyn Sheahan-Bright provides an historical overview of children's publishing in Australia, positing questions in relation to ownership, production, technology, distribution, consumption and the role of the state. Her paper '"This little piggy went to market": Some perspectives on Australian children's publishing since 1945,' examines the tensions existing between commerce and culture in this industry.

In Part II, the papers by Robin Pope and Monica Jarman make use of postcolonial reading strategies. Pope works with the construction of the individual self by comparing subjectivity and the function of place in texts by William Howitt (1792-1879) while Jarman concentrates on the ways in which language is used to delineate Aboriginal and non-Aboriginal relationships in *The children of Mirrabooka* (1997).

The availability of modern technology has rapidly increased the quantity, quality and complexity of children's texts using written and illustrative formats to encode meaning. This in turn has provided a growing number of scholars who are interested in researching these trends. Three papers in this collection have addressed a range of issues in relation such texts. Kerry Mallan's paper uses a neonarrative model as a means to theorise artistic practice and to develop an understanding of the phenomenon of human experience. She argues the need for us to become aware of our own textual identities and strategies by considering the social and cultural positioning of the narrative, the narrator and the listener/reader. Robin Morrow"s paper, 'Neither slogging at tuck or living off the land: Food in Australian picture books' was such a palatable and tasty offering that it was presented as an after dinner feature. It refers to 'landmark' books as she explores the purposes served by food in literature and the associated metaphorical constructions. Alison Halliday's paper moves away from fiction to poetry to tease out the ways in which ideologies and cultural assumptions about the imagination are reflected when different illustrations are used for the same poetry text.

Clare Bradford uses a range of female-authored texts to argue that the representations of female friendships in these texts are far from homogenous in that they produce quite different modes of female subjectivity. Gender identity and the ideologies manifest in writings for young people work to both construct and deconstruct particular political and socio-cultural agendas. By using Constance Mackness as an exemplar, Pam Macintyre examines the role of cultural transmission through stories written for and read by girls, in the construction of gender identity, while the ideology behind the metaphor of animal metamorphosis and its relationship to masculinity is the focus of Jo Coward's paper, 'Masculinity and animal metamorphosis in children's literature'.

The final section of the collection brings together a selection of papers that is representative of the diverse range of interests addressed by conference participants. Jill Holt uses two children's books, *Dreaming of Antarctica* and *Dyptoe, the yellow-eyed penguin* to argue that the literary effect of narrativity in creating 'reality' bears an aesthetic harvest, while Jeri Kroll considers how we understand 'popular' as opposed to 'literary' by closely examining Gleitzman's books, *Water wings* and *Two weeks with the Queen*. The role of elective mutism in a selection of contemporary books provides the focus for Carlisle Sheridan to raise issues relating to the role of language, literature and literary criticism. This collection of papers is brought to a close with John Tingay's paper examining the ways in which late twentieth century re-tellers of traditional tales may be said to leave less to the imagination than the original oral tellings.

As readers, teachers and scholars we are all in touch with some of the 'Neverlands' that children's literature constructs for us, a little like Peter Pan's Neverland on whose 'magic shores children at play are forever beaching their coracles' (Barrie 1911), and like Peter we're here to crow about it.

# Part I

# Theoretical considerations

# 1. Children's literature, text and theory: What are we interested in now?

## John Stephens

**Abstract:** This paper examines current theoretical/critical approaches to children's literature as reflected in issues of recent journals (a total of twenty-four articles). It examines the critical grounding of the articles and suggests that the criticism is dominated by empiricism, reader response criticism, formalism, and historicism, and the predominant concern with fiction tends to perpetuate 'older' critical discourses. Of concepts absorbed from modern cultural and literary theories, the most common is intertextuality, though with the exception of only two writers the term was normally used in the weakened sense of 'textual allusion'.

The paper explores some of the possibilities of the concept *intertextuality*, and it suggests that when employed to its fullest potential rather than as a fashionable term it can open up other ways of thinking about children's literature.

In the course of the 1990s, there has been a steady trickle of notable books which attempt to place children's literature within the context of those modern literary and cultural theories which post-date the various reader response criticisms, or within a particular facet of that newer body of theory (in particular, Hunt 1991; Wall 1991; Stephens 1992; McGillis 1996; Nikolajeva 1996).[1] Some of these books are still too recent to draw many conclusions about their impact by examining, say, citations in major journals dedicated to children's literature, but we might also think of such books as reflecting a more general interest in newer theoretical ideas as well as having a leading or introductory function. In other words, can we look more widely at the framing of text by theory within contemporary critical practice, and discern some answers to the question, What are we interested in now? A further question which remains more or less implicit in the first is, To what extent does current thinking and writing about children's literature conform with what the wider academic community of the humanities and social sciences perceives as 'usual practice' in research procedures? In this paper, I am going to address the question of current theoretical/critical interest by focussing principally on the deployment of the term (and sometimes the concept) *intertextuality* in some recent periodical literature.

Major research projects (monographs; PhD theses) are, nowadays, theory-driven. This entails not just that a work will develop and argue a theory about something, but also that the thesis to be advanced will be situated within some kind of theoretical perspective. At its simplest, this will mean situation of the project within a 'school' of thought, a recognised critical orientation (though perhaps broadly defined – postcolonial criticism; French feminism; cultural materialism), or the ideas of an individual theoretician with contemporary currency.[2] More complex theoretical perspectives evolve when the process becomes more reflexive and interrogates the categories of thought and the discursive practices employed, or when it uses existing theories and moves on to develop further perspectives. It is, of course, a truism that the most mundane short article will reflect a theory about text and world, no matter whether or not its author is conscious of this.

Children's literature scholars are less diffident about the idea of theory than they were a few years ago, but we share a certain reticence about it with other intellectual communities. In *Literary theory: A very short introduction,* Jonathan Culler reproduces a pertinent cartoon, a version of the conventional moment when a young woman introduces her boyfriend to her father. The caption simply reads: 'You're a terrorist? Thank God. I understood Meg to say you were a *theorist*' (p.16). The distinction between the contrasted terms here has often disappeared for the children's literature community during the past thirty-odd years. Having been accused of both vocations myself, I'm obviously interested in why this should be so, and the actual theoretical underpinnings of the criticism which has been (and remains) in practice, the alternative. Culler, quite reasonably, I think, attributes the unease about theory to its endlessness and 'unmasterability' (1997, p.16). There is more of it than any one person can ever know; you embrace it in the hope it will provide 'concepts to organise and understand the phenomena that interest you' (pp.16-17) and then it betrays you by calling into question the conclusions you reach and the premises they were based on.

But all that may only be a lesser element in the terrorist role of theory *vis-a-vis* children's literature. More threatening may be the propensity for modern theory, from social semiotics to psychoanalytic criticism, simply to sweep aside the kind of approach perhaps encapsulated in Peter Hunt's notion of 'childist criticism' (1984; 1991; 1996-97). The theoretical underpinnings of such approaches, I think, are empiricism and reader response criticism. Empiricism – roughly, the idea that we know the world by observing it objectively, and that ideas and concepts are built up by combining and abstracting from sense-data – had a long history in British intellectual life, lived on in literary criticism and historiography long after its influence in philosophy had diminished, and as far as I can see still seems to dominate its criticism of children's literature.[3] It is apt to supplant any other critical perspective, except a residual reader response criticism, whenever actual children's actual *use* of a book becomes the primary criterion of value. Reader response criticism is still theoretically pervasive in secondary school English classes, but its academic swan song was probably as far back as 1980, when both Tompkins and Suleiman and Crosman published major collections of essays in the field. Notoriously, Louise Rosenblatt, the most influential of reader response theorists on children's education, especially in North America, rated only passing mention in those collections, and did not influence academic theory.[4] It will remain to be seen whether the embedded examples of reader response criticism in May (1995) and McGillis (1996) designate a similar swan song for reader response in children's literature criticism.

In North America the intellectual equivalents of British empiricism are formalist analysis/description and historicism, a similarity and difference that can be seen surfacing in Jill P. May's hostile review of Fox's critical anthology *Celebrating Children's Literature in Education* (in *The Lion and the Unicorn* 1998, pp.237-41): her objection, in effect, is that Fox's selection over-represents British empiricism at the expense of North American historicism (which I understand to be a combination of literary history and social history). Slung as it is amongst the poles of formalism, historicism, empiricism and reader response criticism, it is perhaps not surprising that *Children's Literature in Education* is intellectually the most timid of journals. Jill P. May's own *Children's literature and critical theory* (1995) – an eclectic pastiche of New Criticism, historicism, myth criticism, and reader response criticism – is an epitome of North American criticism, inhabiting a curiously untheorised space somewhere in the early 1970s. I should comment that I don't have any special prejudice against historicism – though we should be far enough on from the work of Hayden White on historiography to be self-reflexive about its procedures and conscious of the metanarratives informing historiography. The opening sentence of Kordula Dunscombe's article in *Papers* (1998) on Louisa Anne Merideth is as ideologically fraught a piece of historiography as one might imagine, but it least it wears its ideology on its sleeve:

> It is heartening to look back on C19th colonial literature for children and see, amongst the messages of domination, exploitation and general disrespect for the environment, that other paradigms of the land were also offered to child readers. (1998, p.16)

The author positions herself by overtly favouring one model of land use over another, and one relationship between textuality and social ideology over another, adopting a position widely held in liberal Australian circles, but not necessarily by a majority of Australians. The positioning is obvious in the contrasts within the strongly emotive language ('heartening...disrespect').

So *are* people interested in anything else now? Logically, this could be addressed by looking at some of the current theory books – Maria Nikolajeva, for example, in *Children's literature comes of age* (1996) brings together many of the perspectives from semiotic and narrative theories which have been increasingly, if slowly, seeping into children's literature criticism over the past decade. Instead of following that path, and examining a small number of individual voices (including my own) I've sought a wider representation of practices by taking the most recent 1998 issue of four journals to see what kinds of theoretical, conceptual or critical approaches informed their articles (excluding reviews, regular columns, and other such genres): *Children's Literature* 26, the general issue of *The Lion and the Unicorn* (22,2), *Children's Literature in Education* (29,2), and *Papers* (8,2). This is a small sample of twenty-four articles. I found that if there was a common thread to try to tease out it was the idea of *intertextuality*, which had a central function in some articles, was evoked in others, and seemed to be a significant absence in two where texts had been placed in loose dialogic relationships. Jonathan Culler (with more than a hint of a sneer) refers to intertextuality as 'a fancy name' for the proposition that 'works are made out of other works: made possible by prior works which they take up, repeat, challenge, transform...A work exists between and among other texts, through its relations to them' (1997, p.34). Maria Nikolajeva, in a parenthetic remark in her article in *The Lion and the Unicorn* issue, expresses a preference for Bakhtin's original term 'dialogics' (p.232), but it now seems too late to go back. *Intertextuality* has been a God-send for innumerable people, because they can deploy a fashionable new word without having to absorb a new concept. Instead of saying 'allusion', one can now say 'intertextual reference', and not worry too much about that notion of existence 'between and among other texts' Culler writes of. As I will argue below, there is a strand in contemporary picture book production which presupposes an awareness of intertextuality as meaning situated in the process of interaction between texts, in the spaces between texts (see Stephens 1992, p.88). Very pertinent to such books, too, is Nikolajeva's reminder that the concept is about 'codes' and conversations between art works, rather than about influences and causes (1996, pp.153-54) and that the range of a work's possible intertexts goes well beyond literary or written texts. The concept of dialogism is of enormous importance, and is getting a lot of attention in discussion of picture books, and I will return to it shortly as the focus for the rest of this paper.

Before I do, however, I will briefly characterise what else I found in the journals. What appears in a particular issue is, of course, largely accidental – I discarded the most recent issue of *Children's Literature Association Quarterly* because it was a special issue on medieval literature and effectively committed contributors to a historicist frame. The four I examined confirm that what we are mainly interested in is fiction. *Children's Literature* surprised by including two articles about poetry. One turns out to be a historical study of the distribution of Coleridge's poems in books for children in the nineteenth century, but the other – John Rieder's 'Edward Lear's limericks: The function of children's nonsense poetry' is in terms of its theoretical affiliations – especially in its deployment of Bakhtin's theory of carnival – the most theoretically advanced piece in the issue. *Papers* reprints an article by Robyn McCallum dealing with that equally rare topic, children's film – film gets a passing mention in a couple of articles in *Lion and Unicorn*, but only with reference to content, not as form or genre. We are still not interested in children's drama. That fiction is the predominant focus of discourses about children's literature may in itself largely explain why those discourses are critically oriented towards an 'older' mode – content analysis within the frame of categories such as character, plot, setting, theme, point of view and style.

I categorised the articles according to four descriptors: the focus – author/period/genre studies, or particular text types (fiction, picture book, etc.); whether the writer deployed a theoretical/critical orientation in existence before 1980 – historicism, formalist analysis/description or reader response criticism; the principal socio-cultural discourses that concern criticism of children's literature (ethnicity/race, gender, class, family); and whether the writer deployed analytical concepts that had come into use since the rise of the reader response theories. As far as possible, I attempted to restrict attributions of the fourth category to *systemic* uses of theory or concept, and hence to exclude non-functional citation. For example, Ellerby (*Lion and Unicorn*, p.211) cites Paul Smith's important work on subjectivity, *Discerning the subject* (1988) but this is essentially an ornamental citation, a common vice often to be found in contemporary criticism. Concepts of subjectivity are very pertinent to the focus text here, Rushdie's *Haroun and the sea of stories*, and Ellerby could have found in Smith a useful version of a common formulation of the concept: that an individual's consciousness and sense of identity is formed in dialogue with others and with the discourses and ideologies that constitute the society and culture that individuals inhabit (see also McCallum 1999, Chap.1). An effective reading of *Haroun and the sea of stories* might develop this (it is not a difficult idea, after all) and further relate it to theories of intertextuality and metafiction, but in this case the writer apparently has no functional access to theories Rushdie himself has been manifestly deploying since at least *Midnight's children*, and simply describes content. A contrast is readily available in Nikolajeva's article, which is instead concerned with how contemporary fictions demand a grasp of appropriate theories as a basic step toward understanding them. A third possibility is afforded by Hanlon's paper (in *Children's Literature*) on Jane Yolen's stories. This makes no pretensions to being informed by contemporary theory, but might have been taken beyond a generally descriptive (and over-long) survey nuanced by gender issues if she had deployed a vigorous theory of intertextuality instead of a lightweight 'influences and parodies' model which resides in placing texts side by side and describing them. Hutcheon's *A theory of parody* (1985) offers an appropriate theoretical linking of parody and intertextuality.

It is not my intention either to privilege or to pejorate in themselves the various discourses I identified and attributed, though various strengths and weaknesses are evident. Most of us (and I hasten to include myself in that 'us') ground our critical

**Table 1:** Summary of the distribution of categories.

| Article focus | Theoretical/ critical orientation in existence before 1980 | Socio-cultural discourses invoked (ethnicity/race, gender, class, family) | Theory since reader response |
|---|---|---|---|
| Author, Period or Genre survey (incl. multiple text types) = 9 | historicist and/or formalist analysis | family = 1 gender = 3 | intertextuality = 1 |
| Theory (of fiction) = 1 | | | narrativity (focalisation, metafiction, intertextuality, etc. ); theory of subjectivity; genre |
| Fiction = 3 | historicist formalism | ethnicity/gender/class = 1 race = 1 | |
| Fiction = 3 | formalism | gender = 2 | intertextuality/ psychoanalytic criticism (with gender) = 1 |
| Fiction = 1 | formalism/reader response | | |
| Fiction = 1 | historicism | gender | Intertextuality |
| Poetry = 2 | historicist = 1 formalist analysis = 1 | | Bakhtinian theory (on formalist ground) = 1 |
| Film = 1 | formalism | alienation ethnicity | cultural studies; post-colonial criticism; theory of subjectivity |
| Drama = 0 | | | |
| Picture Books = 3 | reader response [DL] formalism [CB] reader response [LS] | gender [CB] | intertextuality/ metafiction/narrative theory [DL] intertextuality/ feminism [CB] semiotics [LS] |

procedures in some elements of formalism – attention to structures, alertness to complexities of meaning, an interest in the mode of being of a text from moment to moment. This remains the staple of children's literature criticism. Of course it is often quite poorly done, and I might have taken the descriptor to a further degree of delicacy, discriminating between self-reflexive formalisms which are kept informed by reference to current developments in literary and cultural theory, semiotics, linguistics, and so on, and formalisms which collapse into narrative and descriptiveness. The term and concept of *intertextuality* can again be a key indicator here, though it doesn't, in fact, occur in the most theoretically confused of the articles I looked at, that by Lehman and Crook in *Children's Literature in*

*Education.* Declaring itself to slough off the stultifying, practices of formalism (literary criticism 'too analytical, formal, and unspontaneous, p.70) and to embrace instead 'literary literacy' within a reader response frame, the paper offers an exercise in what other people might recognise as aleatory intertextuality (pursuing comparison between randomly gathered texts) and an analytical procedure – attention to themes, language, symbols and structure – which is actually a filleted version of early New Criticism. Once again an immediate contrast is available with the article which follows in the journal, Clare Bradford's careful, well-argued use of formalist analysis as a basis for gender studies, through a precise deployment of verbal, narrative and visual codes in some Anthony Browne picture books, and a deft reading of the self-conscious dialogism of the illustrations. The Lehman/Crook kind of theoretical monstrosity seems rather harmless, as it can be read with the mind at most half engaged and the books remain recognisable. We tend to blench at non-functional theoretical pastiche rather more when some young scholar cobbles together half a dozen incompatible and incomprehensible bits of poststructuralism to teach us old fogies how we should be talking about text. They are equally inept, of course, both failing to grasp a central point about theory: to quote Culler's useful little book again, 'it involves complex relations of a systematic kind among a number of factors' (1997, p.3).

What is disclosed by reading through the sample of twenty-four articles can be stated briefly. We are interested in fiction and literary history, often in tandem; we are not much interested in poetry, film, drama, or theory in itself; we approach texts from historicist and formalist stances; we are modern in our thematic concerns with socio-cultural discourses of ethnicity/race, gender and class (but the fiction itself is apt to dictate that); and critical practice is taking on board some concepts from modern cultural and literary theories. As I said earlier, the most common of these is intertextuality, which is more characteristically deployed in relation to smaller and/or visual texts than to fiction.

The two articles which best demonstrate a systemic absorption of the concept of intertextuality into critical practice are those of Bradford and Lewis in *Children's Literature in Education*, though in Lewis's case it has been implicitly refashioned on the model of the 'telling gaps' filled by readers which is a central plank of reader response theories derived from the work of Wolfgang Iser. The important thing for my present purposes, though, is that the principle is being examined at work in relation to picture books. This has been one of the more exciting features of recent modern books and the critical responses to them, and is why picture book criticism is a site for some of the most adventurous thinking in the area. Anthony Browne and Colin McNaughton are two author/illustrators who habitually produce obviously intertextual artwork, though they are not alone. Browne, however, has received more attention than anyone else, largely through several published and unpublished papers by Jane Doonan. The American author/illustrator Allen Say has produced some remarkable examples, especially in *Grandfather's journey* (1993) and *Emma's rug* (1996).[5] Say was awarded the Caldecott Medal for *Grandfather's journey*, and a more recent Caldecott Medal winner, Paul O. Zelinsky's *Rapunzel* creates some mind-teasing dialogues between the Grimm fairytale and Renaissance paintings illustrating the life of the Virgin Mary. For example, the prince's entry into the tower is modelled on versions of the Annunciation, one of the most frequently depicted sacred incidents; and the final page, depicting the reunited lovers and their two children, is a transformation of Raphael's *Madonna and Child with the Infant St John (La Belle Jardiniere)*. The dialogue must also extend to Tryna Schart Hyman's *Rapunzel* (1982) as well, in that Hyman had also explored the analogy between the entrance of the prince into Rapunzel's tower and the Annunciation. Both texts lead beyond questions of how the world constructs and reacts to a situation in which an 'impossible' pregnancy eventuates, though that is an obvious place to start, and Zelinsky prompts this with an inverted reprise of the 'Annunciation' scene when Rapunzel's stepmother discovers the pregnancy.

The example I want to consider now, however, is Anthony Browne's *Willy the dreamer*. Not only is this perhaps the most exciting yet of Browne's intertextual playing fields, a discussion of it inevitably enters a dialogic relationship with the articles by Bradford and Lewis, through a shared joke about bananas and Browne's own habit of cross-referencing amongst his books. *Willy the dreamer* links both with the earlier books about Willy and with *The big baby*. A central function of intertextuality pointed to in the Bradford and Lewis articles is that it makes connections, referring readers outside the present text to other worlds, and in this case in particular it sets up dialogic relationships amongst the ways audiences negotiate different kinds of cultural formations. Lewis stresses the intertexts in popular culture suggested by McNaughton, but because the focus text, *Oops!* is also a fractured fairy tale, it enters the domain where fairy tale itself mediates popular culture and high culture texts. Zelinsky's *Rapunzel* is only an extreme example pushing in one of these directions. Audiences are encouraged to reflect on how stories work, and how meaning in texts and in the world emerges and evolves in dialogic forms. When the wolf of *Oops!* in pursuit of the pig who has slipped out of the 'Three little pigs' fairy tale and appears instead as Red Riding Hood, recalls alternative versions of wolf-and-pig stories told to him by his mother, it becomes almost unavoidable to invoke Allan Ahlberg's *Ten in a bed* (1983) and Catherine Storr's *Clever Polly and the wolf* series (1955-1990), older versions of wolf-and-dinner stories which are still in print. That audiences may encounter these other texts, before or after this one, emphasises how intertextuality is not a matter of things occurring in a specific order, but existing in a potential or actualised dialogic relationship. Bradford takes the implication of dialogism still further, and demonstrates how the dialogic play of meanings discloses the ideologies which underpin representation.

As Lewis points out, the semiotic conjunction of bananas and pratfalls recurs in *Oops!* The first appearance of the banana skin evokes the conjunction as an absence, as Preston Pig moralises about the danger of misplaced banana skins. In the final pursuit scene, when Father Pig/woodcutter chases the wolf out of the book, the previous banana scene instantiates an expectation that the wolf will slip on the skin where it still lies. He does, but we have to turn to the front cover to see it. The back cover shows the pigs in a heap after Father Pig has tripped over a rock, which is just as evident in the penultimate scene, but not as an instantiated danger. The effect is a small lesson in the principles of teleology, of discerning patterns and final causes backwards from the end, in counterpoint to the pre-textual knowledge of how the Red Riding Hood story should come out. But the intertextual dialogue with Ahlberg and Storr reinforces an insight implicit in the moment when Preston speaks the wolf's lines ('Grandma, what big eyes you've got...'): the relationship between structures and elements within structures is apt to be unstable – the frame may not survive a variation of its parts. In 'Thinking in threes' from *Last stories of Polly and the wolf* (1990), for example, Polly explains to the wolf, with impressively logical illogic, that his plan to trap her by reinstantiating the story of Goldilocks had to fail because the 'rule of three' was broken: there were three bears, but only one wolf.

In *Willy the dreamer*, nothing is immune from turning into a banana, a pattern well established by the fourth opening, where Willy dreams he is a sumo wrestler. This constitutes one of the less explicit intertextual fields in the book. It links to the audience's world knowledge about the sport, gleaned from television, perhaps, to the discourses of wimp and bully in Browne's earlier Willy books, and to inexplicit narratives about the unexpected victory of the little guy. *Oops!* is one such narrative, though that isn't any stronger reason for bringing the two books together than is the coincidence of bananas. Their relationship is aleatory, but the dialogue between them can be meaningful. The crucial banana lies on the floor of the wrestling ring just beside the left foot of tiny Willy's monstrous opponent. It is not just any banana, however. It is a *banana peel* lying where it should not be. The scene depicts great tension, with the vectors formed by the represented spectators' gazes, including those of Willy's beloved Milly and his friend Hugh, fixed in awe on the unseen face of the opponent. Only Willy's left eye is fixed elsewhere, forward off the page, locked in an alarmed reciprocal gaze with the spectator. The spectator is able to extrapolate a possible action in a moment not yet happened. In simple terms, we can predict ahead, on the basis of cues and the wider context. But we cannot know. The closure of *Oops!* demonstrates that teleologies are produced in story, rather than being innate occurrences. As we move further into *Willy the dreamer*, it becomes clear that Willy's dreams are a mixture of fantasy and nightmare, and some may be indeterminate. Hence the sumo wrestler dream constitutes a subtle narrative and ideological complex, teasing us into irresolution, nudging at *our* fantasies, *our* insecurities. I can't offer a resolution, because I think the picture thrusts its spectators into a terrain of unbounded dialogism.

It would be a joy here to examine every opening in *Willy the dreamer*. I have elsewhere commented on the effect of modality shifts in picture books by Browne and by Say, and that is again a particularly interesting facet of this book as pictures interact with those on facing pages, offering, as is Browne's practice, dialogic relations between realism, surrealism and hyperrealism in a foregrounding of representation that keeps spectators engaged with the process as much as the product. But space won't permit such an indulgence, so I will conclude with a brief comment on one of the more nightmarish scenes, the 'strange landscape' picture in which Browne literally constructs a pastiche of three Salvador Dali paintings and one Magritte. (Within the frame painting, Dali's *The persistence of memory*, he embeds Dali's *Sleep*, the memory chest from the Spanish Civil War nightmare *Spain, 1936-38*, and one of Magritte's 'flaming objects', the latter now, of course, a kind of banana flambé.) Close to the centre of the page is an extremely small figure of Willy, once again engaging the spectator in reciprocal gaze and in doing so physically pulling us towards the plane of the page. The objects disconcert by their refusal to resolve into interpretable wholes. The watch which occupied the left foreground in *The persistence of memory* has become a fried egg with a banana-shaped yolk. Other bananas substituted for Dali's objects seem unstable: they are deflated, turning into things, such as a fish, a goose, a horse-head, a paint-brush (?). The chest has undergone a double change: Dali's red handkerchief, a tragic metaphor for war, has become a deflated banana; its shadow, the shadow of a snake. There is an apparent allusion in the alignment of the intruded objects (*Sleep* and the chest) to an opening in *The big baby*, where Mrs Young's shadow is cast, in a different form, over a reproduction of Dali's *Sleep*, replicating the combination of sleep and horror Bradford pointed to in her discussion of that opening (1998, p.91), but shifting the relationship by softening and feminising the face on the *Sleep*/banana figure and transforming the landscape behind it into a tomb-effigy of a sleeping gorilla. In a way, this may be a more focused application of intertextual dialogism, in that we can interpret Browne's pastiche without knowing its sources because Willy, and his obsession with bananas, is centred as a reference point. His world, like the bananas, has deflated, lost reference, entered a space of horror. The dialogic relationship with Dali and Magritte might, at some future time, prove very useful in reading those particular paintings. That, clearly enough, is a further and practical function of intertextuality in children's literature, and one of which authors and illustrators are well aware. For example, the hope of having such an effect is declared explicitly by Zelinsky in the end-note to his *Rapunzel*: 'It would please me if my pictures served in some measure to spur an interest in the magnificent art from which I have drawn' (n.p.).

Finally, a good reason why scholars might well use intertextuality as a stepping-stone towards other aspects of contemporary theory is that it opens windows. An obvious example suggested by *Willy the dreamer*, when Willy dreams of being a painter and a writer, is *metafiction*, with which intertextuality often overlaps. The two pertinent openings are linked by citations of Magritte's *Ceci n'est pas une pipe*; are built on obviously self-reflexive works (a bundle of Magritte paintings; Lewis Carroll's *Alice* books); make outrageous substitutions of gorillas and bananas for familiar art works; and foreground internal modality shifts (the 'Gorilla de Milo' is simultaneously a painting and a sculpture, through a clever dissolution of pictorial plane; Willy the writer has entered the scene he is writing, in a classic metafictive diegetic shift). Intertextuality offers insights into the representation of subjectivity, perhaps the central theme of *Willy the dreamer*. It prompts thoughts about Jung, Freud and psychoanalysis, when Willy the explorer (as Stanley) encounters Freud enclosed within a nuclear family sitting on a pink couch inside a Rousseau painting; it poses questions about the relationships between high culture and low culture in the ways we make sense of the world; and many, many other things. The interest in intertextuality, then, not only responds to what producers of texts are doing, and what readers bring to those texts, but when employed as a thought-provoking concept rather than an ornamental term, can be a stepping-stone to other ways of thinking about children's texts.

## Endnotes

1.  The process had begun in the 1980s, with such works as Jacqueline Rose's *The case of Peter Pan* (London: Macmillan, 1984) and Zohar Shavit's *Poetics of children's literature* (Athens, Georgia: University Press, 1986). Rose has proved the more quotable in subsequent criticism, but the contribution of the book to the theoretical conceptualisation of children's literature is in fact minimal.

2.  Consider, for example, the extent to which Karin Lesnik-Oberstein's *Children's literature: Criticism and the fictional child* is mapped onto Terry Eagleton's *Literary theory*.

3.  At least so it seems from 'outside the culture'. When delivering her Oxford Amnesty Lecture in 1992, Julia Kristeva began by saying she found it a 'perilous enterprise' to talk about subjectivity to 'an English audience – brought up on empiricism and logical positivism' (1993, p.148). Empiricism is what underpins the pragmatism (p.10) of Hunt's *Criticism, theory and children's literature* and makes it such a peculiarly British work.

4.	The classic text for children's literature was Aidan Chambers' 'The reader in the book' (1977). See further Stephens (1992, p.10) and Benton (1996, p.84).

5.	For a discussion of transformations of works by van Gogh, Vermeer, Munch, Bosch and Monet in *Emma's rug*, see my 'Modality and space in picture book art: Allen Say's *Emma's rug*', forthcoming in CREATA.

# References

Ahlberg, A. (1983). *Ten in a bed.* London: Granada.

Benton, M. (1996). Reader-response criticism. In *International companion*: *Encyclopaedia of children's literature*, ed. P. Hunt. London: Routledge, pp.71-88.

Bradford, C. (1998). Playing with father: Anthony Browne's picture books and the masculine. *Children's Literature in Education,* **29**, 2, 79-96.

Browne, A. (1995). *The big baby.* London: Fox.

Browne, A. (1997). *Willy the dreamer.* London: Walker Books.

Culler, J. (1997). *Literary theory: A very short introduction.* Oxford: Oxford University Press.

Doonan, J. (1999). Drawing out ideas: A second decade of the work of Anthony Browne. *The Lion and the Unicorn,* **23**, 1, 30-56.

Dunscombe, K. (1998). In the service of infinitude and glorious creation: The nature writing of Louisa Anne Meredith. *Papers: Explorations into Children's Literature,* **8**, 2, 16-30.

Eagleton, T. (1996). *Literary theory: An introduction.* 2nd edn. Cambridge, Mass.: Blackwell.

Ellerby, J. M. (1998). Fiction under siege: Rushdie's quest for narrative emancipation in *Haroun and the sea of stories. The Lion and the Unicorn,* **22**, 2, 211-220.

Hanlon, T.L. (1998). 'To sleep, perchance to dream': Sleeping beauties and wide-awake plain Janes in the stories of Jane Yolen. *Children's Literature,* **26**, 140-67.

Hunt, P. (1984). Childist criticism: The subculture of the child, the book, and the critic. *Signal,* **43**, 42-59.

Hunt, P. (1991). *Criticism, theory and children's literature.* Oxford: Basil Blackwell.

Hunt, P. (1996-97). Passing on the past: The problem of books that are for children and that were for children. *Children's Literature Association Quarterly, 21*, 4, 200-202.

Hutcheon, L. (1985). *A theory of parody.* New York: Methuen.

Kristeva, J. (1993). The speaking subject is not innocent. In *Freedom and interpretation: The Oxford amnesty lectures, 1992*, ed. B. Johnson. New York: Basic Books, pp.147-174.

Lehman, B. A. and Crook, P. (1998). Doubletalk: A literary pairing of *The giver* and *We are all in the dumps with Jack and Guy. Children's Literature in Education, 29*, 2, 69-78.

Lesnik-Oberstein, K. (1994). *Children's literature: Criticism and the fictional child.* Oxford: Clarendon.

Lewis, D. (1998). *Oops!* Colin McNaughton and 'knowingness'. *Children's Literature in Education, 29*, 2, 59-68.

May, J. (1995). *Children's literature and critical theory: Reading and writing for understanding.* New York: Oxford University Press.

McCallum, R. (1999). *Ideologies of identity in adolescent fiction.* New York: Garland Publishing.

McGillis, R. (1996). *The nimble reader: Literary theory and children's literature.* London: Twayne.

McNaughton, C. (1996). *Oops!* London: Andersen Press.

Nikolajeva, M. (1996). *Children's literature comes of age: Toward a new aesthetic.* New York: Garland Publishing.

Say, A. (1993). *Grandfather's journey.* Boston: Houghton Mifflin.

Say, A. (1996). *Emma's rug.* Boston: Houghton Mifflin.

Smith, P. (1988). *Discerning the subject.* Minneapolis: University of Minnesota Press.

Stephens, J. (1992). *Language and ideology in children's fiction*. London: Longman.

Stephens, J. and McCallum, R. (1998). *Retelling stories, framing culture: Traditional story and metanarratives in children's literature*. New York: Garland Publishing.

Storr, C. (1990). *Last stories of Polly and the wolf*. London: Faber & Faber.

Suleiman, S. and Crosman, I. (eds) (1980). *The reader in the text: Essays on audience and interpretation*. Princeton: Princeton University Press.

Tompkins, J. P. (1980). *Reader response criticism: From formalism to post-structuralism*. Baltimore: Johns Hopkins University Press.

Wall, B. (1991). *The narrator's voice: The dilemma of children's fiction*. London: Macmillan.

Zelinsky, P. O. (1997). *Rapunzel*. New York: Dutton Children's Books.

# 2. This little piggy went to market: Some perspectives on Australian children's publishing since 1945

## Robyn Sheahan-Bright

### Abstract

We are dealing with texts designed for a non-peer audience, texts that are created in a complex social environment by adults. (Hunt 1991, p.45)

This paper will summarise some of the key factors influencing Australian children's publishing industry development, rather than children's literature history. As Curtain (1993) Wilson (1989, 1992) and Haye (1981) have pointed out, very little research into Australian book publishing has been undertaken. Children's publishing history analysis has been even more scant, including brief references in seminal works by Eyre (1978), Saxby (1993), Prentice and Bird (1987), Marcie Muir's research for the 'History of the Book in Australia' project and earlier biographical histories, and profiles of individual publishers.

My research focuses on children's publishing as a media and cultural industry experiencing factors such as: concentration of ownership and globalisation; electronic developments and the influence of the 'other' media; the tension between the production of culture and the market forces which always exists in publishing; and the important relationship between 'institutionalised structure and strategic conduct'. (Cunningham and Turner p.138) I'll attempt to define the influence of this relationship in determining what has (has not!) and will be published, and posit likely directions for the industry in future.

Do Australian companies necessarily focus on Australian cultural product or are they just as likely to match their cloth to the designs of international markets? Does the industry's isolation from the mainstream make children's publishing less or more vulnerable to market forces? What are the key factors which will influence it into the next millennium?

## Introduction

This little pig went to market, This little pig stayed at home,
This little pig had roast beef, This little pig had none,
And this little pig cried, Wee-wee-wee-wee-wee,
I can't find my way home. (Opie & Opie 1989, p.349)

Since 1945 children's books have been 'taken to market' in Australia, in an unprecedented period of growth and change. It has been an era of transition from a local publishing scene dominated by British interests, to a gradual growth of Australian-owned companies, to an age of increasing globalisation with international media conglomerates in control of most of our publishing interests. Australian-originated product is still strong, however, a fact which is illustrated by the growth in numbers of books submitted to the annual Children's Book Council of Australia awards. In 1959, despite post war enthusiasm, 'only fourteen books were submitted and of these seven were published abroad' (Fabinyi 1971, p.7). Now there are several hundred books submitted each year. From 1946-1976 'almost all these books were published by three companies: Angus and Robertson, Oxford University Press and Kestrel/Puffin' (Price 1990, p.16). In the ensuing twenty years, several very powerful lists (including independent publishers) have been established. The marketplace also seems to be witnessing a blurring of the boundaries between the mass market and the library market. Instead of questioning the producers and distributors regarding these developments, however, we have generally addressed our questions to the creators, a somewhat ill-founded exercise. For as Bourdieu has pointed out, the power of individual 'dispositions varies according to the state of the field...the position in the field and the degree of institutionalisation of the position' (Bourdieu 1993, p.72). This paper is premised on the factors of production and consumption, in recognition of a perceived need to position children's publishing, not in opposition to the media as it has been customarily located, but in a symbiotic partnership with it, as one of a range of media industries.

In reviewing the literature pertaining to Australian cultural industries generally and the publishing industry in particular it becomes obvious that, as Wilson (1989, 1992), Curtain (1993) and Haye (1981) have pointed out, 'there are large gaps in the institutional histories of...media: the television and radio industries, advertising, publishing, and music are still waiting for their general historians' (Cunningham and Turner 1993, p.14).

Publishing has, since the seventies, gone through a period of rapid restructure with corporate takeovers and globalisation, highlighting the urgent need for research:

> With each move and merger individuals disappear, and documents (including manuscripts, illustrated letters and artwork) are lost, destroyed and otherwise dispersed...It therefore becomes increasingly difficult to locate detailed information about anything – from economics to changes in ethos and intention. (Reynolds and Tucker 1998, pp.xi -xii)

The framework for my analysis acknowledges Curtain's identification of the three prime characteristics of book publishing: 'the tension between commerce and culture; 'easy entry' and structural complexity' (Curtain in Cunningham and Turner 1993, p.102):

> ...the media are constantly torn between conflicting forces: between responding to local demands or international trends; between taking the cost-effective option or taking the culturally responsible option; between accepting the rhetorics of globalisation or asserting the right for national or local differences to be maintained. (Cunningham and Turner 1993, p.12)

The first of these tensions is the powerful conflict between 'cultural value' and the 'market' – a view which has been played out in a range of arenas, in which publishers have tried to resist being governed by marketing regulations, by maintaining that 'books are different' (Barker 1966). The use of culture as a defence for government assistance to publishing received a damning refutation in the *Australian Industries Assistance Commission report on the publishing industry (1979)* for example, which employed words such as 'elitism', 'paternalism' and accusations of promoting 'vested interests' (p.60) in its recommendation that forms of assistance cease. Definitions are complicated by the fact that publishing is a 'hybrid' which 'has more in common with a craft industry, than with mass industries that are organised along bureaucratic lines' (Coser 1982, p.7). 'Standardised procedures' (p.7) are difficult to monitor in companies dealing with such individualistic product, 'unknown markets', (p.7) and such a high level of risk. Publishing is a business but sometimes a very unbusiness-like one.

'Easy entry', the second factor, contributes to the cyclical nature of industry change (Curtain 1993, p.102). As mergers occur, there are new companies arising as it were, like the proverbial phoenix from the ashes. The relatively low cost of establishing a publishing enterprise as compared to other media companies, means that though mergers may appear to be condensing the industry, small houses are apt to appear (as Australian children's houses did in the eighties), creating both a competitive and a fragmented marketplace in which trends are difficult to isolate (Noble in Compaine 1979).

The third factor in publishing – 'structural complexity' (Curtain 1993, p.102) affects all its components. The dynamic relationship between 'innovation and control' (Turow, in Curran and Gurevitch 1992, p.168) in the mass media structure of publishing is complexified, though, in the children's industry, for non textbook output is divided into 'two separate segments with distinct, generally non overlapping production and distribution outlet organisations...the "library market segment" and 'the mass market segment" with "different client relationships'" (Turow 1978, p.3) though the same 'purported audience' (Turow 1978, p.5) making this a difficult sector to manage. Analysis is further complicated by Hunt's simply put statement of the monumentally difficult fact that: 'We are dealing with texts designed for a non-peer audience, texts that are created in a complex social environment by adults' (Hunt 1991, p.45).

Many questions then, may be asked of publishers – of the structures and the agents who work within them. Many remain to be asked of publishers for young people, for their history is relatively briefer, and has been rarely subject to industry analysis. Literary theorists have even maintained that an analysis of the commercial aspects of book production is not relevant to their aesthetic appreciation or their cultural value. Change is in the wind, though, so that 'the 1990s may mark a moment of theoretical synthesis where text and audience are brought back into the context of industrial and professional production' (Tulloch in Cunningham and Turner 1993, p.155).

Where United States and United Kingdom theorists have begun researching the marketing of children's properties (Turow 1978; McNeal 1992; Duke 1979; Reynolds and Tucker 1998) such research in Australia has been scant, including only brief references (e.g. Eyre 1978; Saxby 1993; Saxby and Winch 1987; Prentice and Bird 1987; Muir 1977, 1982) publishers'profiles in journals (*Magpies, Orana, Reading Time, Australian Book Review* and the *Australian Bookseller and Publisher*) and conference addresses. There are few Australian publishing histories (Sayers 1988; Munro 1998; Dutton 1996) and some 'History of the book in Australia' papers have been published in *Publishing Studies*. On wider industry issues, most authors, save for a few exceptions (e.g. Ker Wilson 1998; Ferguson 1991; Russell 1981; Muir 1996, 1998; Macleod 1998) are silent.

## Why the silence?

1.   This gap is partly a reflection of the industry's brevity. Australia's formal recognition of children's publishing as an entity with Joyce Boniwell Saxby's appointment as the first children's editor at Angus and Robertson in 1963 came some forty years later than in the United States, with Macmillan's appointment of Louise Seaforth Bechtel.

2.   It is also a result of the retarding historical influences which have affected Australian publishing generally (Kirsop 1969). Much of our publishing has been 'dominated by large foreign-owned publishing groups' (Curtain 1993a, p.233) and 'Unlike the press and broadcasting, book publishing is not concerned with news and interpretations thereof, nor is it an industry with a particularly high profile' (Haye 1981, p.2).

3.   Moreover, it is also a product of the isolationist culture in which children's literature in Britain, the United States and Australia has created a similarly thriving industry. In each country, structures (e.g. awards and professional

bodies) 'forged important links in the new system, which secured an independent status for itself at the expense of becoming somewhat isolated from the mainstream' (Marcus 1997, Pt.1).

4.    The importance of women and librarians in this rarified atmosphere meant that: 'Thereafter, few literary critics outside the field deigned – or saw the need – to write about children's literature' (Marcus 1997, Pt.1).

The permanence of women in Australian children's publishing has still to be examined – there is no doubt that men have assumed positions of publishing power whilst the status of these new children's departments remained somewhat inferior to these companies' core business, and that female children's editors' voices were often silenced in boardrooms, and in institutional histories:

> Children's books have been seen as the 'soft' area of the business – the easy bit – and so all the more likely to be left to women…the growing economic and critical importance of children's books will probably mean that men will take this area of publishing more seriously. It is certainly one of the reasons why more women now find themselves in senior positions in publishing companies. (Price 1990, p.17)

5.    And finally, this silence may also be a result of the aforementioned distinction between commerce and culture which has plagued publishing criticism, and in the children's arena has assumed a sort of no-go area. The very notion that books are part of an industry causes anxious enthusiasts to begin hunting for signs that a book is either written for a 'market' or made to look as if it is, to which I can respond no more powerfully than in Sonya Harnett's words: 'any writer who imagines publishing as anything other than a business is not *innocent* but *naive*, and at all times the writer must work around this fact, and sometimes he or she can make use of it' (Hartnett 1998, p.33).

So what is the nature of this business environment? Do Australian companies necessarily focus on Australian cultural product or are they just as likely to match their cloth to the designs of international markets? Does the industry's isolation from the mainstream make children's publishing less or more vulnerable to market forces? What are the key factors which will influence it into the next millennium? Is it still the library market it appears to be? Or are we moving into a mass market and thence towards the targeted market analysed in Joseph Turow's *Breaking up America*? There are distinct signs that we are moving along that self-same yellow brick road towards not so much a frightening future, but an extremely unpredictable one.

# Historical overview

Valerie Haye has defined three periods of Australian publishing growth:

> ...the early days to the Second World War...the second phase, following the outbreak of the Second World War, witnessed a growing market for Australian books...and from 1964 onwards...the third phase...the takeover period. (Haye 1981, pp.93-94)

These serve as a framework for this discussion, focusing on the transition from the second to the third period.

## Phase one

The moribund state of pre-war children's publishing was noted by Hungarian Andrew Fabinyi, arriving in 1939 (later to become director of Cheshire) 'except for the handful published by Angus and Robertson...were contracted, printed and published in England and consequently lacked an Australian editorial or economic involvement (Fabinyi 1971, p.3).

The origins of this dearth may be found in British publishers' practices of using local representatives or offices in the Antipodes. Cassell was first, sending Charles Gardner in May 1884 to establish an office whose 'principal business...has...been the marketing of Cassell publications from London' (Nowell-Smith 1958, p.266). Ward Lock followed suit a few months later in Melbourne. The intentions of these agencies are explained tellingly in Liveing's history of Ward Lock: 'the value to a publisher of establishing an outpost in the Commonwealth does not lie only in furthering the sales of its books' (Liveing 1959, p.96). (Such colonial successes as Ethel Turner and Mary Grant Bruce continued throughout their lives to be published in Britain.) Ward Lock's branch was managed faithfully by William Steele who was given a twentieth fifth anniversary party in 1909 in London, since none of the directors ever ventured south until 1948 when the Chairman 'made a tour of Australia' (Living 1959, p.104). William Collins similarly established a 'warehouse and showroom' in Sydney in 1876 (Keir 1952, p.180), and in 1901, a new office, purely 'to combat the high protective tariff imposed by the Australian government' (Keir 1952, p.217). From such colonialist beginnings was Australian publishing derived.

## Phase two

Several factors, including the shortage of paper and the difficulty of maintaining British imports, created a more fertile publishing atmosphere during World War Two. From a history dominated by British influence, the forties ended with a new national awareness. More fundamentally:

> The 1940s were the last great period of traditional book publishing. Wartime shortages of most consumer products and the closed frontiers had a favourable effect on the sale of books. The war had also preserved bourgeois society – social change came to a standstill for the duration.
>
> (Gedin 1975, p.81)

Nicholas Tucker confirms that 'enduring conservatism' was encouraged by 'British war-time propaganda (which) had concentrated on celebrating shared values dating from the past rather than looking to the future' (Reynolds and Tucker 1998, p.1). These, though European perspectives, have some bearing on the growth of Australia's industry too.

The establishment of the Children's Book Council of Australia in 1945, and of the Australian Publishers Association in 1948, augured well for the future of Australian-originated publishing. At that time, 'about fifteen percent of the books sold in Australia were of local origin' (Curtain 1993a, p.235). An enormous demand for education stimulated by wartime access to literature, and to post-war educational opportunities, drove local educational publishing growth with Cheshire, Jacaranda, Rigby and later, Lansdowne's trade list, catering for a larger literate audience. Overseas companies, too, began to re-enter, and produce for this market. Cassell's Australian branch had during the war published Australian books 'printed in Melbourne and Sydney' (Nowell-Smith 1959, p.267) and even printed English-originated books to be shipped back to England until in 1947 'the Board of Trade prohibited the import of fiction and children's books' (Nowell-Smith 1959, p.267). It appointed Bob Sessions to 'develop an educational and trade list' (Curtain 1993a, p.237) as did other companies, thus maintaining strong ties to Britain, so that by 1953, '24 percent of all British book exports went to Australia' (Curtain 1993a, p.235).

Frank Eyre, sent out in 1950 to establish Oxford University Press's Australian branch, is credited with professionalising the children's publishing industry, discovering writers such as Nan Chauncy and Eleanor Spence. Other post-war influences were increased national cultural awareness and the influence of the Children's Book Council of Australia awards in educating buyers and promoting books. Nevertheless, the fifties saw a gradual decline in the effervescent post-war situation, and decreasing local production again: 'In 1961...Only 4 of the books to be judged were published in Australia, and once again no award could be made for a best Australian picture book' (Fabinyi 1971, p.7).

This led to 'experiments', such as 'The Children's Library Guild of Australia...an advisory board...to produce and sell high quality children's books' (Fabinyi 1971, p.8) for libraries, and the creation of Cheshire's 'Authors and Artists Series for Young Australians' (Fabinyi 1971, p.11). Children's publishing history is littered with such cultural experimentation, e.g. the Children's Book Council of Australia awards are an attempt to favour the cultural over the commercial. The sixties saw *Reading Time* established (1961) and the *Australian Book Review* contained a *Children's Books and Educational Supplement* throughout the decade. Barbara Ker Wilson succeeded Joyce Boniwell Saxby at Angus and Robertson from 1965-74, and: 'it was through her efforts that Angus and Robertson's children's books obtained international recognition: she was the first...to exhibit Australian works at the Bologna Children's Book Fair' (Harper 1988, p.194).

She also published Ivan Southall and Hesba Brinsmead's Children's Book Council of Australia award winning novels. Improved printing techniques and the advocacy of new children's editors in seeking new talents, led later to the creation of quality picture books which were virtually non-existent prior to the seventies.

It is hard to imagine the situation which provoked Cheshire's children's editor, Barbara Buick to assert in 1967 that 'we have produced no picture book worthy of the name since Norman Lindsay's *The magic pudding*' (Buick 1973, p.343). (The Children's Book Council of Australia award was only presented intermittently from 1956-1970.) But the sixties also saw changes with lists such as F. W. Cheshire Publishing Pty Ltd which had produced 'more than 250 titles...since the Second World War ended' (Cheshire 1984, p.105) falling into foreign hands in 1964. It had contributed substantially to Australian-produced books dominating school reading demands, but with the sale of it and Lansdowne Press to a partnership between Wilkie & Co. Ltd, Melbourne printers, and International Publishing Corporation Ltd of London, two companies ceased to be solely Australian.

## Phase three

The late sixties and seventies ushered in 'the age of takeovers', with Angus and Robertson being 'taken over by Gordon Barton's Tjuringa Securities Ltd' (Barker 1991, p.2). Despite lost independence, there was a heartening growth in Australian publishing figures, even by the foreign-owned companies. In 1971 Ann Bower Ingram started a list for William Collins, and Era Publications began. (Van Putten 1996). Rigby had, 'the largest operation of any Australian publishing house' (Haye 1981, p.76). Hodder appointed Barbara Ker Wilson in 1974, and later, Margaret

Hamilton. Lisa Highton, at Nelson from 1977, had by 1980 'managed to produce at least a dozen good books a year' (McVitty 1980, p.250) and specialist editors, such as Rosalind Price and Elizabeth Fulton (McVitty 1982, p.40) further developed the industry. (This period, ironically, has been decried as the beginning of 'local' publishing losing out to overseas domination.)

The period also saw retail price maintenance outlawed in Australia despite the trade's application for 'exemption before the Trade Practices Commission' in 1971 (Curtain 1993a, p.236). Similar representations to defend the Net Book Agreement in the United Kingdom had succeeded in 1962, but in Australia the narrow definition of 'public interest' went against a successful ruling. 'Both the Statement of Terms and Retail Price maintenance were finished in Australia' (Curtain 1993a, p.236). Some attribute to this, the growth of remaindering and diminishing backlists. But Wallace Kirsop puts it much earlier:

> The displacement of Melbourne merchant-importers by agents of European manufacturers has been noted as a major commercial development of the 1880s...We are still paying – a century later – the high price for letting control of book importation slip out of our hands. (Kirsop 1969, p.42)

The takeover trend continued into the eighties: Oxford University Press closed its Australian children's list; Angus and Robertson merged with HarperCollins and became a Murdoch subsidiary: 'In 1979 James Hardie took over the company [of Rigby] unloaded stock, closed departments and sold off much of the valuable real estate' (Bransom 1986, p.41). Mergers created stronger foreign ownership and also increased spending on developing the children's market, e.g. Jenny Rowe at Angus and Robertson, who was 'keen to produce more child-oriented mass market stuff' (Harper 1988, p.195) and Margaret Hamilton at Hodder developed acclaimed Australian lists. Though Penguin Australia in 1963 published its 'first Australian title – *Kangaroo tales*, edited by Rosemary Wighton' (Watts 1994, p.256) it wasn't until the late seventies, under Kaye Ronai, that their list really began. Her 'first children's book contracted, *In the garden of badthings*' by Doug Macleod and Peter Thompson, was she says, 'a gamble' (Ronai 1983, p.126). In 1980, Ronai published '17 new Australian books...Encouraged by their success the program grew to 24 titles by 1985 and to 35 by 1987' (Watts 1994, p.256) when Julie Watts was made children's publisher, and has since developed a stridently Australian list.

Eighties consolidation was accompanied by a surge in independent publishing, notably enormously successful Omnibus with early titles such as *Possum magic* (1983) and *One woolly wombat* (1982). Others were Walter McVitty Books, Margaret Hamilton Books, Random House's Mark Macleod Books, Rosalind Price's Little Ark imprint for Allen and Unwin, and University of Queensland Press Young Adult fiction list and later Storybridge lists (both established by Barbara Ker

Wilson), Greater Glider, and Jam Roll Press, (now an imprint of University of Queensland Press, under the editorship of Leonie Tyle).  Collins/Angus and Robertson continued with editors Cathie Tasker, Brian Cook, and Laura Harris, and titles such as *My place* reflected growth and increased national pride.

Nineties developments have included the establishment of indigenous publisher, Magabala Books (Lands 1991) and the growth of Lothian, with Helen Chamberlin as editor, and Hodder Headline, with Belinda Bolliger.  However, economic downturn has led to rationalisation in small publishing. e.g. Omnibus and Margaret Hamilton are now owned by Scholastic and Walter McVitty Books by Lothian. Even large companies have suffered with Reed selling its children's list to Hodder; and Random's closure of Mark Macleod's list, in the wake of its takeover by Bertelsmann (Waldren 1998; Pullan 1998).  The supposed advantages of mergers such as economies of scale will continue to create a pattern of consolidation and globalisation.  However 'history suggests that in book publishing it is difficult to create a monopoly with staying power, at least if the emphasis is placed on the consolidation of assets rather than on people' (Noble in Compaine 1979, p.256).

Globalism, the worldwide technology revolution, social changes such as feminism. and multiculturalism, and increased government spending and intervention in the publishing sphere have altered the field.  Trends include monopolisation; a focus on marketing and 'name' publishing; a shift away from British to United States and global publishing influences; the increasing power of the Children's Book Council of Australia awards; a nexus between the trade and educational sectors; the growing influence of the electronic media on the 'visually literate' reader; and 'issues-based' publishing.

Perhaps the most revealing influence for the future has been Scholastic Australia. Founded in 1920 in the United States, in 1995 it had multi-media sales nearing $750 million in that country.  'We create a mini Scholastic in any country we go into' (Sanislo p.3). Established here in 1968, it shared the name Ashton with the New Zealand branch.  In 1985 it took over Scholars Choice (Rigby's) Australian Book Fairs, (Stewart 1990, p.133) and now owns magazines, book clubs, book fairs and trade lists.  It is the 'sixth-biggest book publisher' in Australia (Hely 1998, p.19). Scholastic predicted publishing directions earliest, evincing current trends in all its marketing approaches.  These are, 'mass marketing' rather than 'library-oriented' approaches, despite the anomaly that Scholastic admits it's successful because it becomes part of the school culture in every country it invests in.  It nevertheless engages in practices evinced by mass market multinational conglomerates: vertical integration of its media properties, niche marketing (e.g. book clubs targeted to specific age groups) sales through non-traditional outlets, cross merchandising and joint food promotions (e.g. Goosebumps) Internet sales and promotions, and value-added incentives (Sheahan-Bright 1998).  Speculation might only suggest that more publishers will develop similar strategies. Australian Broadcasting Commission Books' success is interesting too, in that it represents a form of monopolisation, operating on multinational principles - those of synergy and convergence - though it is a government owned media company.

## 'Big questions'

And now to formulate brief answers, to dispel some myths, and to develop an investigatory strategy. Wilson (in Kress 1988, p.61) defines the 'industrial aspects of communication' as 'ownership, production, technology, distribution, consumption, and the role of the state', terms here applied to Australian children's publishing in a world context.

## Ownership

It has been suggested that by the year 2000, four companies will control all the world's media. In 1994, it was reported that 'six companies [now] control from 40 to 50 percent of school book sales in the US' (Schuman 1994, p.42). Nobel defines three types of conglomerate or 'congeneric' mergers occurring – 'electronic companies and publishers...welding broad media companies' and 'European publishers seeking to expand worldwide markets as well as greater political stability' (Noble in Compaine 1979, p.261). Such globalisation concentrates power over: 'mass media content, mass media structure and mass media technology' (Turow 1992b, p.211). Regarding these developments, two questions are commonly asked.

Question: Is the 'agent' or the structure the key factor in the development of a publishing house?

Answer: With other artforms, publishing shares a tendency to 'foreground the individual' (Bourdieu 1993, p.29). However, as Turow's table of the partners in media industries demonstrates (Turow 1992b, p.22) they are far from being agent-driven (as publishing is commonly supposed to be) for all are organisations except for the creator and the reader. Moreover, he indicates that mergers have always been a publishing characteristic, balanced by a continual regeneration in new outlets. If: 'The key to successful publishing is people – and their ideas...Economies of scale through merger are most obvious in selling and distribution...and may be nil in editorial' (Noble in Compaine 1979, p.275) then there is evidence to suggest that editorial economies of scale may be one of the real losses incurred in an industry beset by global conglomerisation. However, to understand mass media: 'requires seeing organisations and industries as the creators of meaning' (Turow 1992b, p.163). Too little children's publishing research has recognised that the editor is one cog in the wheel of making meaning. To value the individual's role we need to understand how it is facilitated by the structure of which it is a part: 'the producers of the meaning and value of the work...and the whole set of agents whose combined efforts produce consumers capable of knowing and recognising the work of art as such' (Bourdieu 1993, p.37).

Question: Are small Australian or large multinationals more likely to produce Australian product?

Answer: Valerie Haye's ground-breaking study of the effect of foreign ownership on 70s literary publishing, established that:

> ...there is no evidence of any of the large Australian commercial publishers feeling a cultural obligation to champion quality Australiana...with the exception of the university presses, most of the upmarket (quality) Australian publishing in the 1970s was undertaken by overseas-owned publishers. (Haye 1981, p.87)

She demonstrated that more Children's Book Council of Australia award winners were published during the age of takeovers by overseas than local companies (Hayes 1981, p.91). Lloyd O'Neill, an influential post war Australian publisher, said that: 'the real question is not who owns whom, but who has a demonstrated commitment to Australian publishing' (A'Hearne 1987, p.19). Companies which 'are or were branches of British publishing houses have probably produced more 'Australian' material...than the...local independent publishers' (Wilson 1992, p.121). Another factor worth returning to here is that ease of entry leads to small publishers entering the marketplace but generally not retaining their independence. Eyre says this is more common with children's books, since they are 'more expensive to produce...have to be sold much more cheaply...are much more difficult to distribute' (Eyre 1978, p.99). Thus, he maintains that small children's publishers fail to stay in business for long, a fact evinced by the growth and decline of small presses in Australia in the eighties.

Concentration of ownership will therefore inevitably influence content, and the resultant fallout has contributed to, for instance, the crisis in picture book making in Australia, and the tendency to manufacture appeal in creating too many 'market-oriented' books: 'the market was weakened and fragmented by overproduction' (Covernton 1995). So in one sense a reduction in outlets may also create a greater originality in product.

## Production

Monopolies affect all aspects of production in publishing, printing, binding, paper supplying. 'Book publishing...is the most specialised of present-day media industries' (Noble 1979, p.265).

Question: To understand production, should we consider more than the editor's role?

Answer: Because of the complex web of agencies involved in producing a children's book, it is difficult to assess their role and impact. Traditionally information has been provided reluctantly, and statistics kept with an air of secrecy. More research work needs to be done on the editor's views, but also on the imperatives of dealing with the variant aspects of production − how they influence the editorial and other creative processes.

## Technology

Ownership concentration, problematically, may effect the diversity and accessibility of technology. Companies seek synergies via convergence, concentrating on a few viable properties. They also make decisions concerning the economic possibilities of information resources − decisions which should more properly be the province of public authorities.

Question: Is technology being hijacked by big corporations?

Answer. Yes and no. Again, this development is not as new as it would seem. In the late nineteenth century H.W. Wilson and R.R. Bowker worked to form the American Library Association. 'Bowker, as editor of both the *Library Journal* and *Publishers Weekly* offered an unusually powerful platform from which to speak to both librarians and publishers' (Schuman 1994, p.41). Those who decry the influence of global companies in public policy-making today, are describing a situation which has existed for far longer than the fear of Gates and Murdoch and others suggests. Such concentration affects not only commercial companies, but also government intervention in technology legislation and policy making: 'Many of the private sector companies lobbying for privatization of government information are multinational conglomerates' (Schuman 1994, p.42).

Monopolisation of technology ownership is prevalent, but how that manifests itself may provide positive and negative benefits. Big companies saturate and synergise, and can potentially provide huge markets for essentially regional or local product, acting as powerful agents for change in market tolerance for product.

Question: Is technology a threat to publishers?

Answer: Some publishers seem to be running scared. 'For the first time in half a millennium, publishers may lose control of their package' (Engelhardt 1997, p.2). Media interests are blurring the boundaries between the variant media formats, and publishers will need to acknowledge this or fall victim to their resistance to change. Many have embraced the potential for technology to promote and enhance the publishing process.

Question: Will technology destroy the book as theorists like Sven Birkets (1995) and Neil Postman (1995) have suggested?

Answer: Media changes have influenced both the reader and the content and packaging of books, and it is here that publishers are, or should be, doing more market research. Today's reader 'is often more committed to technology than to reading, but...has had the benefit of exposure to cinema and other media techniques and...is computer literate' (Saxby 1995, p.36). The products marketed to them need to reflect their experience, and to recognise their buying power (McCaughan 1994, p.16).

## Distribution

This is one of the most crucial, problematic aspects of publishing: 'An inquiry into distribution...in 1968 disclosed that for many of the larger publishing firms between 6 and 10 percent of their customers accounted for 90 percent of their business' (Barker and Escarpit 1973, p.78) and that: 'The reader expects a book to be available in circumstances which would be considered economically absurd by other trades, and furthermore the book trade expects and tries to provide this service' (Barker and Escarpit 1973, p.79).

Such a high concentration of energy on non-profitmaking exercises makes the question of whether publishing is a business or a craft, a vexed one. Monopolies in distribution are legion, affecting every outlet – warehousing, wholesale, retail, centralised buying practices of libraries and school supply services. To this trend is added the effect of the mass marketing ploys now increasingly used by companies like Scholastic. How could the distribution of books be streamlined? Again the practices of Scholastic which 'controls much of the distribution network for children's books' (Hely 1998, p.19) are worth considering, as is the fact that Panorama Bookfairs, 'a joint venture by Pan Macmillan and Penguin' (Hely 1998, p.25) has just been launched in Melbourne. Whether Australia needs a national distribution network is a question to be examined again.

Question: Is children's publishing reliant on schools and on library-oriented assessment of books for purchase?

Answer: The two separate sectors, of the 'library market…of nonprofit patron institutions…(and) the commercially oriented mass market…dominated by department, chain and bookstore patrons' (Turow 1978, p.3) are in competition. Evidence suggests that the library market does not wield the influence it once did. United States theorists agree: 'there's been a shift away from institutional to individual buyers' (Latrobe 1996, p.2) and 'the conglomeration of children's books has moved into the implementation phase – the mass merchandising of children's books' (Roxburgh 1992, p.1). Duke said twenty years ago that 'The library market is a steady one, but it is not growing itself' (Duke 1979, p.10) primarily because of government funding cutbacks. The shrinkage of the teacher librarian's promotional role caused by 'budgetary and staffing cutbacks during the 80s' (McVitty 1990, p.168) has led to a decline in library buying and, 'there are many signs that this market may have been oversupplied' (Macleod 1998, p.6). Though increased efforts in the United States have attempted to better the relationship between librarian and publisher (Schuman 1994), these two gatekeepers may be missing the point – that in an increasingly technological environment, gateways will be multiple paths to information and leisure, and in future there may be less need for gatekeepers at all.

## Consumption

Audiences are changing and with libraries losing their stranglehold the market is more unpredictable.

Question: How do we gauge the consumption of books whose buyers are often not the readers?

Answer: Some suggest that rather than 'reach out to non-readers', we should 'concentrate on increasing sales to the existing core market where there is already such a wellspring of commitment to the book' (Burn and Tredinnick 1994, p.100). To do that we need to know who and where those readers are, and why and what they are buying, reading and viewing. Two Australia Council reports (1990, 1995) have assessed reading patterns, but: 'Population, school enrollment, illiteracy, children's television viewing habits and economic conditions…rising prices, unemployment, declines in…tax funding, the energy crisis' (Duke, 1979, pp.44) are just some of the acknowledged factors which affect children's books and reading, and which might also be studied.

## Role of the State

Children's publishing is affected by a general trend to legislate cultural industries, though the offering of stopgap subsidies is allied to an increasingly hostile resistance to the notion that books are necessarily deserving of special treatment.

Question: Should governments protect the book industry and if so, how?

Answer: We've witnessed, for example, the uphill battle fought to preserve Public Lending Rights (PLR) and to introduce Educational Lending Rights (ELR) in Australia, and the dwindling of the Book Bounty. 'Australian government intervention in the book publishing industry has been proactive and limited to a concern with titles and ownership rather than industry ownership' (McLaren 1988 p.240).

The aforementioned Industry Assistance Commission report (1979) recommended cancelling all supports and pre-empted the 1995 ruling to make Australia 'an open market for books' as its 'clearly preferred option' (Prices Surveillance Authority 1995, p.113). Literature Fund and state ministries' individual project grants and subsidies have avoided addressing infrastructure support necessary to prop up an industry. Children's writers have fared less well in these forums than 'grownup' writers, and illustrators have until fairly recently been ignored (Macleod 1992). Other suggested areas of legislation have been library purchase of Australian materials (McLaren 1988; Isaacs 1988), required readings on school lists (Wilson 1992), postal rates and copyright regulations. Though some suggest that an industry needing props might best be left to be hoist by its own petard, the inarguable fact is that government has a mandate to investigate manufacturing industries' needs, and that children's books have two powerful claims to consideration. One is the potentially quantifiable economic benefits to be gleaned from a 'growth industry', and the other is the unquantifiable, yet inarguable cultural benefits.

## Conclusion

Question: Have we entered a phase of crass commercialisation which denies culture a voice?

Answer: We presume that the book has only recently been commercialised by trends such as the author tour and the value added product. And yet, such trends are more cyclical than chronological: 'criticism of commercialisation has been common at almost every phase of the book industry's history' (Coser et al. 1982, p.363). In the nineteenth century the literary press bemoaned the bestseller and rampant promotion e.g. the author reading tour popularised by Dickens, led in Australia, to such events as the Penny Readings in Victoria 'between 1865 to 1870' (Askew in Borchardt and Kirsop 1988, p.134) and the 'public lectures which were a feature of the colonial life of the colonial communities' (Askew in Borchardt and Kirsop 1988, p.133). Another early commercial success was E. R. Cole and his Book Arcade who could be said to have invented the book marketing campaign in Australia, and which when it closed in 1929 had produced *Cole's Funny Picture Book* in its 'fifty-eighth edition…(with) claims that 630,000 copies had been sold' (Muir 1996, p.37). Yet another was Cheshire's practice of 'advertising on the back of tram tickets…' which 'ran into over the one million mark' (Cheshire 1984, p.63). 'Everything old is new again' would seem to be one possible assessment, though the picture is full of surprises as well.

While changes are evident in the publishing climate, there are just as many factors which are part of a familiar pattern of decline and regeneration. Commerce and culture have always vied for supremacy in the complex environment which is publishing. Instead of decrying the daunting nature of globalisation, which, after all, has been a distinctive pattern for much of the last century, we should be making greater efforts to understand it. The mass market has been a pervasive influence in the growth of publishing and its trends bear closer investigation in terms of the future of Australian children's publishing. One of the primary business tactics is to analyse the factors which determine market growth. We have left the corner store and have entered a vastly different marketplace where, if we are not very careful we will be sold short:

> To market, Supermarket,
> To buy a full quart;
> Home again, Open it;
> measure is short. (Merriam 1969)

Mass market industries rely on three advertising functions: 'creative persuasion, media planning and buying, and market research' (Turow 1997, p.14). Children's publishers, too, need to develop such skills, or it's more than likely that this little pig – the Australian children's book – might very well be forced to stay at home.

# References

A'Hearne, K. (1987). Good culture and good business. *Australian Society*, **6**, 18-19.

Australia Council (1990). *Books – who reads them? A study of borrowing and buying in Australia 1990*. Sydney: Australia Council.

Australia Council (1995). *Books: Who's reading them now? A Study of book buying and borrowing in Australia*. Research Report. Sydney: Australia Council.

Barker A. (1991). *One of the first and one of the finest. Beatrice Davis, Book Editor.* Carlton, Victoria: Victorian Society of Editors.

Barker, R. E. and Davies, G. R. (eds) (1996). *Books are different.* London: Macmillan.

Barker, R. and Escarpit, R. (eds) (1973). *The book hunger.* London: Unesco Press.

Birkets, S. (1995). *The Gutenberg elegies.* Boston: Faber & Faber.

Borchardt, D.H. and Kirsop, W. (eds) (1988). *The book in Australia. Essays towards a cultural and social history.* Melbourne: Australian Reference Publications in Association with the Centre for Bibliographical and Textual Studies, Monash University.

Bourdieu, P. (1993). *The field of cultural production.* Cambridge: Polity Press.

Bransom, V. (1986). Rigby remembered. *Australian Bookseller and Publisher,* October, 38-41.

Buick, B. (1973). An indigenous children's literature. In *Children and literature: Views and reviews*, ed. V. Haviland. Glenview, Ill.: Scott, Foresman & Co., pp.340-344.

Burn, J. and Tredinnick, M. (1994). Knowledge is power: The case for consumer research in book publishing. *The Australian Library Journal,* **43**, 2, 81-103.

Cheshire, F. W. (1984). *Bookseller, publisher, friend.* Melbourne: The National Press.

Compaine, B. M. (ed.) (1979). *Who owns the media: Concentration of ownership in the mass communication industry.* White Plains, N.Y.: Knowledge Industry Publications.

Coser, L. A., Kadushin, C. and Powell, W. W. (1982). *Books: The culture and commerce of publishing.* New York: Basic Books.

Covernton, J. (1995). *Unpublished response to survey.* Conducted by Robyn Sheahan for *Magpies* articles, 1996.

Cunningham, S. & Turner, G. (1993). *The media in Australia.* Sydney: Allen & Unwin.

Curtain, J. (1993a) Distance makes the heart grow fonder. *Media, Culture and Society,* **15**, 233-244.

Curtain, J. (1993b). Book publishing. In *The media in Australia,* eds S. Cunningham and G. Turner. Sydney: Allen & Unwin, pp.102-118.

Duke, J. S. (1979). *Children's books and magazines: A market study.* White Plains, N.Y.: Knowledge Industry Publications.

Dutton, G. (1996). *A rare bird: Penguin Books in Australia 1946-96.* Ringwood, Victoria: Penguin.

Engelhardt, T. (1997). Gutenberg unbound: Publishing execs no longer feel the book, as a freestanding entity, is sustainable. *The Nation,* **264**, 10.

Eyre, F. (1978). *Oxford in Australia 1890-1978.* Melbourne: Oxford University Press.

Eyre, F. (1978). Whither children's books! In *Readings in children's literature: Proceedings of the Second National Seminar on children's literature.* Frankston State College, pp.96-108.

Fabinyi, A. (c.1971). *The development of Australian children's publishing. MS 2600 Box 37 Folder 79.* Canberra, ACT: National Library of Australia.

Fabinyi, A. (Pica, P.) (1963). The production of children's books. *Australian Book Review, Children's Book and Educational Supplement,* **5**.

Fabinyi, A. (Pica, P.) (1962). Standards of Australian book production. *Australian Book Review, Children's Book and Educational Supplement,* **7-8**.

Ferguson, J. (1991). Future directions: Where to now? In *Children's literature and contemporary theory: Proceedings of a Children's Literature Conference held on 13 April, 1991,* ed. M. Stone. Wollongong: New Literatures Research Centre, pp.15-23.

Gedin, P. (1975). *Literature in the marketplace,* trans. G. Bisset. London: Faber.

Harper, S. (1988). Angus & Robertson's involvement with the children's book scene. *Orana,* **24**, 4, 191-6.

Hartnett S. (1998). In defence. *Viewpoint,* **6**, 1, 33-4.

Haye, V. *The impact of foreign ownership on Australian publishing of the 1970s*: A thesis submitted in partial fulfilment of the requirements for the degree of Master of Arts, La Trobe University, November 1981.

Hely, S. (1998). The unfunny end of kids stuff. *The Australian Author, 30*, 2, 19-25.

Hunt, P. (1991). *Criticism, theory and children's literature.* Oxford: Blackwell.

Industries Assistance Commission (1979). *The publishing industry report.* 17 October. Canberra: AGPS.

Isaacs M., Emmett, L. and Whyte, J. P. (1988). *Libraries and Australian literature: A report on the representation of Australian creative writing in Australian libraries.* Melbourne: Ancora Press.

Keir, D. (1952). *The House of Collins: The story of a Scottish family of publishers from 1789 to the present day.* London: Collins.

Ker Wilson, B. (1998). Children's book publishing: reality and virtuality: Where are we going? Part One. *Magpies, 13*, 4, 10-13.

Kirsop, W. (1969). *Towards a history of the Australian book trade.* Sydney: Wentworth Books.

Lands, M. (1991). Magabala Books: The beginning of a publishing house. *The Lu Rees Archives: Notes, books and authors, 13*, 27-8.

Latrobe, K. and Schwartz, P. (1996). Bodies corporate: The new face of children's publishing. *Emergency Librarian, 24*, 1, 14+.

Liveing, E. (1959). *The House of Ward Lock 1854-1954.* London: Ward, Lock & Co.

McCaughan, D. (1994). Kids stuff. *Marketing, 57*, 21, 14-17.

Macleod, M. (1992). *The artist and the bureaucrat: Unpublished paper.* Delivered at the Artists' Day Luncheon, sponsored by Arts Qld, Brisbane 13 October.

Macleod, M. (1998). Marketing books for young people. *Viewpoint, 6*, 3, 5-7.

McLaren, J. (1988.) Publishing in the twentieth century. In *The book in Australia Essays towards a cultural and social history*, eds D. H. Borchardt and W. Kirsop.

Melbourne: Australian Reference Publications in association with the Centre for Bibliographical and Textual Studies, Monash University, pp.66-109.

McNeal, J. U. (1992). *Kids as customers*. New York: Lexington, 1992.

McVitty, W. (1982). Australian children's literature: Some thoughts on three decades of change. *Orana*, **18**, 2, 39-42.

McVitty, W. (1980). Children's publishing in Australia. *The Bookseller,* **3891**, 245-50.

McVitty, W. (1990). Publishing for children in Australia: A thriving industry. *Children's Literature Association Quarterly*, **15**, 4, 167-171.

Marcus, L. S. (1997). Mother Goose to multiculturalism Parts One & Two. *Publishers Weekly Interactive*, July 1.

Merriam, E. (1969). *The inner city Mother Goose.* Simon & Schuster.

Muir, M. (1996). Children's publishing before the war. *Publishing Studies*, **3**, 37-43.

Muir, M. (1998). Australian children's books after World War Two. *Publishing Studies*, **6**, 31-37.

Muir, M. (1977). *Australian children's book illustrators.* Sth. Melbourne: Sun Books.

Muir, M. (1982). *A history of Australian children book illustration.* Melbourne: Oxford University Press.

Munro, C. (ed.) (1998). *UQP: The writers press.* Brisbane: University of Queensland Press.

Noble, J. K. (1979). Books. In *Who owns the media: Concentration of ownership in the mass communication industry,* eds B. M. Compaine et al.White Plains, N.Y.: Knowledge Industry Publications. pp.251-291.

Nowell-Smith, S. (1958). *The House of Cassell 1848-1958.* London: Cassell.

Postman, N. (1995). *Technopoly: The surrender of culture to technology.* New York: Vintage.

Prentice, J. and Bird, B. (1987). *Dromkeen: A journey into children's literature.* Knoxfield, Victoria: Dent.

Price, R. (1990). Children's book publishing. *Australian Women's Book Review*, **2**, 3, 16-17.

Prices Surveillance Authority. *Prices Surveillance Act (1995). Inquiry into book prices and parallel imports.* Report No. 61, 28 April. Melbourne: Prices Surveillance Authority.

Pullan, R. (1998). Random Haus. *The Australian Author*, **30**, 1, 17-20.

Reynolds, K. and Tucker, N. (1998). *Children's publishing in Britain since 1945.* Aldershot: Scholar Press.

Ronai, K. (1983). Complexities of children's publishing. In *The imagineers: Writing and illustrating children's books*, eds B. Alderman and L. Harman. Marrickville: Reading Time, pp.113-131.

Rowe, J. (1987). How does the garden grow: The management of an established children's list. An edited transcript of a talk given on 29 September 1984 at the Canberra Children's Book Council Seminar on Writing and Illustrating for Children. In *The inside story: Creating children's books*, eds B. Alderman and S. Owen. Reeder Canberra, CBC (ACT Branch), pp.95-106.

Roxburgh, S. (1992). A publisher's perspective. *Horn Book Magazine*, January/February, 105-108.

Russell, J. L. (1981). *Children's book publishing in Australia with an emphasis on editorial policies June 1981.* Brisbane: Kelvin Grove CAE.

Sanislo, G. (1995). Scholastic Inc.: 75 years strong. *Publishers Weekly*, **242**, 46.

Sayers, S. (1988). *The company of books: A short history of the Lothian Book Companies 1888-1988.* Melbourne: Lothian.

Saxby, M. (1993). *The proof of the puddin': Australian children's literature 1970-1990.* Sydney: Ashton Scholastic.

Saxby, M. (1995). Changing perspectives: The implied reader in Australian children's literature, 1841-1994. *Children's Literature in Education*, **26**, 1, 25-38.

Saxby, M. and Winch, G. (eds) (1987). *Give them wings: The experience of children's literature.* Sth Melbourne: Macmillan.

Schuman, P. (1994). Librarians and publishers: An uneasy dance. *Wilson Library Bulletin,* **69**, 40-43.

Sheahan, R. (1996). Australian children's books 1985-1995. *Magpies,* **11**, 1, 14-17; **11**, 2, 33-35; **11**, 3, 20-22; **11**, 4, 22-24; **11**, 5, 18-19.

Sheahan-Bright, R. (1998). *Touting for business: The manufacture of appeal in Australian children's publishing.* A paper to be delivered at the Australian Association for Creative Writing Programs Conference, 9 October 1998, Adelaide.

Stewart, D. (1990). Bringing books and children together: Ashton Scholastic's contribution to children's literature and reading. *Orana,* August, 129-134.

Turner, G. (1994). *Making it national: Nationalism and popular culture.* Sydney: Allen & Unwin. .

Turnley, C. (1974). *Cole of the Book Arcade: A pictorial biography.* Hawthorne, Victoria: Cole Publications.

Turow, J. (1997). *Breaking up America.* Chicago: University of Chicago Press.

Turow, J. (1978). *Getting books to children: An exploration of publisher-market relations.* Chicago: American Library Association.

Turow, J. (1992a). A mass communication perspective on entertainment industries. In *Mass media and society*, eds J. Curran and M. Gurevitch. London: Edward Arnold, pp.160-177.

Turow, J. (1992b). *Media systems in society: Understanding industries, strategies, and power.* New York: Longman.

Van Putten, V. (1996). Era Publications celebrates 25 years. *Reading Time,* **41**, 2, 17,18.

Waldren, M. (1998). Written off? *The Weekend Australian,* March 28-9, p.29.

Watts, J. (1994). From little acorns…the growth of an Australian children's list. In *Creative connections: Writing illustrating and publishing childrens books in Australia: Papers of the Canberra CBC Seminars 1987-1993,* eds B. Alderman and P. Clayton. Melbourne: Thorpe, pp.255-266.

Wilson, H. (1989). Australia and the international publishing industry. In *Communications and the media in Australia,* eds T. Wheelwright and T. Buckley Sydney: Allen & Unwin, pp.117, 137.

Wilson, H. (1992) Marketing the canon. *Discourse,* **12**, 2, 116-126.

Wilson, H. (1988). Communication as an industry. In *Communication and culture: An introduction,* ed. G. Kress. Kensington, NSW: New South Wales University Press, pp.55-77.

# Part II

# Postcolonial tensions

# 3. Challenging places: England vs the Antarctic end of the world

## Robin Pope

**Abstract:** In 1852, aged 60, William Howitt came to Australia for two years with his wife and two sons, to visit his brother. *A boy's adventures in the wilds of Australia* and his later novel for adults, *Tallengetta, the squatter's home* (1857) constitute two early works of significance about Australia. Howitt had already spent three years living in Heidelberg in the 1840s, and in his later years spent his summers in the Tyrol and the winters in Rome. As an educated and observant man of the world, it makes an interesting study to compare two of his works for children, *The boy's country book* (1839) written in England for an English audience, and *A boy's adventure in the wilds of Australia, or, Herbert's notebook* (1854) which had a wider audience in England and Australia (and was translated into German). Drawing on cultural studies and postcolonial ideas, this paper will compare the subjectivity each text offers its readers, and the functions of 'place' (including time and culture) in the world of the text and the world of its reception, which contribute towards this construction of the individual self.

William Howitt (1792) and his wife Mary (1799-1888) enjoyed enormous popularity as writers of works of history, nature, description, spiritual experiences, poetry and novels for both children and adults. In 1839 William's *The boy's country book* was published, which ran into several editions 'in the course of a few years' according to Herbert Strang who later had it re-issued as one of his Herbert Strang Library series, in the early decades of this century. I will compare this work with his later *A boy's adventure in the wilds of Australia or, Herbert's notebook* (1854) which he wrote after spending two years in Australia, noting particularly the functions of 'place' as geographical, historical and cultural spaces within the two texts.

In showing that discourse constructs our sense of reality, Michel Foucault said, 'We must not imagine that the world turns towards us a legible face which we would only have to decipher. The world is not the accomplice of our knowledge; there is no prediscursive providence which disposes the world in our favour.' That is, our reality is linguistically constituted, because discourse constitutes objects for us by the systematic nature of its ideas. It delineates the field for us by setting the limits of inclusion and exclusion, and by its internal structure and rules. Pecheux extends the idea to point out that discourses 'do not exist in isolation but in dialogue, in relation to or, more often, in contrast and opposition to other groups of utterances' (Mills 1997, p.11). Pecheux thus stresses that ideological struggle is the essence of discourse (Mills 1997, p.14).

In examining Howitt's two works we can see different discourses at work, constituting different sets of ideas in relation to 'place'. One discourse is appropriate for 'place' which represents the centre of empire, but another discourse comes into play for the marginal outposts of empire as constituted by Australia.

*The boy's country book* mines a range of discourses which were available to an English male naturalist, writing for younger males of his culture: masculine discourse, scientific discourse, historical and 'national' discourses intersect to produce a text which is a combination of celebration and advice concerning English country life. It does not need to specify its locality, for it is firmly located in England, which it describes and where its audience is situated. It is a fascinating insight into a world on which the irrevocable changes of industrialisation has made its stamp, as his section headed 'Town vs country life for the working lad' verifies. There is a strong sense, however, that while the towns may be changing, certain country practices will continue indefinitely:

> ...the fact is, that while there are boys and birds' nests, there always will be birds'-nesting. There always was since the foundation of the world, and I verily believe there always will be till its end. It is an instinct, a second nature, a part and parcel of the very constitution of a lad. (p.50)

Howitt implies in this declaration of male determinism a sense of belonging *now* to a community with other boys who collect birds' nests, birds' eggs and young birds too; and in having links with a community of past birds' nesters, the boy knows he is engaging in an unchanging activity which connects him strongly to his geographical, historical and cultural location. In England, this is what boys do; and this what boys have always done. Hence 'place' in this text is much more than a mere geographical location where a particular activity takes place. It connects the reader with a community. It operates as an extension of what it is to be an English boy, in the past, the present and the future.

The connection with place is powerfully present in Howitt's celebration of the pleasures of various other pursuits open to any who reside in the country – activities such as gardening, cowslip-gathering, hay-making, wasp-nesting and acorn-gathering. And when towns were smaller and the countryside closer, town dwellers might have had access to many of the activities too. He writes with joy of specific winter amusements, such as riding horses – or, failing a horse, he advises that a large dog, goat, pig or cow will do! – rat-hunting, and the keeping of rabbits, pigeons and dogs. His advice seems directed at any boy, regardless of class, although 'working lads' seem to be the focus of his address. While recognising some of the discomforts of life, he judges them to be minor when compared with the miseries of city, and factory life:

No, I have no pity for country lads in general. They have, it is true, to blow their fingers over turnip-pulling on a sharp, frosty day...they get bumps on the ice, and chillblains to plague them o'nights when in bed, and masters rousing them up in the dark, just as their chillblains get easy, to fodder and be off to plough; but bless me! what are these things to a cotton mill! – to a bump on the bare head with a billy-roller, or the wheels of a spinning-jenny pulling an arm off! (p.106)

There are ritual activities too, to connect the young readers with a specific time in their history, such as Guy Fawkes night when the countryside was cleared of old rotting posts, and roots as the 'lads' went from house to house chanting:

Pray remember
The Fifth of November!
A stick or a stake
For King George's sake,
Timber or coal
For the bonfire pole. (p.81)

This event reminds the readers of their place in a culture established on firm foundations. Guy Fawkes night recalls the monarchic rule that has survived centuries of change and challenge. It is part of a political discourse which encourages citizens to celebrate their good fortune in being part of such a strong culture. It is also a marker of permanence, for this repeated ritualised activity acts as an annual reminder of the enduring nature of the monarchy.

Drawing on the discourses used to describe nature, Howitt offers advice calculated to alter some of the more brutal practices found among young country boys. He attempts to raise the sensitivities of his readers in his plea for the enthusiastic birds' nester not to inflict pain on the wild-life:

Lads are not naturally cruel, but they are thoughtless, and grasp at whatever pleases their fancies, without the smallest idea of the pain they inflict. This is the grand lesson that parents should everywhere teach –THAT ALL LIVING CREATURES ARE SENSITIVE LIKE THEMSELVES, and that while they admire the beauty of bird or moth, or any other living thing, they must have a care of inflicting pain upon it. (p.51)

In addition, the idea of guardianship over the natural resources is incorporated in several pages advising against taking young birds from their parents. He concludes with these words which are based on a desire to preserve the natural wonders so accessible to the English country boy:

It follows then that boys may take eggs only...If there are three or four – five is the average number of eggs in general – take only one or two...for birds are no arithmeticians, they can't count their eggs; and while they have one or two left they seem perfectly contented as if they had a dozen. (pp.54-55)

The young reader is reminded of other responsibilities which form part of his masculine subjectivity, and which are incorporated in the masculine discourse of the text. Apart from the pleasures already listed, there are accomplishments which he has to acquire, which pertain to nobler, imperial goals. One of these accomplishments is swimming:

> ...it is highly desirable that every boy should, both for his health and security through life, learn to swim early and learn to swim well. Without this knowledge a man is always in danger when he has to cross the water; and loses moreover the noble opportunities of assisting and saving his fellow-creatures in moments of peril. (p.66)

There is a hint here of the dangers which have to be confronted in travelling beyond the safety of England's island-fast borders to reach distant parts of her empire. At this time when few could swim and there were real risks of ships foundering on some distant reef or rock, courage and skill in peril might be required.

So this text constructs a place, an England, which is known, lived, shared by its readers and recognisable to them by the invoking of the discourses they use themselves to describe activities and observations similar to those found in the text. Place is a construct of spatial, temporal and cultural dimensions which have resonances in the lived experiences and perceptions of readers' lives.

In 1852, aged 60, Howitt came to Australia for two years with his wife and two sons, to visit his brother. He wrote two significant early Australian texts as a result of this experience. *Tallangetta, the squatter's home* (1857) was written for adults; while the text I will discuss here, *A boy's adventure in the wilds of Australia or, Herbert's notebook* (1854) was written for children. This text had a wider audience than *The boy's country book*, being of interest to readers in England and Australia (it was even translated into German), and again it is directed at a largely male audience, although girls may well have read copies too.

As the sub-title suggests, the novel takes the form of a notebook or journal, which was a favoured form of travelling writers and explorers. Paul Carter sees these journals not as 'an objective slice through geographical reality, but a critical equivalent of the explorer's spatial experience' (Carter 1987, p.74). In Carter's sense *A boy's adventure* is Herbert's personal spatial experience. It is a story purportedly written by Herbert, with entries dated from November 1852 to January 1854. The preface tells us the narrative 'was written amid the scenes and characters which it describes, and the desire of the author has been to afford to Herbert's contemporaries a reflection, as it were, of his own great enjoyment.' Herbert's journey is a conglomeration of descriptions of life in Australia, various 'adventures' experienced, and even some potted history on the early explorers and settlers. For about half of the 376 pages Herbert follows the fortunes of the Popkins family whom they meet en route, and traces the progress of the two Popkins cousins, Jonas and Phineas.

Paul Carter extends Foucault's idea about our preconceived notions of the world when he writes, '...historically speaking, the country did not precede the traveller: it was the off-spring of his intentions...he found what he was looking for' (Carter 1987, p.34). Howitt brings to Australia his set of imperially constituted ideas about Australia. As an educated man with an interest in the natural sciences, he is familiar with the discourse of that discipline, but in addition, as this text demonstrates, he is also familiar with imperial discourse with its assumptions that European 'success' has been due to their superior civilisation and consequent strength. He brings to Australia a set of preconceived notions which he expects to confirm, such as the evident superiority of his own culture, the weirdness of new species of flora and fauna, the freedom to enjoy certain privileges closed to him in England, and opportunities to behold new scenery.

Pam Morris has pointed out that 'what is other does not have identity in its own right, it often acts as an empty place to be ascribed whatever meanings the dominant group chooses (Morris 1993, p.14) and we see this principle at work in this text. From the opening pages Herbert reminds his readers that this place, Australia, is Other.

> Strange it is that while I shall be busy writing, the folks at home are all fast asleep in bed; but no wonder for I am turned topsy-turvy on the outside of the antarctic end of the world...first of all I remark that things are very fond of flying in this country. The squirrels fly; the grasshoppers fly; the mice fly; and I see all sorts of seeds flying at a great rate; I shall therefore let my thoughts and observations fly on paper to Old England, for it is an old proverb, 'that at Rome you must do as the Romans do'. (p.2)

The imperial centre, where life is lived the right way up, is the benchmark by which all the new sights and objects are measured. Despite his claims of doing 'as the Romans do', he and his companions trundle about the countryside as proud models of British propriety, setting up their rough tables with plates and glasses and tea-cups so that even the diggers are astonished. For the purpose of his English readers Herbert tries to erase difference by creating a sense of familiarity:

> Our journey is just like a long picnic. What great fun anybody would think it in England to take a tent in a cart, with provisions and everything one can want for cooking and eating, with beds and blankets for sleeping and set off right away into some forest and there camp! (pp.8-9)

Like *The boy's country book,* Herbert's notebook draws on masculine discourse, but here it intersects with imperial discourse which establishes Australia as amusingly different and curious.  The business of empire is the business of the male, whose skills and knowledge are necessary for the empire's civilising mission.  Although Herbert is temporarily de-centred, he has a specific task to record the official history of his group.  His journal is not an 'objective slice through geographic reality' (Carter 1987, p.74) but his record of his spatial experience.  Through his writing he is able to quickly establish a temporary colonial subjectivity for himself, for his skills provide the necessary record to take back to the imperial centre as authentic evidence of their journey.

A large part of Herbert's entries comprise descriptions of the 'new' flora and fauna they see.  These 'discoveries' serve the purpose of filling in the blank spaces about what wildlife Australia has: they contribute to constructing an identity by ascribing qualities to objects.  Contrary to the careful warnings in *The boy's country book* about preserving sufficient birds' eggs for the species to survive, Herbert is proud of his dog Prin, who 'is very much admired by the gentlemen here' and who 'is quite mad about opossums, and often goes scouring about the woods after them all night' (p.6).  Prin turns out to be a 'capital water-dog too, and fetches out the ducks and other birds that are shot' (p.6).  The many descriptions of hunting various animals contain no sense that there ought to be any controls.  Howitt has the imperialist's attitude towards naturally occurring objects as curiosities with little intrinsic value.  This is emphasised by contrast when he regrets that a 'rascally dog' has devoured two of three 'fine European swans' in the Botanic Gardens.  'There were plenty of ducks nearer that he might have killed, and they could speedily have been replaced; but no! nothing would serve him but to destroy these beautiful creatures...' (p.73).  It comes as no surprise when we recall that the first protected species in Australia were imported ones (Griffiths 1996, p.16) and that acclimatisation societies formed for the purpose of introducing European species to Australia, flourished in the nineteenth century.  A kind of biological imperialism is evident in the opinion that if 'the animals of the colony could not protect themselves, they were unfit to live in Australia'.  It was a belief many colonists held (Griffiths 1996, p.16) and possibly shared with Howitt.

The culture of hunting in nineteenth century England carried markers of class, for the stringent British Game Laws meant that only the privileged classes had access to game – edible game was only in the possession of the land-owner.  The lower classes could only engage in the lowly pursuits listed in *The boy's country book,* such as rat-hunting.  Hunting was an elite social activity, and was a sign of 'advanced culture' (Griffiths 1996, p.12) in contrast to the activity carried out by the indigenous inhabitants of the colonies, who hunted out of necessity.  This, too, was a marker of their lower form of civilisation.  Hunting was a sign of masculinity, symbolising the qualities of bravery and skill which males needed, and which made them expert pioneers. In other colonies such as South Africa and India, big game hunting fulfilled the imperial notions of manhood. Australia was a disappointment in offering no fierce predators, but many colonists found compensation for this shortcoming in the fact that there were no restrictive game laws (until about 1860 in Victoria) so that for the first time they could legally enjoy the 'sport of kings'. Herbert's notebook expresses this joy, especially through Prin the inestimable dog who enjoys hunting the 'native cats', 'assuredly because they showed more determined fight' (p.194). Prin is indifferent about bandicoots because they 'are killed without any resistance' (p.194). We see here the intersection of masculine and imperial discourse: the valuing of the activity for reasons which are justified in the name of sport, or science. Herbert's party often shoots an animal or bird to get a better look at it.

Hunting often results in the collection of trophies or souvenirs, such as the skin of the platypus they shoot in the river and judge a 'very queer animal' (p.374). Such a trophy exists in the text as traces of the Authentic Australian Experience, a souvenir of an event that is reportable. In the discourse of Herbert's narrative, the platypus skin is a signifier of Australia as a wild untamed place, and arises from the prior masculine discourses of the hunt and from imperial discourses about the Otherness of the colony. Susan Stewart sees exotic souvenirs such as these as representing 'distance appropriated' (1984, p.147). They stand as signs of the owner's survival outside his familiar context, and as signs of taming and subduing (p.148), which is the proper activity of one who visits the outposts of empire.

Space allows me only one other example of how place is constructed in this Australian text, and that concerns Howitt's representation of the Aborigines. Discourses consist of truth claims which are constructed by the dominant group who holds the power. Herbert reiterates many of the truth claims about Aborigines he has heard from other colonisers. In addition, his report is given added status by recourse to the discourse of science and the words of authority figures, lending his own assessment an enhanced authority such as when he reports, 'Travellers and writers agree in considering the Australian blacks as very low in the scale of humanity' (p.297).

Herbert's opinions are given truth value by some quotations from Leichardt's reports on the Aborigines in the Gulf of Carpentaria. Leichardt's assessment of some two-storied huts he observed caused him to conclude that 'these natives were evidently of a more advanced class, and probably came from New Guinea', thus confirming the commonly held belief expressed above, and showing how Leichardt also found what he was looking for, as Paul Carter suggested. Herbert even mocks the Romantic view of the noble savage by describing an encampment of the 'natives of Victoria' (p.316). He emphasises their lack of material possessions, the lack of civilised habits – 'they eat all their meat half raw' – and the dirt of the European clothes they wear:

> Many of them have blankets, and always of that dingy hue which those of
> gipsies have; others, only shirts or jumpers, black as months or years of
> unwashed wear can make them. Old hag-like women are crawling about,
> supporting themselves on tall sticks, like so many old fortune-tellers or black
> Meg Merrilies. All this is a picture of savage life which would not, I think,
> enchant even a Rousseau! (p.317)

He is ignorant of the fact that these are not Aborigines 'in their savage state' at all,
but a dispossessed people already dependent on the handouts of their dispossessors,
eking out a miserable existence as marginal outcasts of the now dominant white
society, like the gipsies to whom he likens them. This is confirmed by his own
admission:

> We are living here in a land of savages; a few years ago, comparatively
> speaking, it was inhabited only by savages, and yet the English are now so
> completely at home in it that they do not seem to think any more of the native
> blacks than we used to do in England when we saw a wandering party of
> gipsies. (p.297)

A belief in the inevitable demise of the Aborigines because of their lack of
civilisation or advancement is another truth claim Herbert perpetuates:

> The Australian natives have wandered for ages over these vast regions, and
> have left no monuments, or lasting traces of their abode amid them. They
> have been always wandering, but never seem to have advanced, and when
> they are all gone they will leave no memory behind them; they might never
> have been. (p.298)

The persistence of this particular truth claim from the discourse of race is shown in
the echoes of the same sentiment in George Hamilton's book, *Experiences of a
colonist forty years ago*, published in 1880. He wrote, 'Here was a country without
a geography, and a race of men without a history' (p.38, 1974 reprint).

Finally, the utter impossibility of Aborigines either surviving, or attaining a
civilised state is made clear when Herbert calmly tells his readers:

> ...the women show no want of natural affection for their children in general,
> though they do kill and eat them occasionally...their killing their children is
> attributed in a great degree to the impossibility almost of the women dragging
> them and all their household stuff about the country on their continual
> wanderings. (p.313)

Herbert actually knows no Aborigines, is mostly reliant on the reports of others and
is able to see only what imperial discourses allow him to see. He writes with the

authority of the imperial centre on a subject which has already been thoroughly discussed and the ideas effectively disseminated. It is tragically inevitable that his construction of the indigenous people shackle him to a set of fixed beliefs which still emerge in various debates today.

So Herbert's perception of Australia as a place is always filtered through the discourses of the imperialist. Australia is forever Other, until such time as the last Aborigines die and it can be remade into the likeness of England. For William Howitt, the ideological struggle between England as a place and Australia as a place has been a no-contest. Australia only exists as a place in order to confirm its need for the civilising influence of the imperial centre.

# References

Carter, P. (1987). *The road to Botany Bay: An essay in spatial history.* London: Faber.

Foucault, M. (1981). The order of discourse. In *Untying the text: A poststructuralist reader,* ed. R. Young. London: Routledge Kegan Paul.

Griffiths, T. (1996). *Hunters and collectors: The antiquarian imagination.* Cambridge: Cambridge University Press.

Hamilton, G. (1974 [1880]). *Experiences of a colonist forty years ago.* Adelaide: Libraries Board of South Australia.

Mills, S. (1997). *Discourse.* London: Routledge.

Morris, P. (1993). *Literature and feminism.* Oxford: Blackwell.

Stewart, S. (1984). *On longing: Narratives of the miniature, the gigantic, the souvenir, the collection.* Baltimore: Johns Hopkins University Press.

# 4. Postcolonialism and language use in Australian children's literature: A case study of *The children of Mirrabooka*

**Monica Jarman**

**Abstract:** *The children of Mirrabooka* (Arthy 1997) is significant in Australian children's literature because it is the first non-Aboriginal authored novel to include positive and explicit reference to Aboriginal land rights. In fact, *The children of Mirrabooka* seems to promise the narrativisation of indigenous land rights. This promise, and its betrayal, will be critically examined in this paper. Moreover, strategies with which to examine the presentation of Aborigines and Aboriginality will be introduced to facilitate this critical examination.

Firstly, postcolonialism will be presented as a framework within which to read *The children of Mirrabooka*. A postcolonial framework facilitates study of the negotiation of the centre-over-periphery hierarchy in colonial and postcolonial era texts. Its use will enable examination of the relationships between Aborigines and non-Aborigines as they are portrayed in the text.

The encoding of Aboriginal and non-Aboriginal relationships in the language of *The children of Mirrabooka* will be examined through exemplary extracts from the text. However, in order to unpack the linguistic encoding of relationships recognisable to a postcolonial framework, the framework needs to be augmented by a systematic approach to the description of language. Select elements of systemic functional linguistics will be utilised to describe the relationships between Aborigines and non-Aborigines in the extracts from *The children of Mirrabooka*.

A closer reading of the language of *The children of Mirrabooka*, within a postcolonial framework, will enable problematisation of the uneasy relationship between Aborigines, non-Aborigines and land in this novel.

The critical reading approaches outlined in this paper are applicable to both colonial and postcolonial era texts. It is to be hoped that this paper encourages the critical and closer reading of the presentation of Aborigines and Aboriginality, Aboriginal relationships with land, and Aboriginal and non-Aboriginal relationships in colonial and postcolonial era Australian children's literature.

*The children of Mirrabooka*, written by Judith Arthy and published early 1997, is significant in Australian children's literature because it is the first non-Aboriginal authored novel to include positive, explicit and extended reference to Aboriginal land rights. In fact, *The children of Mirrabooka* seems to promise the narrativisation of land rights. This promise and its subsequent betrayal are the focus of my examination. Arguably, *The children of Mirrabooka* is exemplary of a specific trend in contemporary Australian children's literature. In this paper I want to explore strategies with which to examine the encoding of the promise and denial of Aboriginal land rights in *The children of Mirrabooka* by focusing upon the presentation of Aborigines and Aboriginality in the text.

There is one constant in Australian children's literature attendant upon the appearance in fiction of Aborigines and Aboriginality: that is a preoccupation with the proprieties of European land acquisition and ownership. *The children of Mirrabooka* shares this preoccupation. The earliest Australian children's literature often excludes any explicit mention of indigenous people in relation to land and land ownership, according to the narrative of *terra nullius.*[1] However, towards the close of the nineteenth century a definite theme of anxiety is discernible. References to invasion, war, Aboriginal resistance, military-style operations and the minimal rights of indigenous subjects under British law are present in children's literature of the last two decades of the nineteenth century.[2] Nevertheless, these novels conclude uniformly with the triumph of the non-indigenous/European land appropriator. The potential for the continued prosperity of the appropriator, usually agricultural, is guaranteed by the close of the novel. The removal, the 'dispersal' of the local Aboriginal population is integral to the security of this conclusion.

I have just briefly outlined the typical narrativisation of the land relationship between the indigenous and non-indigenous in the children's literature of the nineteenth century. It is a narrative that one would *not* predict the appearance of in a late twentieth century novel, published in a context energised by the general currency and critique of the narrative of *terra nullius* and the conciliatory gestures and actions complementary to that critique. Through the course of this paper I would like to problematise *The children of Mirrabooka* and in particular the presentation of Aborigines and Aboriginality in relation to land, utilising select extracts and strategic ways of reading text.

The first strategic way of reading *The children of Mirrabooka* I would like to explore is postcolonialism. Postcolonialism has meanings and theoretical applications that are diverse and distinct across disciplines.[3] In general terms it is a response to the disintegration, predominantly through the second half of the twentieth century, of the major colonial empires. And this is the first of two usages of postcolonialism that are most relevant to this discussion. Postcolonialism denotes a chronology that distinguishes between two periods in modern history: the colonial era and the postcolonial era, which provides the context to this paper, *The children of Mirrabooka* and contemporary society.

The second feature of postcolonialism concerns its theoretical application to literary study. This application is once again extraordinarily diverse according to the context and the purpose of the study.[4] For my purposes, postcolonialism is a framework for examining literature that responds to relationships before, during and after the collapse of empire. Literature that responds to this collapse generally explores, examines, and critiques the relationship between the indigenous-colonised and the non-indigenous-coloniser. The postcolonial framework enables examination of the fictive presentation of the relationship between the colonised periphery and the colonising centre. For example, I have previously described nineteenth century, that is, colonial era, Australian children's literature as typically encoding the narrative of *terra nullius*. In this narrative, I can identify an imbalance in the relationship between the indigenous periphery and the non-indigenous centre: that is, a hierarchical relationship is established with the centre situated as being powerful over the periphery. In postcolonial era literature, one could predict the typicality of this hierarchical relationship to be negotiated and revised, if not thoroughly critiqued.

For example, the colonial relationship between the indigenous-colonised and the non-indigenous-colonisers in land is explored in the postcolonial era novel *The children of Mirrabooka* through a reference unusual in contemporary Australian children's literature.

> Something had occurred to me, something I saw in a new light, now that I was in the middle of this countryside. 'Dad', I began, 'you know how you said the government gave all this land to the settlers?'
>
> 'Ye-es,' Dad admitted in a tone that implied he knew what was coming next.
>
> 'Well, how could they do that? I mean how come they could just give it away or sell it or whatever?'
>
> 'It was all Crown land. That's what it was called – "Crown land" – it belonged to the Queen of England.'
>
> 'You mean they took it.'
>
> 'Took it?'
>
> 'From the Aborigines.'
>
> He looked mildly uncomfortable, which surprised me. 'Well, I suppose you could say that,' he conceded at last. 'But the Aborigines didn't own it, not the way we own things. I mean they didn't have fences or crops or real houses or anything. They wandered about hunting. The white settlers needed the land to farm and raise animals to feed people. That's what our civilisation is about.'

'My teacher said they did own it, and they had their own special tribal lands. They only looked as if they "wandered about."' Dad was looking really uncomfortable by now, as though he'd rather not be having this discussion. 'It's not as simple as all that,' he said firmly. 'I know you kids get taught all sorts of new things these days, and there's all this push for land rights going on. But these things happened a long time ago. That's the way things were then. We can't keep going back into the past'. (Arthy 1997, pp.28-29)

In the extent of my reading, the content of this quotation is unprecedented in non-Aboriginal Australian children's literature for its inclusion of a discussion of land rights and the endorsement of land rights through the narrative voice. This extract represents a fictional contribution to current Australian revisionist histories of the colonial treatment of Australia's indigenous people, especially with regard to the expropriation of land. Nevertheless, as I stated earlier, ultimately the novel betrays this acknowledgment, or what I have called the promise of land rights. A closer examination of a second extract from the novel will clarify the encoding of this betrayal.

This betrayal is, I think, symptomatic of the assumption that the novel depicts relationships distinct from those of the colonial era because produced in a postcolonial context, in the postcolonial era. The postcolonial chronology, which seemingly distinguishes and categorises on the basis of publication date alone, does not encourage recognition of, or critique of, or resistance to, colonial era fictive presentations of Aborigines and Aboriginality in postcolonial era texts. The postcolonial chronology encourages the assumption of a uniform improvement over time in the fictive presentation of Aborigines and Aboriginality.[5] The next extract, and the strategic way in which I will read it, will enable critique of the postcolonial chronology, through an examination of the choices in language.

Language is, obviously, a further concern of literary postcolonialism. Historically, colonisers invested heavily in control of the production, distribution and consumption of oral and written language as a carrier of culture, and as a means of establishing and consolidating the centre-over-periphery hierarchy. Indigenous cultural dislocation, dispossession and alienation was effected by the colonialists' homogenisation and standardisation of language at the centre and the periphery during the colonial period (Kachru 1995; Schmidt 1990). Simultaneously the suppression of indigenous languages was effected.

The focus of contemporary postcolonialist studies of literature and language has been upon choices about language, resulting from the impact of colonisation upon language use, survival and transformation. Choices about language are generally discussed with regard to the indigenous author's decision about her/his indigenous and colonial inheritances. For example, a common question asked of and by the indigenous postcolonial writer is: which language? That is, which language is being emphasised as the one of identification. The resultant choices may be regarded as a statement of subversion, or of complicity, with either the centre or the indigenous, the periphery. An exemplary and problematic product of this debate would be *Alitji in Dreamland* a Pitjantjatjara version of *Alice's adventures in Wonderland* (Shepherd 1992).

Choices about language and in language are not restricted to indigenous writers. Non-indigenous writers also make choices concerning language and language practices within a postcolonial context. For example, stereotypical presentations of Aborigines as noble savages, cannibal heathens or as faithful retainers in the model of Man Friday are no longer acceptable or possible in literature. However, reading colonial era texts within a postcolonial context I would expect certain choices in language, certain linguistic patterns, to be present in the text; choices that would reflect the colonial hierarchy.[6] Similarly, I would predict choices in language in postcolonial texts to represent a changed and changing relationship between the colonised-indigenous and the colonising-non-indigenous.

Before examining another extract from the novel, I would like to elaborate on its co-text. *The children of Mirrabooka* is narrated in the first person by twelve year old Jenny Blair, who is set to inherit her great aunt's substantial cattle property upon that aunt's imminent death. The possible sale of the property to an eco-tourism consortium triggers Jenny's apprehension of the past. She travels back in time, on only one occasion, to witness the rounding-up, murder, imprisonment and forced removal of the Aboriginal people local to her family's property. Later in the narrative we are informed that there are absolutely no Aboriginal survivors from the round-up.

The narrator travels from the postcolonial era to the colonial era and back again. The time traveller, Jenny, is a privileged focaliser, witnessing past events, and acquiring information previously disregarded as unimportant, information that is not available to all characters in the narrative, but available only to the main focaliser, Jenny, and the reader. A reader could expect time travel in *The children of Mirrabooka* to enable a contrast between the colonial past and the postcolonial present. This contrast would then enable the narrative, the narrative voice, and the model reader, to not only revise fictionalised past events, but also to revise fictionalised present events with the additional information provided by the revelatory function of the backward time travel.

The extract prepares the climax to the novel, and the climax to Jenny's time travelling sequence. She and the model reader are witness to the rounding up of the local Aboriginal people in 1905, before their removal to a mission. The removal of Aborigines enabled further land expropriation.

Then the riders set fire to the dismantled gunyahs and soon the whole camp was alight.   I saw an old man standing alone amidst this destruction, his waddy raised in his hand.  One of the horsemen rode at him, knocking him to the ground.  The rider then leapt off his horse, and bound the man's arms and chest with a thick rope, tethering him to a tree.

More Aboriginal men came running into the camp in response to the women's cries.  The horsemen raised their carbines and fired above their heads.  The display was enough to cow the tribe and soon they were taken prisoner and bound by fetters, each to the others in a long line.  Some of the women had returned, and they, too, were bound by the wrists and linked together in a human chain. (Arthy 1997, p.127)

Of course, there is an obvious relationship between the riders and the Aborigines, which reflects the centre-over-periphery hierarchy which was firmly in place in 1905 in Queensland where the novel is set.   However, how is this relationship realised by the choices *in* the language of the text?   One way of answering this question is to consider what the participants do, and more particularly what they do to each other in order to effect a relationship that replicates the colonised-coloniser hierarchy.  Obviously the language has to reflect the domination of the settlers over the Aborigines.

Look at what the riders and horsemen, the settlers, do *to* the Aborigines:

| Agent | Process | Medium |
|-------|---------|--------|
| the riders | set fire | to the gunyahs |
| | Stood | an old [Aboriginal] man |
| the horseman | rode at | him |
| [the horseman] | knock[ed] | him to the ground |
| [the rider] | Bound | the man's arms |
| [the rider] | tether[ed] | him to a tree |
| | came running | Aboriginal men |
| The display | [cowed] | the tribe |
| | had returned | the [Aboriginal]women |
| | were bound | they [Aboriginal women] |
| | were linked | [Aboriginal women] |

From the table the following pattern emerges:

The rider set fire to the dismantled gunyahs [and the camp]
the horseman rode at him [the old man with the waddy]
[the horseman] knock[ed] him [the old man with the waddy] to the ground
[the rider] bound the man's arms and chest
[the rider] tether[ed] him to a tree
The display cowed the tribe

In each case the settlers, the horsemen and riders, and their display, produce an effect upon the Aborigines or their property. The Aborigines are ridden at, knocked, bound, tethered, and cowed by the settlers, and their gunyahs are set fire to by the settlers. Here is a linguistic pattern that realises a relationship that reinforces the hierarchy of the colonial over the indigenous which was dominant during the colonial period. This linguistic pattern has been identified by others as common to imperial adventure stories (Knowles and Malmkjær 1996).

And what do the Aborigines do? Do their actions, standing, running, and returning produce an effect upon the settlers?

> the old man stood
> Aboriginal men came running
> the women returned
> they [Aboriginal women] were bound
> [Aboriginal women] were linked together

Although active, visibly engaged in activity, the Aborigines are ineffective. And this linguistic pattern contrasts strongly with the affectivity of the settlers. The settlers' complete domination of effective activity in the passage is realised in the language choices *in* the text.

Presumably this relationship of settler impact upon Aborigine is encoded in this postcolonial text deliberately. Remember, our narrator has travelled back in time to witness this traumatic colonial event to gain important information that explains present postcolonial circumstances. Part of that information requires her to know not just that Aborigines were rounded-up by the settlers, but, also that they were rounded-up in a thorough manner. The text borrows the language of colonial children's literature in order to convey the colonial period.

However, why is this elaborate plot, these linguistic patterns, and the temporal displacement of the primary focaliser, necessary? In other words, what is the function of the time travel and how do these two extracts relate?

The first extract initiates a certain discourse of land rights, and the second extract facilitates the diffusion of the possibility of land rights. By travelling back in time with the narrator, the model reader is also able to witness the complete destruction of the Aboriginal people local to Jenny's inheritance. The presentation of this destruction is reinforced by the linguistic features of the text, as outlined above. Remembering Jenny's initial inclination towards the legitimacy of Aboriginal land rights, one could expect her experience of the round-up to at least provoke a reappraisal of the fragmentation of Aboriginal peoples and their culture. However, this is not forthcoming.

Aborigines and the potential for land rights claims are removed from the present of the text, and, most importantly, from Jenny's property. Any responsibility for the lack of the bestowal of land rights is removed from the present to the past. This appears to reinforce an ethical distinction between the colonial and the postcolonial – where 'we' would, if we could, grant Aboriginal land rights, 'they', the colonial, would not, even though they had the means and opportunity. The elision of contemporary Aborigines and Aboriginality diffuses the land rights issue, and the need to actively confirm land rights, safely within the terms of the novel. Here is a final statement on the matter from the novel:

> ...the families of all the white people who had come into the area were still here, and pleased to be descendants of pioneers. Like me. And the worst thing was that the damage could not be undone. The tribe was gone forever.
> (Arthy 1997 p.141)

Consequently, the colonial conclusion is secured. The potential for continued agricultural prosperity is guaranteed by the close of *The children of Mirrabooka* due to the elision of contemporary Aborigines and Aboriginality. This elision is usual in colonial era literature. Unfortunately, *The children of Mirrabooka*, is a more direct example of a general tendency in other postcolonial era Australian children's literature to elide contemporary Aborigines and their culture.[7]

The critical reading of the presentation of Aborigines and Aboriginality in Australian children's literature has been the intention of this paper. The first strategic way of reading text, postcolonialism, although flawed, does focus attention upon relationships of power between the indigenous and non-indigenous. Nevertheless, the use of a strict chronological categorisation of distinct colonial and postcolonial periods has facilitated the assumption of a uniform improvement over time in the fictive presentation of Aborigines and Aboriginality. Not only is this chronological approach overly descriptive, and in the scholarship of Australian children's literature redundant, such an approach does not enable critique of the fictive presentation of the colonised-coloniser relationship in postcolonial era texts. More significantly, a descriptive chronological approach does not allow the problematising of the colonial-postcolonial succession; but instead creates a new hierarchy, privileging the postcolonial product over the colonial, and favouring a feeling of complacency about the real position of contemporary Aborigines and Aboriginality.

The assumptions of postcolonialism in the reading of both colonial era and postcolonial era texts, may be checked by a suggestion contained within postcolonial literary studies. That is, attention to the choices in language realised by the text. For this, a theory of language is required, and in recent children's literary criticism, systemic functional linguistics has been suggested as appropriate (Knowles and Malmkjær 1996; Williams 1988). Certain aspects of systemic functional linguistics concentrate, as I did in the analysis of the linguistic patterns of the second extract, upon who is doing what to whom, when, where, why and how. A systemic analysis of the linguistic patterns in text, and their function, ensures that contradictory ideologies within the one text are not overlooked.

## Endnotes

1.  *Terra nullius* (empty land) is a key narrative of the colonial era. In this narrative the colonised indigene is completely elided from European conceptions of spatio-temporal dimensions, narrative, history, culture and society.

2.  Examples include, Fenn 1892; Ferres 1896; Rowe 1880; Sargeant 1865 and Timperley [1892] 1908.

3.  *The post-colonial studies reader,* eds Ashcroft et al. 1995, spans a variety of approaches and disciplines in the theory and practice of postcolonial study.

4.  An introductory volume of postcolonialist approaches to literature is best served by Ashcroft et al. 1989.

5.  The most recent example of this assumption is evident in Bradford 1997.

6.  In their study of an exemplary work by G. A. Henty, *For name and fame* (1886) Knowles and Malmkjær (1996, p.107) have identified elements of this pattern.

7.  Recent examples include Maddocks 1996; Marsden 1998; Masson 1996 and Wrightson 1994.

## Bibliography

Arthy, J. (1997). *The children of Mirrabooka.* Ringwood, Vic.: Penguin.

Ashcroft, B., Griffiths, G. and Tiffin, H. (1989). *The empire writes back: Theory and practice in post-colonial literatures.* London: Routledge.

Ashcroft, B., Griffiths G, & Tiffin, H. (1995). *The post-colonial studies reader.* London: Routledge.

Bradford, C. (1996). Centre and edges: Postcolonial literary theory and Australian picture books. In *Writing the Australian child: Texts and contexts in fictions for children,* ed. C. Bradford. Nedlands, WA: University of Western Australia Press, pp.92-110.

Bradford, C. (1997). Representing indigeneity: Aborigines and Australian children's literature then and now. *Ariel: A Review of International English Literature*, **28**, 1, 89-99.

Fenn, G. M. (1892). *The dingo boys; or, The squatters of Wallaby Range*, illus. W.S. Stacey. London: W. & R. Chambers.

Ferres, A. (1896). *His first kangaroo*, illus. P.F. Spence. London: Blackie & Son.

Jarman, M. (1998). A 'Luminous fantasy still glowing?' Relations between postcolonialism and language use in Patricia Wrightson's *Shadows of time*. M. Phil. Sydney University: Sydney.

Kachru, B. B. (1995). The alchemy of English. In *The post-colonial studies reader*, eds B. Ashcroft, G. Griffiths and H. Tiffin. London: Routledge, pp.291-95.

Knowles, M. and Malmkjær, K. (1996). *Language and control in children's literature*. London: Routledge.

Maddocks, J. (1996). *Streetwise*. St Lucia, Qld: Queensland University Press.

Marsden, J. (1998). *The rabbits,* illus. S. Tan. Port Melbourne: Lothian.

Masson, S. (1996). *The sun is rising.* St Lucia, Qld.: Queensland University Press.

Mudrooroo and Trees, K. (1993). Postcolonialism: Yet another colonial strategy? *Span,* **36**, 1, 242-264.

Rowe, R. (1880). *Roughing it in Van Dieman's Land.* London: Strahan & Co.

Sargeant, G. E. (1865). *Frank Layton: or, An Australian story.* London: Leisure House Office.

Schmidt, A. (1990). *The loss of Australia's Aboriginal heritage.* Canberra: Aboriginal Studies Press.

Sheppard, N. (1992). *Alitji in Dreamland; Alitjinya Ngura Tjukurmankuntjala: An Aboriginal version of Lewis Carroll's 'Alice's adventures in Wonderland'*, illus. D. Leslie, trans. N. Sheppard. East Roseville, NSW: Simon & Schuster.

Timperley, W. H. (1908). *Bush luck: An Australian story, 1892.* London: Religious Tract Society.

Williams, G. (1988). Naive and serious questions: The role of text criticism in primary education. In *Language and literacy in the primary school*, eds M. Meek and C. Mills. London: Falmer Press, pp.151-167.

Wrightson, P. (1994). *Shadows of time.* Sydney: Random.

# Part III

# Representing the visual

# 5. Constructing neonarratives: An approach to research of artistic practice

## Kerry Mallan

**Abstract:** Inquiries into the nature of artistic practice, and, in particular, into the lives of artists have long intrigued researchers. Since the 1980s, the range of publications focusing on Australian and New Zealand illustrators of children's books has extended from those aimed at school students and teachers to the more critical commentaries written for professional and academic readers. Consequently, the quest to discover the many layers of artistic and personal behaviour, in all its cognitive and creative forms, has resulted in an array of understandings, portrayals and stereotypes.

This paper provides an approach to the research of artistic practice by using a neonarrative model. The focus of the paper will be a description of the model and its application to my research into five Australian illustrators of children's picture books. Broadly this will include a discussion of the research process, approaches to data analysis, and the implications of this model for further research.

My argument is that the neonarrative model provides researchers with a means for theorising artistic practice and developing an understanding of the phenomenon of human experience. In this sense, it has the potential to incorporate an understanding of the complex relationships of the meaning and process of artistic practice and its embeddedness in cultural influences, personal experience and desire.

## Introduction

There is a long tradition of research into artistic practice. Such inquiries have attracted the attention of psychologists, art historians, art critics, and biographers. Research into the artistic practices of children's book illustrators has drawn from a similar range of disciplines including education. Whilst the purposes for investigations into artists and their art vary, the method by which research is undertaken tends to be centred around the interview. The interview provides a context for an exchange of narratives. Narratives told by the artist are ways of passing on knowledge: knowledge about the artist and about his/her art. This knowledge is rarely questioned nor does it need to prove itself to be true. As Alexander suggests, 'It is so because it is so. It has been thus decreed by the narrative' (Alexander 1992, p.77). This form of narrative knowledge is considered to be just as valid as scientific knowledge. According to Bruner, both narrative and scientific knowledge are 'distinctive ways of ordering experience' but the two are ultimately 'irreducible to one another' (Bruner 1986, p.11). The researcher then provides another narrative account when writing up the interview. These new narratives (neonarratives) may be either antagonistic or agreeable to the original narratives. Whilst the interview process has its own set of problems, it is the textual practice of writing up the research and the complex issue of representation that form the basis of this paper.

It was in considering the form by which research is conducted and written that the neonarrative approach seemed to offer an interesting possibility. On closer inspection, however, this approach may run the risk of becoming another Enlightenment project if the emphasis on the individual and his/her achievements is highlighted without reference to the ways culture shapes and positions both the artist and the art. According to Stewart, 'the Neonarrative approach is guided by narratology, the study of narrative, as a qualitative method which offers an interpretive reconstruction of an aspect of a person's life' (Stewart 1996, p.40). It is this issue of the individual-self and its modernist associations of unity and authenticity, themes challenged by poststructuralists, which needs to be addressed. By taking into account poststructuralist considerations, the purpose of any methodology can be seen as not to uncover an underlying truth, but to seek alternative 'truths'. It is also necessary that assumptions about the nature of knowledge are questioned and unsettled, and that notions of identity and representation are problematised.

Research into artistic practice celebrates the individual as the origin of the work. Poststructuralism denies origin and argues that the meaning of any text cannot be 'authoritatively' revealed through reference to the source of its production. Poststructuralism also considers the human self as multiple and fragmented. Therefore, in investigating 'the artist-self', there is a merging and intersecting of other selves with the artist-self at various points. It is by accepting that the self is not unitary and stable, but multiple and shifting, that the complexity of the artist-subject can be realised (Cahoone 1996). The potential of neonarratives lies in the notion that there can never be a complete account of the individual as each new context brings different ways of being. Consequently, each new story, or re-storying of experience, may provide the reader with opportunities to view the subject from changing and different perspectives.

These issues, and others, will be explored more fully in the course of the paper. As a starting point, the discussion considers research into artistry before focussing on the neonarrative method as a both a process and product of inquiry into picture book artists and their art.

# Inquiry into artistry

Perhaps in keeping with Barthes' (1977) proclamation of the 'death of the author', or in this case the death of the artist, there has not been the same *critical* interest in looking at the artist as the creator of the picture book as there has been into the nature of the text itself. There remains, however, a *curiosity* about picture book illustrators. This curiosity has been aroused and sated to a large degree by publishers, booksellers, academics, teachers and conference organisers. Picture book illustrators have been the subject of several books, articles and conference papers (see Nodelman 1988; Graham 1990; Children's Book Council of Australia 1992, 1994, 1996; Alderman and Clayton 1994). Illustrators, along with writers of children's books, often are asked to speak and write about their works. This apparent need to hear and see the artist 'in person' (as evidenced by conferences, book signings, media interviews, school visits, artists' residencies) is explained by Derrida (1976) as a perception in Western thought that speech has privileged access to meaning and 'truth' over the written word (or the image) because of the presence of the speaker.

For many readers it may still appear that the text itself is not enough and that the 'true meaning' of a text can be authoritatively revealed through reference to the author's/illustrator's intentions. Whilst poststructuralists argue that authorial/artistic intentions are no more relevant to understanding the text than any other considerations, many teachers and students may indeed feel that the accessibility of writers and illustrators in person or in written or media commentary, will provide them with the answers to their questions regarding purpose, form, and meaning. Such thinking persists, despite critical theories about the ways texts (written and visual) are produced and received. The lingering vestiges of a structuralist tradition are evident in the ways art education is approached in schools (see Rizvi 1994). Such a tradition continues to pursue the goal of determining how meaning is produced by investigating artistic practice within a set of hierarchical oppositions – nature/culture; innate/learned; form/content; literal/metaphorical – without deconstructing these by attending to the discourses which shape them.

There is another aspect of inquiry into artistry that needs to be mentioned: the expert-novice relationship. As Hawke comments, 'The recognition of practising artists as exemplars has always underpinned the conduct of professional art education in tertiary education' (Hawke 1996, p.32). Similarly, teachers have used the work of picture book artists as a means for teaching students in both primary and secondary schools about various artistic styles, media and techniques and for encouraging their students' imitation of these. This model of learning based on the practice of artists harks back to the romantic tradition and has been influential in shaping the expressivist approach to art education which focuses on developing students' innate aesthetic capabilities (Hawke 1996; Rizvi 1994). There is perhaps more interest in and financial support than ever before for artist-in-residence programs at both the school and tertiary levels. Whilst there is evidence to suggest that some artists feel that their 'professional expertise was exploited' by schools which conducted residencies (Mason 1995, p.23), Hawke suggests that, at least in university settings, there is a growing need in art courses to address the theorising about art and to understand the phenomena of human experiences. The nature of research into artistry then is increasingly addressing personal artistic practice.

Research into personal practice has become a significant feature of educational research. The teacher as reflexive practitioner has become both the subject and object of research (see Connelly and Clandinin 1990). Similarly, research of personal artistic practice has also become an important field of inquiry whereby the artist undertakes reflective inquiry into his/her own artistic endeavours, and the student of art is provided with access to the world of the artist. Research into picture book illustrators has been, on the whole, less rigorous and often results in satisfying a reader's curiosity about the artist by providing biographical sketches and personal anecdotes (see Hamilton 1993; *Authors and illustrators scrapbook* 1991).

## De/constructing neonarratives: Process and product

Alexander (1992) considers 'neonarratives' in the context of policy formation and contends that the discussion documents circulated throughout bureaucratic organisations are 'stories without endings' and that 'the endings come from neonarratives' (Alexander 1992, p.71). He provides an example of how he sees neonarratives emerging:

> A narrative is started with a focus on a particular policy matter. Practitioners and other interested people interpret the narrative in what are often idiosyncratic and disparate ways in an attempt to provide meaning necessary for practice to begin. The result is that many meanings will emerge, thereby challenging the original meaning signalled by the initiators within the bureaucracy. An interactive process among the secondary meaning-makers will ensue until common meaning is established...subjecting a narrative to the processes of change often culminates in a neonarrative.
>
> (Alexander 1992, p.78)

Stewart (1996) who cites Alexander, adopted neonarratives in her research into artists and art educators. Whereas Alexander saw neonarratives as the eventual outcome of collaborative restorying of the original narrative, Stewart developed neonarrative as both a method and product of inquiry into artistic practice: 'It was designed to describe and explore the major themes or tensions in their [artists' and art educators'] visuality and the transmission of that visuality to others' (Stewart

1996, p.39). 'Visuality' is a term used by Stewart to refer to 'the cultural framing of visual perception' (Stewart 1995, p.37). To this purpose, Stewart considered the effect of the social and political environment on artistic practice and production.

Stewart considers the neonarrative approach as comprising 'a pluralistic amalgam of views which are appropriate within postmodern theoretical constructs' (Stewart 1996, p.39). Whilst she is aware of the need to bring 'pluralistic approaches to cultural analyses' (p.39) Stewart reverts to a Modernist position by claiming that the formation of neonarratives 'give *cohesion* to the otherwise disparate narratives' offered by the subjects (p.39, emphasis added). Furthermore, she naively claims that neonarrative method is 'a process for analyzing what *actually happened* according to the people involved' (p.39, emphasis added). This slippage between modernist and postmodernist stances is symptomatic of the nature of any investigation into artistic practice. The meaning of an illustration or painting is not what the artist had in mind at some point during its composition, or what the artist thinks the work means after it is completed, but rather what he/she succeeded in embodying in the work (Culler 1997). Artists' statements about their art, however, may prove to be valuable additional texts which can be read in relation to their work and may provide points of contradiction, extension, and subversion.

Stewart suggests that the neonarrative method is guided by narratology which 'offers an interpretive reconstruction of an aspect of a person's life' (Stewart 1996, p.40). According to Stewart, this reconstruction is possible if a 'plurality of approaches' (p.40) such as narratology, autobiography and interview, are employed. Narratology is the study of narratives according to their structure or elements. Narratologists examine story and describe its 'grammar' in terms of universal conventions, rules, structures, categories and themes. In drawing on narratology, Stewart analyses the themes which emerge across the different narrative accounts offered by the artists.

Stewart's regard for historical contextualisation through a subject's reflection on the past is not at odds with poststructuralism (though history is often absent from many poststructuralist perspectives and vice versa). This reflection on the past enables the subject to consider the discursive 'cycle of intentions and effects' (Hall 1986) on his/her decisions and actions over time. However, Stewart does not consider the constructedness of perception nor the unreliability of memory in dealing with biography. For her, the autobiographical process provides a means for the artist to '*uncover* reflexively their personal and cultural influences concerning general relationships with family, nature, educational and social conditions, and material things' (Stewart 1996, p.40, emphasis added). Such 'uncovering' suggests a true essence which lies buried beneath the layers of memory.

The interview is seen as a process for explaining 'why people act the way they do' (p.40). The implicit message of a rational, stable identity tends to override any suggestion that the subject has multiple subjectivities which are achieved through discursive practices and social relations with others (Davies 1993). Furthermore, Stewart misguidedly describes the interview process as 'a straightforward method of trying to discover what people think' (p.41). Such a view is a legacy of the positivist approach and not consistent with a postpositive/poststructuralist perspective which alerts one to the slipperiness and instability of the interview. As Scheurich suggests:

> What a question or answer means to the researcher can easily mean something different to the interviewee. What a question or answer means to the researcher may change over time or situations. What a question or answer means to the interviewee similarly may change. What occurs in a specific interview is contingent on the specifics of individuals, place, and time. (Scheurich 1995, p.24)

Stewart identifies five phases in the neonarrative research process: 'the identification of the research method; the establishment of the collaborative process; the conduct, transcription and review of interviews; the follow up procedures; and the analysis of data and synthesis into neonarratives' (Stewart 1996, p.45). This process is not dissimilar to other qualitative approaches, however, it is in the final phase that the neonarratives evolve through a process of re-storying based on emerging themes from both the literature review and the subjects' interview data. The subjects are provided with the opportunity to review the neonarratives of their experiences and a final edit is undertaken to accommodate their concerns. Figure 1 provides an overview of the research process:

Stewart is aware of her authorial hand in this process and she cautions other researchers that they:

> ...should be mindful of the characteristic personal genre which each participant presents as they collaborate in the research process. The process attempts to create, in their narratives, a style which complements their individual personalities. (Stewart 1996, p.46)

Nevertheless, Stewart's coining of 'characteristic personal genre' and 'individual personalities' evokes a humanistic subject.

Whilst the description of the re-storying phase has not been given full attention in this paper, it is sufficient to provide a sense of the research process which is in itself open to further elaboration and modification by different researchers. What needs to be given further consideration, however, are the issues which have emerged from this preliminary deconstruction of the method. The following section signals some

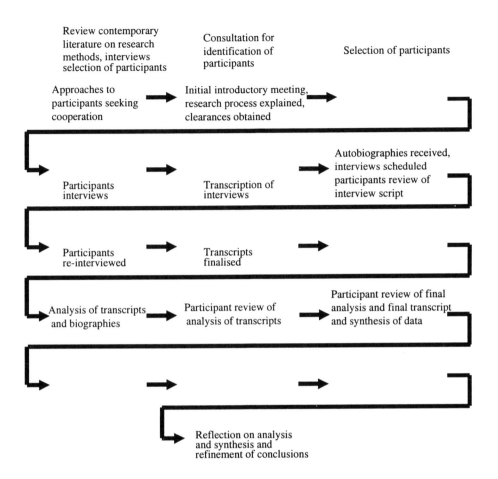

**Figure 1:** Overview of the research process (Stewart 1996, p.45).

of the worrying points of this method while at the same time considering its potential strengths.

## Narrative, identity and representation

As the neonarrative approach draws heavily on narratology for its theoretical basis and on personal history (story) for its method of investigation, it is within the wider field of (auto)biography that the subject is able to situate and contextualise experience within an historical framework. Whilst McCooey (1996, p.5) argues that it is these very issues of 'historicity, reference and individuality' which are intertwined in people's everyday experiences, it is also the reliance on memory and the act of narrating which give rise to the claims that there is no distinction between autobiography and fiction. This view of the fictional status of autobiography is made by critics such as Elbaz (1988) who claims that in writing one's memories of personal experiences, one is imaginatively reconstructing the past as a means of reordering the truth. It is because of idealistic and romantic notions of '*the* truth' and '*the* stable self' that the criticisms surrounding the autobiography/fiction debate are hinged. Bruner reiterates Derrida's (1976) position on the complexity of representation by claiming that autobiography does not provide a transparent window to the 'real world' of the subject nor does it offer an essentialist form of history, but rather points to the constructedness of subjectivity and personal accounts of life experiences:

> Perceiving and remembering are themselves constructions and reconstructions. What is 'laid down' in memory is not some aboriginal encounter with the 'real world', but is already highly schematized. There is no mental reference shelf of our aboriginal 'real world' encounters, any more than there is an aboriginal real world 'out there' made available to us by means of them. (Bruner 1993, p.40)

There appear to be two main thrusts involved in the argument of autobiography's fictional status. One is concerned with the way knowledge is represented and the other is concerned with form. On the former, there is perhaps a misconception by many that knowledge of an artist's life and intentions will provide the reader/viewer with a privileged point of access to the text. Knowledge in this sense is seen as unmediated. The latter view considers the narrative aspect of autobiography as the feature which arouses suspicion of its fictional status. As McCooey argues, 'rather than assuming that narrative falsifies experience, we should consider whether or not "experience" is inherently narratological' (McCooey 1996, p.10). This view is supported by Bauman (1986, p.5) who proposes that rather than consider narrative as a form which shapes 'the raw flux of reality' (Jameson in Sarup 1989, p.141) an alternative is to consider that events are themselves 'abstractions from narrative'.

Lyotard (1984) claims that, ultimately, all knowledge is narrative knowledge, as all knowledge depends for its 'truth' or legitimacy upon a discourse which is constructed and confirmed through the process of telling. It is through narrative knowledge that we locate ourselves in the storylines of our cultures. It is this point of making knowledge explicit through narrative that is the basis of understanding stories of artistic practice and a means for considering the complex notions of identity and representation.

Hall makes the point that the concept of identity 'isn't founded on the notion of some absolute, integral self and...clearly can't arise from some fully closed narrative of the self' (Hall 1987, p.45). Hall's observation speaks to the danger of Modernist stories which seek to fix identities within their closed, universal storylines. This is particularly pertinent when researching artists from different cultural backgrounds, for as Gunew (1994, p.9) suggests, it is by considering the intersections of poststructuralist and postcolonial theories that there is the opportunity to redefine the 'aesthetic legacy of the master narratives of Modernisms' by listening to the voices from the margins (themselves of course are not authentic or authoritative). Neonarratives need then, to be carefully considered so that in restorying the stories of the subjects the researcher does not fall into the old trap of speaking on behalf of others. Such ventriloquism is one of the key sticking points of this methodology which needs to be carefully considered and deconstructed. It is the politics of representation which have plagued and continue to plague the writings about and by marginalised groups. The accusatory finger can easily be pointed at the researcher (or editor) who needs to be mindful of the dangers of a monological authorial voice which can muffle and distort the stories of the subjects throughout the various stages of the writing process. It is through these very stages of editing, organising, selecting of material that the stories of artists are continually shaped and framed by either the idiosyncratic whims or scrupulous actions of the researcher.

There have been examples of feminist researchers who have explicitly blended the voices of the subject and the researcher in order to provide a polyvocal text (see Brettell, 1997). In addition, this 'blending of voices' is seen by Gmelch (in Brettell 1997, p.225) as as being able 'to portray the collaborative and interactional nature' of the research and to reveal the researcher's relationship with the subject. Whilst the notion of blended voices (a harmony or polyphony?) is enticing there are still the lurking shadows of dominance and power of which the researcher needs to be ever mindful. Claims of authenticity and objectivity, therefore, need to be reconsidered in the light of poststructuralism's abandonment of the idea of objectivity and recognition that all speaking/writing is within a particular social, cultural and political framework. To take seriously a poststructuralist's perspective is to expose the folly of claiming an authentic voice or a true account of the self. It is perhaps more viable to take up Lyotard's call for 'little stories' (*petits recits*) and in this regard the neonarratives of artistic practice have the potential to offer readers stories of difference rather than totalising 'big stories' of sameness which can occur when writing about a particular art movement or genre. In the case of children's book illustrators, it would seem that there needs to be a balanced treatment and space given to illustrators based on gender, race and ethnicity.

The discussion to this point has relied on the written account of the artist's life and experiences. There is an alternative to this form of representation, namely, the self-portraiture. Although there are arguments for and against the comparison of the painted image and autobiography (see McCooey 1996), the two forms can offer insights into the subject. Whilst one is contained by the fleeting moment in time, the other offers a series of selected moments of a lifetime. Allen Say's account of his family's cross-cultural experience (Japan-America) in *Grandfather's journey* (1993) offers an example of how biography and autobiography can be conveyed through portraiture of self and others in a picture book form. Whilst only highlighting selected events, Say nevertheless conveys the dual nature of belonging/not belonging experienced by immigrants living in a different culture.

It is perhaps indicative of the changing form of the genre of autobiography and their refusal to accept the standard form of the dominant culture that indigenous writers and illustrators such as Daisy Utemorrah and Pat Torres (1990) and Ian Abdulla (1994) can provide telling narratives of a life through both illustrations and words. Though not self-portraiture, their illustrations provide glimpses of the subject in relation to family and geographical place.  The attachment between subject and place is presented in both words and illustrations and may offer to the reader a visceral, even spiritual kind of identification between the artist/writer and the physical environment.  It is this entwining of the 'I' and the geographical location which is a feature of many texts, both literary and pictorial, by writers and illustrators who see their identities and sense of belonging as being forever fused with place.  Such fusion is of course at odds with poststructuralism's notion of shifting subjectivities.   Whilst poststructuralism has opened up the space for marginalised groups to be heard, it is the dismissal of identity that has caused a point of divergence between poststructuralism and the project of Aboriginality (Brewster 1995).  Many artists incorporate traditional colours, patterns, motifs, and techniques in order to portray the setting and characters who live there.  Examples can be seen in the picture books created by Dick Roughsey and Percy Trezise who use red, yellow and ochre pigments from the soil along with charcoal in their Dreaming stories centred around the Quinkin country and other parts of northern Australia; Junko Morimoto's illustrations of Japanese legends are executed in the Sumie style; Ed Young uses calligraphy, Chinese panel art, Oriental paper cutting – the art forms of his birth place, China – in his illustrations of Chinese folktales (Saxby 1993).   These examples are not meant to assert that there is an unproblematic equivalence of place and artistic form.  They do, however, highlight the cultural positioning of the artist and the way art is embedded in culture.

There is a danger in offering these pieces of personal background as they may confirm a view that the text alone is not enough and that understanding comes with knowing more about the artist – his/her life, background, and influences. Undoubtedly, such snippets of information provide the reader with a second look at the illustrations: an opportunity to look more closely and to read the illustrations with this information in mind.  Whilst such information does not determine meaning, it may provide additional understanding of the artistry behind the pictures prompting questions about form, cultural influences, and ways of re-presenting self in relation to others and setting.   It may also remind the reader of the interrelatedness of verbal and visual images in a picture book and of how the two media can complement, extend, and displace one another.  Ultimately, both words and images add to the storytelling experience of reading picture books.

# Neonarratives or second-hand stories?

Many societies have, with fervour, taken to storytelling and personal anecdote. This trend is evident in qualitative research methods which rely on storying as a process and product of inquiry, and is also apparent in the media where people willingly tell the most intimate details of their lives to an ever-attentive studio audience and a still wider viewing/listening audience. Even the President of the United States felt compelled to tell-all, or at least a version of his tale of promiscuity, to his country folk and the world, on international television. This topical example has significance when understood in terms of Foucault's comment regarding confession and sexuality. For Foucault (1979) the dissolution of a cultural group's identity depended increasingly upon the ability and willingness of the individual to reflect upon and speak about personal experience. Modern societies were able then to regulate and discipline their peoples by sanctioning the knowledge claims and practices of such groups as teachers, doctors, and judges. It would appear that television and radio talk-show hosts can now be added to the list. The confession, as a form of autobiography, is not a modern invention as its roots lie in the eighteenth century when Rousseau's *Confessions* was published (though an earlier classical model dates back to Augustine's AD 397-9, *Confessions*). Denzin notes that the confession 'reifies the concept of self and turns it into a cultural commodity' (Denzin 1992, pp.8-9). Whilst this paper has not focussed on the confessional mode of neonarrative inquiry, such statements of an artist's honesty in admitting and describing past mistakes (albeit in an artistic sense) often emerge as part of the interview or reflexive process. Each revelation about the narrated self ensures that the public has further invested in the artist-celebrity as a cultural commodity.

Goodson (1995) argues that the life story runs the risk of silencing critical analysis. The power of storytelling to sustain an audience's interest and to reveal the personal is a means by which an audience becomes enraptured by the teller and his/her tale. Often it is the familiarity of the story that makes it hard to resist. As artists tell their tales, and depending on the number of times they have been interviewed or shared their stories before, the emphasis often is placed on 'telling a good story' first and foremost. After all, the way they 'story' their life (artistic) experiences draws inevitably on the storylines and motifs derived from the cultural, historical and political circumstances in which they are situated. It is of little surprise then that members of the literary/artistic community are able to 'dine out' on tales of artists. Researchers who embark on similar projects of finding out about the artists' world also have opportunities, through their publications and conference presentations, for dining out on the tales of their subjects of inquiry. Researchers, like their subjects, also need to ensure that they tell good stories if they are to have their research accepted, read and remembered by the academic community.

It is at this point that the question posed at the beginning of this section needs to be given consideration. Britzman suggests that her ethnographic study of student-teachers comprised '*secondhand stories*...grounded in the worlds and the words of those who live in teacher education' (Britzman 1995, p.233 emphasis added). On reflection, Britzman concedes that these second-hand stories produced a 'humanistic ethnographic subject' whereby even the titles she gave her stories 'promised a unitary narrative, a noncontradictory and essentialised subject, and, of course, a cohesive account' (p.234). This notion of a 'cohesive account' corresponds to Stewart's claim cited earlier regarding neonarratives. However, both Britzman and Stewart acknowledge the influence of poststructuralist theories in understanding the constructedness of meaning and identity. For Britzman, it means that ethnography is 'a regulating fiction...a particular narrative practice that produces textual identities and regimes of truth' (p.236). Stewart concedes that the neonarrative approach 'is interpretive and postmodern in that no certainties are promised, rather the design presumes tentative pluralistic outcomes' (Stewart 1995, p.38). Whilst Britzman's metaphor of second-hand stories suggests narratives which have been told before and are retold perhaps without a freshness of insight, Stewart's neonarratives promise new stories which are 'more representative than those they replace' (Stewart 1995, p.38). Once again, there is the underlying assumption that representation equals truth and that, by logical extension, neonarratives provide a more truthful account of experience than that first offered by the teller (subject).

Research of artistic practice is not a simple matter of revealing the words of wisdom uttered by the artist. Inquiry into artists and artistry began centuries ago while inquiry into picture book artists and their art has received only relatively recent attention. Given the prominence of the picture book in education and publishing circles, it is likely that interest in the genre and its creators will continue to grow. It is important that research is rigorous and shifts from a predominantly humanistic mode of valorising the artist to one which considers both the artist and the text as cultural commodities. Narrative methods provide a valid means of inquiry into human experience and knowledge. The need to story experience is something which people find irresistible. However, as McLaren notes, 'we can't escape narratives...but we can resist and transform them' (McLaren 1995, p.89). In looking to tell new tales, neonarratives perhaps, we need to take seriously McLaren's point of resisting and transforming narratives. How we choose to write (or read) artists' stories of artistic practice depends on our access to different discourses and our preparedness to question how truth becomes legitimated as knowledge. It also requires us to become aware of our own textual identities and strategies, and to be willing to resist a mimetic representation by considering the social and cultural positioning of the narrative, the narrator, and the listener/reader.

# References

Abdulla, I. (1994). *Tucker.* Norwood: Omnibus.

Alderman, B. and Clayton, P. (eds) (1994). *Creative connections: Writing, illustrating and publishing children's books in Australia.* Port Melbourne: Thorpe.

Alexander, D. (1992). Discussion documents as neonarratives. *Journal of Education Policy,* **7**, 1, 71-81.

*Authors and illustrators scrapbook.* (1991). Norwood: Omnibus.

Barthes, R. (1977). *Image, music, text.* London: Fontana.

Bauman, R. (1986). *Story, performance, and event.* Cambridge: Cambridge University Press.

Beyer, L. (1996). The arts as personal and social communication: Popular/ethical culture in schools. *Discourse: Studies in the Cultural Politics of Education,* **17**, 2, 257-269.

Brettel, C. (1997). Blurred genres and blended voices; life history, biography, autobiography, and the auto/ethnography of women's lives. In *Auto/ethnography: Rewriting the self and the social,* ed. D. Reed-Danahay. Oxford: Berg, pp.223-246.

Brewster, A. (1995). *Literary formations: Post-colonialism, nationalism, globalism.* Carlton South: Melbourne University Press.

Britzman, D. (1995). 'The question of belief': Writing postructural ethnography. *Qualitative Studies in Education,* **8**, 3, 229-238.

Bruner, J. (1993). The autobiographical process. In *The culture of autobiography: Constructions of self representation,* ed. R. Folkenflik. Stanford: Stanford University Press, p.40.

Cahoone, L. (ed.) (1996). *From modernism to postmodernism: An anthology.* Cambridge, Mass.: Blackwell.

Children's Book Council of Australia (1992). *At least they're reading!* Port Melbourne: Thorpe.

Children's Book Council of Australia (1994). *Ways of seeing: Story from different angles.* Port Melbourne: Thorpe.

Children's Book Council of Australia (1996). *Claiming a place.* Port Melbourne: Thorpe.

Connelly, F. M. and Clandinin, D. J. (1990). Stories of experience and narrative inquiry. *Educational Researcher*, **19**, 5, 2-14.

Culler, J. (1997). *Literary theory: A very short introduction.* Oxford: Oxford University Press.

Davies, B. (1993). *Shards of glass: Children reading and writing beyond gendered identities.* Sydney: Allen & Unwin.

Denzin, N. (1994). Postmodernism and deconstructionism. In *Postmodernism and social inquiry*, eds D. Dickens and A. Fontana. London: UCL Press, pp.182-202.

Derrida, J. (1976). *Of grammatology*, trans. G. Spivak. Baltimore: Johns Hopkins University Press.

Doonan, J. (1993). *Looking at pictures in picture books.* Stroud, Glos.: Thimble Press.

Elbaz, R. (1988). *The changing nature of the self: A critical study of the autobiographic discourse.* London: Croom Helm.

Foucault, M. (1979). *The history of sexuality; Volume one; An introduction.* London: Allen Lane.

Goodson, I. (1995). The story so far: Personal knowledge and the political. *Qualitative Studies in Education,* **8**, 1, 89-98.

Graham, J. (1990). *Pictures on the page.* Carlton: Australian Reading Association.

Gunew, S. (1994). Arts for a multicultural Australia: Redefining the culture. In *Culture, difference and the arts*, eds S. Gunew and F. Rizvi. St Leonards: Allen & Unwin, pp.1-12.

Hall, S. (1987). Minimal selves. *The real me: Postmodernism and the question of identity*, ICA Documents 6, 44-46.

Hamilton, M. (1993). *The picture people.* Sydney: Margaret Hamiliton Books.

Hawke, D. (1996). Autobiography as an approach to research of artistic practice. *Australian Art Education,* **19**, 3, 31-36.

Lyotard, J. (1984). *The postmodern condition.* Manchester: Manchester University Press.

McCooey, D. (1996). *Artful histories: Modern Australian autobiography.* Cambridge: Cambridge University Press.

McLaren, P. (1995). *Critical pedagogy and predatory culture.* London: Routledge.

Mason, R. (1995). Contribution of professional artists to art education in schools. *Australian Art Education,* **18**, 3, 19-24.

Nodelman, P. (1988). *Words about pictures. The narrative art of children's books.* Athens: University of Georgia Press.

Rizvi, F. (1994). The arts, education and the politics of multiculturalism. In *Culture, difference and the arts*, eds S. Gunew and F. Rizvi. St Leonards: Allen & Unwin, pp.54-68.

Sarup, M. (1989). *An introductory guide to post-structuralism and postmodernism.* Athens: University of Georgia Press.

Saxby, M. (1993). *The proof of the puddin': Australian children's literature 1970-1990.* Sydney: Ashton Scholastic.

Say, A. (1993). *Grandfather's journey.* Boston: Houghton Mifflin.

Scheurich, J. (1995). A postmodernist critique of research interviewing. *Qualitative Studies in Education,* **8**, 3, 239-252.

Stewart, R. (1995). (Re) positioning art in art education; visuality, production and agency. *Australian Art Education,* **19**, 1, 37-50.

Stewart, R. (1996) Constructing neonarratives: A qualitative research process for the visual arts. *Australian Art Education,* **19**, 3, 37-47.

Utemorrah, D. and Torres, P. (1990). *Do not go around the edges.* Broome: Magabala Books.

# 6. Neither slogging at tuck nor living off the land: Food in Australian picture books

## Robin Morrow

**Abstract:** Food in literature can serve many purposes: it can have magic properties, it can indicate acceptance and community, it can be a marker of ethnicity or social class; food can be for pure indulgence, or can mark celebration, or it can represent survival. For all of these six categories I have cited 'landmark' books which have influenced writers (and readers) of children's literature. Picture books which were Winners or Honour Books in the Children's Book Council of Australia awards from 1988 to the present, and some important others, were examined under these six headings. I was surprised to find very little treatment of food as sheer indulgence or for survival. Only in the depiction of Aboriginal Australia is food for survival a serious issue.

Books have long been regarded as food. The metaphor of a reader 'devouring' knowledge, and of books as nourishment for mind or soul is an ancient one.

> Just as writers speak of cooking up a story, rehashing a text, having half–baked ideas for a plot, spicing up a scene or garnishing the bare bones of an argument, turning the ingredients of a potboiler into soggy prose, a slice of life peppered with allusions into which readers can sink their teeth, we, the readers, speak of savouring a book, of finding nourishment in it, of devouring a book at one sitting, of regurgitating or spewing up a text, of ruminating on a passage, of rolling a poet's words on the tongue, of feasting on poetry, of living on a diet of detective stories. (Manguel 1996, p.170)

This metaphor was made familiar in the English speaking world by the words of the old Church of England collect for the second Sunday in Advent, which exhorts the congregation to 'hear [all holy Scriptures and] read, mark, learn and inwardly digest' them (*The book of common prayer* 1662, p.13).

The idea of reading as nourishment is particularly prevalent in discussion of children's books. In her paper at the Children's Book Council of Australia Conference, Adelaide (May 1998) on the 'Morals, messages and medicines' panel, Jenny Pausacker referred to 'wholesome' books and 'junk food' literature. She pointed out that although we all disapprove of a diet of nothing but junk food, even carrots can be harmful–she had seen someone turn yellow as a result of eating too many of them! She concluded that as in eating, so in reading: it is best to have a balanced diet.

As well as books-as-food I was tempted to stray into the area of books-*and*-food, a topic dear to the heart of all librarians and booksellers. (Remember the poster which used to be popular in libraries saying: 'Please do not feed the books'?) I could spend quite some time listing the foods discovered among book pages: the chewing gum, the phenomenon of the teabag bookmark, the challenge of the hot chip.

But I must not be diverted from my *real* topic, which is food as subject matter in children's books. I have divided this into six categories, six different ways in which writers portray food in their work. In each case I shall remind you of a 'benchmark' book, a classic which has influenced writers (and readers) of children's literature. Then I shall refer to Australian picture books, especially the Winners and Honour Books in the Children's Book Council of Australia awards over the last ten years.

## Food as indulgence

[Rat appears] staggering under a fat, wicker luncheon-basket...

'What's inside it? asked the Mole, wriggling with curiosity.

'There's cold chicken inside it' replied the Rat briefly; 'coldtonguecoldham coldbeefpickledgherkinssaladfrenchrollscresssandwidgespottedmeatgingerbeerl emonadesodawater –'

'O stop, stop,' cried the Mole in ecstasies: 'This is too much!'

'Do you really think so?' inquired the Rat seriously...(Grahame 1908, p.13)

This is the scene evoked for me by the phrase 'food in books'; and although I have spent most of my life reading children's books (so should have known better), I misguidedly expected to find many more such scenes in the contemporary books I was investigating.

To give another example from the past: two years after the publication of *The wind in the willows*, a book was published by an Australian author, Joseph Bowes, entitled *Pals: Young Australians in sport and adventure*. This is how the local cricketing team and their visitors enjoyed themselves during the luncheon adjournment:

The Dingdongla's mothers were determined that, whoever won, the boys of both sides should have a rippin' feed. A stuffed sucking pig, whose savoury odour filled the room, lay at one end. Roast wild duck and cold pigeon-pie balanced it at the other. An immense round of spiced beef, standing in the centre of the long table seemed to say: 'You may cut and come again.' Potatoes and pumpkins smoked in big bowls, and all the available space was filled with cakes, puddings and pies. Needless to say, the onslaught was terrific. They were all sloggers at tuck. Meats, puddings, cakes, tea, and ginger-beer disappeared like magic. (quoted in Saxby 1998, p.126)

As long ago as 1966 critics were suggesting that food in children's books replaces the interest which sex provides in popular adult fiction (Tucker 1966, pp.33-40). John Stephens has included in his study of the Carnivalesque in children's books the observation that, 'The carnivalesque children's feast – whether "midnight feast" or birthday party or food-fight – celebrates a temporary liberation from official control over the time, place and manner in which food is consumed' (Stephens 1992, p.122).

But where, in the modern picture books, were the scenes of 'slogging at tuck'?

The nearest I found were the exploits of Wild and Woolly (or Julie and Boris as they are named in the French edition) in Alison Lester's *The journey home,* who journey from one magical place to another (Lester 1989). First they meet Father Christmas who serves roast turkey and plum pudding; then the Good Fairy who gives them angel cakes and sugar kisses for supper; at Prince Charming's they eat royal trifle and rhubarb fool, and so on. Most comforting of all are the mugs of hot chocolate given them by their own parents on the completion of their journey, a homely pleasure after the exotic dream worlds of imaginative childhood.

There is an indulgent side to this consuming of good things, but the foods and drinks do more than just satisfy the young travellers' physical appetites, they round off the experience of each fantastic microcosm. Indulgent, yes, but all quite orderly and sedate, and not a food-fight to be seen.

It is interesting to speculate on the relative inability of the picture book as a medium to present the sensuality evident in the passages quoted from *The wind in the willows* and *Pals*. Each of these quoted passages is a 'catalogue' of attractive foods, gaining from the cumulative effect of such a seemingly endless list, but also offering an entry point for the individual reader at the mention of their favourite food. Visual illustrations of such banquets may be either too static, if purely in 'still life' form, or they may lose their idealised quality if characters are depicted in the act of consuming the food.

## Food as magic

*Alice in Wonderland* has some famous scenes of the power of magic food and drink. Early in the story, just after falling down the rabbit hole, Alice found a bottle marked 'DRINK ME'.

> Alice ventured to taste it, and, finding it very nice (it had, in fact, a sort of mixed flavour of cherry-tart, custard, pine-apple, roast turkey, toffy, and hot buttered toast), she very soon finished it off.' [and she shrank, and then noticed a little glass box under the table]...' she opened it, and found in it a very small cake, on which the words '*EAT ME*' were beautifully marked in currants' (Carroll 1865, pp.10, 12).

She ate it and grew taller; and later, in chapter 4, found another bottle from which she drank and grew tall inside the house, and a cake which shrank her so she could get out; and in chapter 5 met the caterpillar on the mushroom who told her to eat from this mushroom: 'One side will make you grow taller, and the other will make you grow shorter' (Carroll 1865, p.64).

Sometimes the magic food in children's stories does nothing but harm, such as the Turkish Delight given by the White Witch to Edmund in *The lion, the witch and the wardrobe*, which was '...enchanted Turkish Delight, and...anyone who had once tasted it would want more and more of it, and would even, if they were allowed, go on eating it till they killed themselves' (Lewis 1950, ch. 4).

Such descriptions of magic food undoubtedly influenced the writing of *Possum magic*, the bestselling picture book (Fox 1983) in which Hush the invisible possum is restored to visibility, gradually, by eating a number of foods described by Clare Bradford as 'foods associated with colonisation' (Bradford 1996, p.101). Interestingly the foods listed in *Possum magic* have often been considered funny, jokey foods, not to be taken seriously. Following is a list of all the foods mentioned as tried by Grandma Poss and Hush in the effort to restore the young possum's visibility:

> Anzac biscuits
> mornay and Minties
> steak and salad
> pumpkin scones
> vegemite [sic, no capital letter] sandwich
> a piece of pavlova
> lamington

The last three are the most significant, apparently, as the book concludes: 'But once a year, on her birthday, she and Grandma Poss ate a vegemite sandwich, a piece of pavlova and a half a lamington, just to make sure that Hush stayed visible forever. And she did.'

Even by 1983, the year of publication of *Possum magic*, all these foods had to varying degrees become the source of humour. Pumpkin scones, which Hush ate 'in Brisbane', were associated with the folksy character of Senator Flo Bjelke Petersen. And the 'big three' Aussie foods which reassured Poss that she would not fade from sight had all become part of comedy routines such as those of Barry Humphries in his satiric role of Edna Everage. These foods have in common a lack of subtlety – one (Vegemite) is too salty for the taste of most people who have not been reared on it, and the other two, pavlova and lamington, are of a degree of sweetness usually associated with foods for children, not for adults. The laughter evoked by mention of these foods is embarrassed laughter, because many Australians recognise that these foods are seen as 'typical' Australian foods but are unsophisticated in the extreme. These foods 'associated with colonisation' in Bradford's phrase, serve their ideological purpose well: there is a sense of unease that such foods are probably viewed as odd by those at the 'centre'.

So the role played by the foods in *Possum magic* is a mixed one. At first sight, they are simply magic foods just like Alice's cake, plot devices to make something mysterious happen to the main character. But they also act as clear indicators of nationality. If the feelings of national identity evoked by these foods are mixed with laughter, and if this laughter contains a measure of embarrassment, it has not been enough to prevent many thousands of adult Australians from buying copies of *Possum magic* both for their own children and to send as gifts to families in other countries.

## Food as sign of acceptance and community

> A peculiar thing about the Puddin' was that, though they had all had a great many slices off him, there was no sign of the place whence the slices had been cut.

> 'That's where the Magic comes in,' explained Bill. 'The more you eats the more you gets. Cut-and-come-again is his name, an' cut, an' come again, is his nature. Me an' Sam has been eatin' away at this Puddin' for years, and there's not a mark on him...' (Lindsay 1918, p.23)

The book is entitled *The **magic** pudding*, and it is the two qualities – of constant replenishment, and its ability to change flavour on demand – that make the puddin' so valuable. However, unlike the food and drink in *Alice*, the puddin' has no magical effect on the eaters. Bill Barnacle and Sam Sawnoff are their mundane selves even after (apparently) living off the puddin' for years. The book as a whole is not a magical story, but a tale of mateship. To be offered a slice of Albert, the puddin', is to be accepted, to be a 'good bloke' (and certainly only a bloke: there are no female characters in this ideal Australian world of mateship and adventure). First Bunyip Bluegum, and later several minor characters, are invited to tuck in to a slice of puddin'. Each character met on the road by Bill and Sam is put into a category of acceptable (to be offered food and friendship) or unacceptable (the puddin' thieves, and those others quickly judged not worthy of friendship, such as the 'low larrikin' Kookaburra). The world of *The magic pudding* is a world of little boys playing gang games, or more accurately of men relaxing after having survived trench warfare in a deadly serious gang game. The puddin' serves as a currency of acceptance and friendship, and his other chief function is to be fought over! Albert is both rations and plunder.

There are a few passages describing the delicious meals enjoyed by the puddin' eaters, but these are not so many or so detailed to put the book into the 'food as indulgence' category. Sitting around the campfire and singing are dwelt on as activities just as pleasurable as actually eating a hearty meal.

A recent picture book with a similar treatment of food is *Greetings from Sandy Beach* (Graham, 1990) an account of a family holiday. The narrator is a young child who goes with parents and baby brother to a campsite by the sea.

As they set out, 'Mum started on the toffees before we even left our street', which sets a carefree holiday mood. The next spread is a traffic scene, in which the family car is dwarfed by a huge poster for an (unbranded) hamburger, the universal advertised food. Does this represent the consumer world from which the family is escaping by the sea? If so, there is irony in the mention of the dinner that night: 'Dad cooked the dinner – Camp Stew out of a tin'. The fact that the young narrator comments on this suggests that there is novelty in the situation: it is a 'father takes over to give Mum a rest' meal, but sadly the work of a father lacking in cooking expertise.

Food also figures in the relationship of the narrator's family with the Disciples of Death. At first the parents warned the children to keep away from these bikers. Later the bikers showed the family how to put up their tent, while Dad 'looked nervous and smiled at them a lot'. The ice-cream sticks of The Disciples were used for an ice-breaking game of boats. Then, as the family was about to leave for home, 'The Lady Disciple bought us a raspberry Icy Pop each'. The narrator's family is already obliged to the bikers for their help with erecting the tent; now the child narrator's mention of the food gift from the biker is apparently innocent, but loaded for the adult reader – and for the perceptive child reader also – with realisation that the family is now completely in debt to the bikers, unable to treat them as threatening, alien, or as anything but holiday companions.

The picture book *Where's mum?* (Gleeson 1992) shows a family with young children and contrasts the world of humdrum reality with the rich imaginative world of 'what if?' Dad is shown bringing home the three children and the shopping. Scenes of cheerful domestic chaos alternate with pictures of what *may* be happening to Mum as she hurries home too. These imaginary scenes are peopled with characters from nursery rhymes and tales, beginning with Humpty Dumpty who seems to have been evoked by the eggs which Dad dropped as he unpacked the shopping. There is real food in the real kitchen – orange juice and bread for after-kindergarten snacks – and imaginary porridge which Mum *may* be going to eat with the Three Bears. But the main refreshment scene is the very last illustration, in which Dad is shown passing a tray of mugs and cups to the visitors who have crowded in the door with Mum. This is sharing and acceptance with a difference, for the human and animal characters receiving the cups of tea or coffee are all from the story world – the troll, Henny Penny and so on – and the gesture of giving them all a welcoming cuppa is a bridge between the worlds of reality and fantasy. There is humour for a young reader who can see the fun: if these trolls and bears are drinking coffee with Dad, they *must* be real!

*Rose meets Mr Wintergarten* (Graham 1992) is a picture book rich in intertextual references (Oscar Wilde's story *The selfish giant* is an obvious one, and also the visual references to the film version of *Little Lord Fauntleroy*). The story reads like a folk tale or fable, with its extreme contrast between the Summers family and Mr Wintergarten. The text tells us that the Summers family produced 'a carpet of flowers' on the day they moved into their new house, and that their next door neighbour lives in a house that 'the sun never touched'. The illustrations depict an even greater contrast: nothing but greys and black for the Wintergarten side of the fence, bright greens, yellow, red and pink for the Summers family and the children visiting them. When Rose bravely visits Mr Wintergarten to ask for the ball that went over the fence, several pictures use colour contrast dramatically – as Mr Wintergarten is seated alone at his huge dining table, the browns and greys are relieved by two points of colour: Rose herself in three of the pictures, and, after she has left his house, the colourful flowers and plate of cakes she has left on the table.

These cakes are one of the most powerful foods to be found in the world of Australian picture books. Rose's mum is dressed in a pure white dress when she takes them out of the oven.

> 'Well, honeybunch,' Mum said, 'you can get your ball back. Why don't you just go and ask him?'

'Because he eats kids,' said Rose.

'We'll take him some hot cakes instead,' said Mum.

'And maybe some flowers.'

When Rose eventually reaches the interior of the gloomy next door house, she says 'I've brought some flowers, and hot fairy cakes from my mum.' The cakes have now had three adjectives associated with them – firstly, as the affectionate name of '*honeybunch*' has moved forward in the reader's mind to link with the cakes themselves, secondly that they are '*hot*' (and we can see in the illustration that Rose's Mum has just taken them from the oven), and finally '*fairy cakes*'.

Rose sees Mr Wintergarten's meal:

> His dinner was cold, grey and uninviting, with bits of gristle floating in it and mosquitoes breeding on top.  But Rose could see that he wasn't eating children.

The contrast between this meal and the cakes sits squarely in the tradition of fairy tale.  There are practical reasons why Mr Wintergarten may not have had inviting food to eat, but in fairy tale terms it is the lack of human companionship that has made his food 'grey'.  His acceptance of the fairy cakes causes a turnabout in Mr Wintergarten: he gathers the strength and interest to kick her ball over the fence, and as the book ends, the reader is left confident that a spell has been broken, that Mr Wintergarten will enter the world offered to him by the Summers.  Any lingering doubt about this happy resolution is put to rest by the final endpaper scene, of the opening up of Mr Wintergarten's house and demolition of the fence dividing it from the Summers'.

So the hot, 'honey', fairy cakes are magical food, but they are also signs of simple neighbourly acceptance.  The turning point for Mr Wintergarten is the thoughtful moment when, 'He sat on his front step in the sun.  "No one has ever asked for their ball back," he said to himself.  "Or brought fairy cakes."'

## Food as marker of class or ethnicity

> She struck another match.  It flared up brightly; where it shone, the wall became transparent as gauze.  She could see right into the room where the table was laid with a shining starched white cloth; on it were dishes of finest porcelain.  A delicious hot fragrance rose from a roast goose stuffed with prunes and apples.  The goose seemed nearer and nearer – she could almost

touch it. Then the match went out. All she could see and feel was the cold unfriendly wall. (Andersen 1986, p.63)

This is, of course, *The little match girl*. Not only is there an abundance of food inside the house in contrast with the little match girl's starvation, but this food is laid out on the 'finest porcelain' on a 'starched white cloth' while the match girl is barefoot and in rags. Andersen could say with Sophie Tucker 'I've been poor and I've been rich. Rich is better,' and he knew in fine detail all the markers of this difference.

This difference is hard to find in Australian picture books. *Let's eat!* (Zamorano 1996), declares itself from the very title as a book about meals. The opening sentence states, 'In my family there are seven of us', so we can assume that the book will be about family meals. And the first spread shows the youngest child, the narrator, holding a bowl of salad while his sister Alicia carefully carries a big blue jug. Where are they all going? To the meal table of course. 'When we are all at the table Mama is happy'. The narrative is a neat and predictable one, with each day of the week offering a different dish (chickpea soup, empanadas, sardinas...) and each day one member of the extended family unable to be at the lunch table. On Saturday it is Mama who is absent, in hospital with the newborn baby, Rosa, and the story ends with the Sunday meal a week later, when the complete family shares a huge pan of paella. 'How wonderful that everyone is eating together!' are the final words of the story. In the words of the Children's Book Council of Australia judges 'The circular meal table, seen from many perspectives, symbolises the close family circle. Everyone is connected; nobody is left out' (Van Every 1997 p.26).

The book celebrates family life, birth, and sharing, and particularly Spanish life and is one of the few not set in Australia to be honoured by the Children's Book Council of Australia awards. (Of the 96 books honoured in the Picture Book category up to and including 1997, ten were set in other countries.) The (adult) reader at first may think *Let's eat!* is about a Spanish-Australian family, until mention of the 'village' and its 'fiesta' and, later, the architectural clues in the illustrations. A child reader meeting the book alone may persist in imagining the setting as Australian. The listing of Spanish foods and the glossary of Spanish words, and the fact that the main meal of the day is at 2 pm, do not of course reveal *where* these Spanish-speaking characters live. Food in the book is a marker of Spanishness, not necessarily of living in Spain.

Many Australian children are familiar with a range of ethnic foods and with the idea that another child's family eats differently from one's own. *Let's eat!* may have been honoured by the Children's Book Council of Australia judges not so much as a book about Spanish families and their meals, as a book that presents a warm family group of an ethnic group other than traditionally 'mainstream' Australian.

If *Let's eat!* at first appears to be a 'peasanty' book, a closer reading reveals that the narrator and his siblings have every human need fulfilled: love, care, fun as well as excellent home cooked food. Nowhere in the typical Australian picture book today could I find a little match girl or even a slightly needy child.

## Food for celebration and reward

> She [Dickon's mother, Susan Sowerby] had packed a basket which held a regular feast this morning, and when the hungry hour came and Dickon brought it out from its hiding place, she sat down with them under their tree and watched them devour their food, laughing and quite gloating over their appetites...(Burnett 1911, p.237)

The amazing fact of the newfound hunger of both Mary and Colin, the spoiled yet deprived children of Misselthwaite Manor, is cause enough to make this meal a celebration. It hardly matters what is in the basket, although the contents can be guessed at from earlier accounts of Susan's baking. What we can be sure of is that it is wholesome food from the humble Yorkshire cottage, and that it is being shared by those brought together in joy at the healing power of the magic (Burnett 1911, p.206). The scene is an exemplary one of closure in children's literature, according to John Stephens' statement that, 'Aesthetic completeness is achieved in children's literature through representation of symmetries or movements from states of lack to states of plenitude...' (Stephens 1992, p.42). Here the *lack* has been not food itself, but appetite, and Mary and Colin demonstrate in their appetite for food that they have both now developed an appetite for life itself. And beaming over the whole scene is the mother figure, Susan Sowerby.

*Each peach pear plum* (Ahlberg 1978) has become a favourite in the Australian market, although illustrated by that most English of artists, Janet Ahlberg. The traditional rhyme has been reworked into a picture puzzle book for very young readers, preferably those with some knowledge of nursery rhymes and folk tales. The book ends with, firstly, an anticipatory page which shows a large, steaming, crusted pie invitingly displayed on a picnic cloth on the grass. Observant readers will pick out the characters met earlier in the book, who are all now hiding in the orchard.

## Plum pie in the sun

*I spy*...reads the text, not so much inviting a page turn as demanding it. The final spread has just one word of text: '...EVERYONE!' and the illustration shows the complete cast of characters helping themselves and each other to the pie. There is a feeling of indulgence in the scene, but a strong sense of community also: Mother Hubbard and the Wicked Witch enjoy cups of tea and preside benignly over all, suggesting tasks completed, riddles solved, and quarrels settled. A superficial reading would suggest that the pie is itself magical, having appeared from nowhere, complete with cream jug and serving spoon. But the ending of *Each peach pear plum* is like the ending of *Where the wild things are* (Sendak 1963) in that it is the benevolent mother figure who has set everything to rights: both books end with food kindly and apparently ungrudgingly provided, in one case by a mother not seen at all in the later part of the book, in the other by a Mother figure whose foot and apron have been glimpsed as she appeared at the side of the spread, struggling under the weight of a pile of pie dishes.

*Drac and the gremlin* (Baillie 1988) is a celebrated Australian picture book, admired for the dual narratives of words and illustrations. According to the pictures, everyday children play out everyday games in a suburban backyard (although here too I would claim that the children depicted are very favoured ones, with a seemingly endless garden to play in); but the text recounts a science fiction/fantasy adventure of heroic proportions. At the end of the book, the text states, "'You have saved the planet' says the White Wizard. "We are very grateful. Please accept as your reward our highest honour, the Twin Crimson Cones of Tirnol Two.'"

The illustration shows the two children reaching out for delicious-looking pink ice creams in cones. The White Wizard, who has appeared not at all in the pictures and only marginally in the text, is clearly the mother, dealing out treats at the end of playtime. Celebratory meals in children's books require a mother figure whose provisioning skills are well in evidence even if she herself is barely glimpsed.

## Food as survival

Last of all I come to the subject which I thought would be common to many stories: food as survival.

*Robinson Crusoe* is the classic story of 'making do'. Crusoe was able to ferry back to the shore from his wrecked ship many useful items which were to help him in the months to come. After he had made his makeshift raft to transport these things, he gathered up; 'bread, rice, three Dutch cheeses, five pieces of dried goat's flesh...[and] several cases of bottles belonging to our skipper, in which were some cordial waters, and, in all, about five or six gallons of rack' (Defoe 1719, p.36).

A pretty good start, but of course he had to look ahead to when these stores would run out. It was the saving of a gun which really ensured Crusoe's survival.

> The first time I went out [with the gun], I presently discovered that there were goats in the island, which was a great satisfaction to me; but then it was attended with this misfortune to me, viz., that they were so shy, so subtle, and so swift of foot, that it was the difficultest thing in the world to come at them. (Defoe 1719, p.45)

Eventually Crusoe was to breed goats and keep them in an enclosure. His experience with cereal crops was somewhat different. He had forgotten that he had emptied out a bag containing dust and husks, and was surprised when, 'I saw about ten or twelve ears come out, which were perfect green barley of the same kind as our European, nay, as our English barley.' This discovery occasioned an interesting burst of theological reflection. 'It startled me strangely, and I began to suggest that God had miraculously caused this grain to grow without any help of seed sown, and that it was so directed purely for my sustenance on that wild miserable place.' When he realised that the barley had appeared where he had emptied out the bag 'my religious thankfulness to God's providence began to abate too' (Defoe 1719, p.58) until he at last concluded that it *was* the work of Providence that he had emptied the bag in a place where conditions were right for the barley to germinate and grow.

*Robinson Crusoe* is, after all, the archetypal story of colonisation, and at no time do we expect Crusoe to learn to eat the local plants. He needs not just European but *English* barley to feel secure about his diet.

*Robinson Crusoe* was to influence hundreds of writers of books for the young, and a special label, that of 'Robinsonnade' (Carpenter and Prichard 1984, p.458) is given to a book modelled on the famous survival story. In the eighteenth century, Australia seemed a suitable place to set such a story, as Saxby comments:

> Many of these [writers of Robinsonnades], including the Frenchman, Jules Verne, saw in Australia (without ever visiting) an ideal environment for adventure: survival and success over what could seem to be overwhelming odds. Increasingly, visitors to Australia and then residents joined the ranks of overseas writers. But because literature was still supposed to instruct as well as entertain, many of the books...still included a great deal of information – and, not infrequently, misinformation – about the country in an attempt to provide authenticity and verisimilitude. (Saxby 1998, p.79)

One would expect the idea of food purely for survival to dominate for a long time in Australian children's books. Early white settlers behaved as Shane Warne, the cricketer, was reported to have done on his recent visit to India, stocking up with the foods they trusted. They took their bully beef into the wilds, often perishing in ignorance of the bush tucker all around.

By the late twentieth century, however, the idea of food for survival is rare in children's books. The picture book of Banjo Paterson's *Waltzing Matilda* (Paterson 1970) reproduces the tale of a swagman desperate enough to steal a sheep for his 'tucker bag'. This picture book won the Children's Book Council of Australia Picture Book award in 1971, and Desmond Digby's illustrations gave the song a new lease of life, but no claim could be made that the book was an attempt to portray contemporary life in the early 1970s.

The most desperate scene of food deprivation in an Australian picture book occurs in *Let the celebrations begin* (Wild, 1991). This book is set in a concentration camp of the European holocaust. To depict the *absence* of food in the camp, the author and illustrator show a meal composed of memory and imagination. First the narrator comments on the skinniness of the four year old David: 'The chickens running in our yard were fatter'. This leads to memories of eating chicken, and leaving the skin and fat. The narrator, Miriam, fantasises about enjoying a chicken meal, and making sure David has lots of helpings. The illustration extends this fantasy by showing Miriam as healthily plump, licking the plate after such a meal. But the reality is that there is *no* food, and the women are occupied in sewing some toys from rags, taking action in an area they can do something about. At the end of the book, at the liberation scene, there is a picture of the women grouped around large metal containers. The only food visible is a crust of bread at the edge of a dixie, but the text tells us that they are eating chicken soup.

Of recent picture books, *Where the forest meets the sea* (Baker 1987) and *Not a nibble!* (Honey 1996) are the two which show any degree of 'living off the land'. Both books show, to be accurate, living not off the land but from the sea, and both, I suggest, show only a transitory and artificial experience of such survival, an interlude in a life which is clearly quite different at other times. The father and son in *Where the forest meets the sea* arrive by dinghy (with outboard motor attached) to visit a place in the rainforest. The ancient past of the forest is referred to in their conversation, and also in the illustrations where we see the 'ghosts' of earlier inhabitants, both human and animal. Towards the end of the book the narrator walks towards his father.

> My father has made a fire and is cooking the fish he caught.

> I like fish cooked this way.

The reader can reasonably assume that the father and son will leave the beach at the end of the day and return to the comforts of a late twentieth century lifestyle, just as we assume that the fire was lit on the beach with the help of a modern packet of matches (and we have not witnessed how the fish were caught in the first place). The book is a plea to leave areas of rainforest undeveloped, but it is not a tale of surviving without technology. The outboard motor and matches of today are just as useful as Robinson Crusoe's gun and barley seeds were in the early eighteenth century to enable the characters to act out readers' fantasies of managing with nothing but the resources of nature.

The family fishing holiday depicted in *Not a nibble!* is also an escape to a more natural environment, although in this case it is shared with other holiday makers. In the camping area, neighbouring tents and caravans are clearly visible, and the nearby shopkeepers figure in the story. Each day (except for one, when it is raining) the father of the family and one or more of the children try their luck at fishing. The rocks, an old swing bridge, the lee of a boat and a jetty all provide peaceful settings for their fishing. The author/illustrator has provided a close up illustration of the 'big black frying pan' with the first day's assorted catch in it, and we can assume that the fish caught on other days end up in the pan, too. But at no time is the reader given cause to worry that no catch would mean starvation: other foods, such as pies and chips and bacon and eggs are mentioned, and the mood throughout the text and illustrations suggests fishing as pleasurable play rather than a serious hunt for food.

To find a serious food hunt in a recent picture book it is necessary to turn to a book of Aboriginal experience. It is the Aboriginal artist, Ian Abdulla, who succeeds in showing what food for survival really means. His first book, *As I grew older*, (Abdulla 1993) is an account of his early life by the Murray River. Here is one activity recalled:

> While living at Winkie we would go [to the] slaughter yards…to buy some sheep heads. There we used to watch the men at work in the sheds. To kill the sheep the men would cut the sheep's throat, and after a while we would buy the sheep heads for about one or two shillings a head.

> We would take the sheep heads home so we could skin them with a razor blade. After we finished, the heads would be put in the oven or on the stove to be boiled up for eating.

The afterword to this book, by John Kean, states:

> [The mid-1950s] was a time of few permanent employment opportunities for Nungas. Ian's family, like others along the river, relied on traditional Aboriginal skills to survive away from the mission and the prevailing government policy of assimilation.

Ian Abdulla's second book, *Tucker* (Abdulla 1994) is as the title implies, devoted fully to the matter of living off the land. The foods mentioned include yabbies, several kinds of fish – pilaki (callop), pondi (Murray cod), thukeri (bony bream) and catfish – swans, quondongs, blue tongue lizard, and, once again those sheep's heads.

> One night when we were camping along the creeks and everyone had gone to bed, I went down to the creek to check the hand line. It must have been a good fish – a pondi, or Murray cod – because when I pulled it in I broke the line. It took the hook and everything. That fish was supposed to be for our breakfast the next morning. We'd cook 'em on the coals on a grid iron.

There is no suggestion here that the young narrator's family will duck down to the shops to buy a MacDonald's breakfast to replace the one that got away. This is a book about food that *really* means survival. And in the words of Paul Greenaway, writer of the foreword: 'If "tucker" is food, then this...book...is tucker for the mind, the heart and the soul...it will give pleasure to many; and it will also serve to empower the poor, the oppressed and the dispossessed.'

It seems fitting that the last word on this topic should come from a representative of the first inhabitants of our land:

> When I was working for the government we used to go to Coober Pedy, and while I was up there the government paid for all my food, which was white man's food.

> When the men from Coober Pedy went out hunting they would come home with kangaroo which was cooked for a while in the ashes. Kangaroo cooked this way, and even goanna, was very tasty. I would swap tins of bully beef for the food they cooked in the ashes. It was so much better for eating.

# References

Abdulla, I. (1993). *As I grew older*. Norwood: Omnibus.

Abdulla, I. (1994). *Tucker*. Norwood: Omnibus.

Ahlberg, J. and Ahlberg, A. (1978). *Each peach pear plum*. Harmondsworth: Kestrel.

Andersen, H. C. (1986). *The flying trunk and other stories from Andersen: A new English version*, ed. N. Lewis. London: Andersen Press.

Baillie, A. and Tanner, J. (1988). *Drac and the gremlin*. Ringwood: Viking Kestrel.

Baker, J. (1987). *Where the forest meets the sea.* Sydney: Julia MacRae Books.

Bradford, C. (1996). Centre and edges: Postcolonial literary theory and Australian picture books. In *Writing the Australian child: Texts and contexts in fictions for children,* (ed.) C. Bradford. Nedlands, WA: University of Western Australia Press.

Burnett, F. H. (1988). *The secret garden.* London: Victor Gollancz.

Carpenter, H. and Prichard, M. (1984). *The Oxford companion to children's literature.* Oxford: Oxford University Press.

Carroll, L. (1980). *Alice's adventures in Wonderland.* London: Macmillan.

Defoe, D. (1995). *The life and adventures of Robinson Crusoe.* Ware: Wordsworth Editions.

Fox, M. and Vivas, J. (1983). *Possum magic.* Norwood: Omnibus.

Gleeson, L. and Smith, C. (1992). *Where's mum?* Norwood: Omnibus.

Graham, B. (1990). *Greetings from Sandy Beach.* Melbourne: Lothian.

Graham, B. (1992). *Rose meets Mr Wintergarten.* Ringwood: Viking.

Grahame, K. (1971). *The wind in the willows.* London: Methuen.

Honey, E. (1996). *Not a nibble!* St Leonards: Allen & Unwin.

Lester, A. (1989). *The journey home.* Melbourne: Oxford University Press.

Lewis, C. S. (1950). *The lion, the witch and the wardrobe.* London: Geoffrey Bles.

Lindsay, N. (1972). *The magic pudding.* Sydney: Angus & Robertson.

Manguel, A. (1996). *A history of reading.* Hammersmith: HarperCollins.

Paterson, A. B. and Digby, D. (1970). *Waltzing Matilda.* Sydney: Collins.

Saxby, M. (1998). *Offered to children: A history of Australian children's literature 1841–1941.* Sydney: Scholastic.

Sendak, M. (1963). *Where the wild things are.* New York: Harper & Row.

Stephens, J. (1992). *Language and ideology in children's books*. London: Longman.

*The book of common prayer*. (1662). Oxford University Press.

Tucker, N. (1966). Problems. *Use of English,* **18**, 1, 33-40.

Van Every, S. (ed.) (1997). *Notable Australian children's books 1997*. Adelaide: Children's Book Council of Australia.

Wild, M.and Vivas, J. (1991). *Let the celebrations begin*. Norwood: Omnibus.

Zamorano, A. and Vivas, J. (1996). *Let's eat!* Norwood: Omnibus.

# 7. Double vision: Poem, picture and imagination

## Alison Halliday

**Abstract:** The relationship between picture and text in picture books has been explored by critics such as Nodelman (1988) and Stephens (1992) but the nature of this association may be very different when the text is a poem. These texts may be picture books, offering a synthesis of word and text but more often the relationship is tenuous or even coincidental rather than one which intensifies and expands the poem. Rosenblatt (1978) has discussed the theoretical process of reading poems and Benton (1988) mapped how the child reads poetry, suggesting a parallel with the 'reading' of pictures. Using different pictures for the same poetry text the balance, or imbalance between text and illustration reveals not only the ideology of each but also reflects cultural assumptions about the imagination. The simplicity of the poem also allows the age of the implied reader and its possible dual nature, often neglected as Bradford points out (1993), and its oral purpose to be placed against the ideology of the child's imagination.

The usual paper is made up of an argument in a sequence of connected statements illuminated by cogent examples. But as Lissa Paul (1989) demonstrated it is often the footnotes, the sub-text and the diversions, paths not taken and the references to other associated theories and work that are equally interesting and relevant. She saw the footnote as presenting a contrapuntal harmony to the main text, it was the sub-text writ large. I may have decided here to put in a footnote to the effect that it is the expressed desire of Oliver Sacks, neurologist and writer, to create a text which has more footnotes than main text and even footnotes for the footnotes. If you have read any of his work you will appreciate that he is working steadily towards fulfilling this aim.

However this is not a paper of footnotes but one which reveals openly its 'head-notes'. In using this name for these particular types of text I wish to suggest not only where they come from but also their relative position in the research process. The 'head-note' is usually in the form of a question. The questions that prompt any research are usually unspoken, unwritten but this is not to deny their existence it just leaves them to be assumed. Throughout this paper I wish to make the questions obvious because it is the assumptions of common understanding and the consequent tacit agreement as to the parameters of the concept that I wish to explore.

I began with two questions: first; what is the relationship between poetry and illustration or picture? and second; what is this thing called 'imagination'? and what bearing does any possible answer have on the first question? I will argue that it is necessary for the second question to be taken first for the association of poem and illustration is a function of the matrix of assumptions behind the concept of imagination.

If a comment is made: 'that's very imaginative' or 'she suffers from too much imagination' (in a tone of kindly indulgence) the statements are essentially positive, along the lines of you can't have too much of a *good* thing; but the remark: 'she has no imagination' is essentially condemnatory, and possibly to the extent that this is an irreversible situation. I would suggest that the first, more positive statements are more often found in talking about children while it is adults who are more likely to be found lacking.

So what is this 'imagination', or to put it more usefully, how has our culture defined the concept of 'imagination'? What are its necessary inclusions and parameters?

I found some clues in a rather eclectic group of books that I have been reading recently; these are *The pleasures of the imagination*, subtitled 'English culture in the eighteenth century' by John Brewer (1997) *The eye of the soul*, subtitled 'Australian writers for young adults and children discuss the imaginative process' by Stephen Matthews (1998) and *The book of the Hob stories* by William Mayne (1984, 1997).

The first of these is a complex exploration of the interaction of literary and artistic endeavour, its means of production and dissemination and the movement of 'high' culture from the court to the public. Writing from the late twentieth century Brewer's perspective of this period of 250 years ago is possible only with the framing of the 'imagination' generated by Coleridge in the early 19th century. It is here that the present parameters of the concept of the imagination may be found.

In his *Biographia literaria* of 1815 Coleridge shifts the position of the imagination and gives it primacy in the creative process. He distinguishes it from fantasy, seeing the imagination as the power which shapes and modifies experience. It is the process which results in original art, and it is the same process which enables the viewer or reader to appreciate the artist's and poet's imagination, through the work they produce, that is, through the work the reader not only appreciates the imagination of another but has his/her own imagination nurtured. As Coleridge said on reading Spenser: 'it was the union of deep feeling with profound thought; the fine balance of truth in observing with the imaginative faculty in modifying the objects observed' (1906, p.48). It is not surprising that Coleridge gives primacy to the poet's work as the epitome of the imaginative process, much of his argument was formulated in response to the poetry and comments of Wordsworth.

Coleridge defines the imagination with a cluster of ideas: it is active, it is associated with 'the act of thinking' (p.72), it is associated with the ability to perceive and to sense or be aware, it is the essence of creativity.

All of this may be seen as stating the obvious, but that is only because it is so familiar, and it is this very familiarity that allows for assumptions of common understanding. Since Coleridge there have been two shifts in the defining parameters of the imagination: first, the imagination is linked with the production of the 'high' arts and thus by implication it has, until recently, not been associated with other endeavours in areas such as science. Hence the work of Edward de Bono is described as 'lateral' thinking rather than 'creative' or 'imaginative'. The scientist 'invents' rather than 'creates', 'thinks' rather than 'imagines'.

This exclusive association is underlined in the second example I mentioned earlier. Matthews (1998) discusses the writing process with a number of writers for children and young adults but in so doing both he and the writers reinforce the mystery of this concept. The writers describe the process in terms such as: 'imagination is never lying', 'I write when the feeling takes me', 'it's like alchemy...a miracle', 'it's about the transformation of feelings'. I do not wish to denigrate the work of these writers, or the truthfulness with which they attempted to answer Matthews' questions, but both the question and the answers reinforce the imagination as special, personal and something that is not only not fully understood but which they do not wish to understand or think too much about in case it disappears or loses its potency. Coleridge linked the poet and the poem: what is poetry? is so nearly the same question as, what is a poet?, that the answer to one is involved in the solution to the other. For it is a distinction resulting from the poetic genius itself, which sustains and modifies the images, thoughts and emotions of the poet's own mind (1906, p.173). The writers that Matthews interviews are the heirs to Coleridge. They are their work, and the link is the imagination.

The second development of the concept of the imagination is a result of the link between the product of the imagination and its effects on the reader, viewer or listener. This link involves the reader in the creative process, not by making the text meaningful or by understanding it, but by a more mysterious association between imagination and creativity. At one extreme it may be that to participate in this imaginative process it is only necessary to read a poem or to look at a painting. A cynic might say that this is merely a process of osmosis, but the shift in the position of the imagination is rather more than this. Because most people do not write poetry, paint pictures or (even) write fiction for the young reader (although we can all visit galleries, listen to music and read books) at the other extreme the result of the imagination is so restricted it has become valued. Our society may value the product of the artist (even if not economically) but this same product of the imagination is now available to many rather than the few. This ease of access has meant that other ways have to be found to valorise the exclusiveness of the imagination. It brings us to the child reader and to the third example of the imagination.

I would argue that this has been done by locating the imagination within the parameters of childhood, and then framing it in certain ways. Just as we have all been children and left childhood behind, it is assumed that as adults most of us have lost the imaginative powers ascribed to the child. In William Mayne's *The book of Hob stories* (1984, 1997) Hob is a small friendly household spirit who copes with the trivial and seemingly normal accidents and everyday mishaps that occur in any house or family. Stephens (1989) points out that not only is Hob a creature of the child's imagination but that he *is* the imagination. I wish to take this idea a little further. Hob is visible to, and known by, the children in the family. He is helpful but also elusive, tricky and devious. He lives in his own place but it is within the house. Despite his strengths he is also dependent upon the children for they have, unknowingly, the power to send him away if they happen to reward him with a gift of clothes. To the adults in the family, even those who acknowledge his existence (usually in a rather jocular tone), he is invisible and has to be taken on trust. Thus the imagination is unique to childhood, the adult may remember its existence and even be a little fearful of it but in most cases they are unable to do more than this, they cannot make use of it, control it or make it active (to use Coleridge's term). For the child the relationship with the imagination may be problematic, one of mutual interdependency. The imagination dwells within the child but it may be wilful and difficult to control. It is intrinsic to the being of the child but may be referred to as having an existence and function that is almost independent of its host. As the child becomes an adult, scepticism, logic and reason will dress Hob and he will vanish. Thus in our society we have positioned the concept of the imagination where it is both important and safe, protected but confined.

At this point that I wish to turn to the first question: that of the relationship between poetry and picture.

Poetry is offered to children, read to them, and by them, for many reasons which may be summed up as those that are involved with pleasure and enjoyment, and those that relate to their imagination. Lewis (1975) advocated the significance of imagination as the main reason for giving fiction to children and I would argue that it is equally if not more strongly used as justification for giving poetry to children. The assumptions are that through reading poetry the child is not only responding to the imagination of another but that their own response will be one of their imagination, and may even result in their own creative act; thus reinforcing the connections suggested by Coleridge.

Poetry texts for children in the last twenty years have been dominated by those that include pictorial material, this may vary from decorative line sketches to detailed and colourful full page illustrations. The presence of pictorial material has not only become commonplace, but recently poems have been re-published as picture books. The dominance of the illustrated text may be for a number of reasons. First there are all those factors associated with technological developments in publishing and printing which have meant the replacement of tipped-in colour plates with full colour printing on the same page as the printed text. Second there is the tension between the cultural position of poetry as a valued discourse and market forces (which while acknowledging the need for poetry, find these books hard to sell). They have to be made eye-catching and be seen to be valuable and valued. Third there is the ambiguous position of poetry itself. It may be approached with enthusiasm and delight but the more common reaction, especially with the dollar-bearing adult purchaser, is one of hesitancy at best and fear and distrust at worst. Illustrations do not seem to pose the same challenge that poetry does, they are a reassurance that the text will be able to be made meaningful. They literally make the text attractive. Smerdon (1975) suggests that the child reader has no preference for realistic or for more abstract or stylised drawings. It seems that it is not the style of illustration which may be a significant factor in determining the possible responses, but the existence of an illustration.

If these two factors are brought together, the importance of the imagination and the association of poem with picture, it is possible to ask what is being implied about poetry, about illustration and about the imagination of the child reader. A comment from the poet Agnia Barto (1979, p.17) quoting the response of a seven year old reader to one of her poems, not only links poem and picture but reinforces the multiple functions of the imagination: 'Here is my drawing for your poem. I know it's not very good, but my imagination might end. Mummy says that it begins to end from the age of six, and it'll soon be my eighth birthday.'

Bradford (1993) in discussing various tensions and ambiguities in picture books makes two points which are relevant to the poetry picture book: first the importance of the dual implied reader, which for poetry is likely to consist of one older, or more probably, adult reader 'something that is rarely discussed in relation to the picture book, the notion of dual readership' (p.13). The reading of these books is a shared and social event. This may be more true of poetry than of fiction, for the school room is the most common place for the child to encounter poetry. Second it is no longer possible to assume that the picture book is exclusive to the younger child, in fact as Bradford says '[it] offers so many possibilities for ironic interplay and multiple constructions of meaning that it inevitably crosses boundaries between younger and older readers' (1993, p.14). The two poems discussed in this paper would have readers of significantly different ages, but the different illustrations for each may reduce or increase the age of the implied reader/s.

I wish to look briefly at two pairs of illustrated poems. I would argue that it is no coincidence that the poems that form the text for picture books are those that recall the ballad form: the role of oral presentation, the importance of listening is underlined by the strength of the patterning of sound. These poems are not lyrics, the poetry that has come to dominate poetry in the second half of the twentieth century, they are less complex, less figuratively dense, more readily understood by the young listener. In other words the choice of poem is an implicit acknowledgment not just of the level of textual comprehension possible by the child but also of the dual implied reader. While these texts are described as picture books they do not have the same relationship between text and picture that characterises the picture book discourse. I have deliberately used the term 'illustration' to indicate that the poem is the primary part of these texts. In fact both these poems had an initial existence independent of any illustration.

*The owl and the pussy cat* by Edward Lear is a poem for a young reader, the text being humorous and a rather subversive mixture of materialism and hedonism. In both examples the illustrations are a pictorial representation of the text. The artists meet the challenge of words that seem meaningless: 'bong' tree and 'runcible' spoon. Closer comparison of the two illustrations shows that the illustrations are doing something more: they are limiting and confining the possible responses of the reader. They are a visual control over the imaginative possibilities within the poem. The nurturing of the child's imagination may be the prime reason for reading poetry but the illustrations limit and control this concept; they construct an ideology that reconstructs the poem. It is also apparent that the illustrations have overt culturally specific ideologies that go beyond those suggested by the poem, these are most clearly seen in relation to the implications of 'married'. Kubick's (1996) illustration confirms the traditional accoutrements of a western wedding with a wedding veil and bridal bouquet, their existence made more apparent by the quasi-realistic depictions of the animals despite the upright position of the cat. The wedding icons are given greater incongruity than that of the association with animals by the definite oriental positioning of 'the land where the bong tree grows'. They dress Hob so that he disappears. The illustration by Voce (1991) seems at first to be more absurd, perhaps more in keeping with the humour of the poem but here too the cat is carrying a wedding bouquet, even though one flower may be thought of as a token. In both texts the existence of the flowers resolves the problem of determining gender, an issue that the poem totally avoids. The disparity in size of the owl and the cat and the continuing presence of a beatific smile serves to underline the absurdity of the poem rather than establish the animals as anthropomorphised beings. While Voce's illustration may be seen to be more sympathetic to the humour of the poem nonetheless it has a similar function to that of Kubick: love and the ritual of marriage defines the utopian.

*The highwayman* by Alfred Noyes is a poem for the older implied reader, one who might be reading the poem as a solitary rather than a shared activity. This poem is also about a love affair but it is a passionate and highly romanticised depiction of a doomed love that has become almost a cliché of the narrative poem.

The unattributed illustration in Hamilton and Colvin (1991) removes the sexual implications of both the soldiers and of the heroine. This illustration not only downplays the role of the soldiers and their lechery but makes the heroine an unlikely sexual object. She is shown as very young and it is improbable that this girl ever plaited 'a dark red love-knot into her long black hair'. This illustration is doing more than just defusing the sexuality that is fundamental to the whole story, it is denying it. On the other hand Keeping's illustration in Harrison and Stuart-Clark (1990) revels in the melodrama. The soldiers see her as an object of thwarted desire, their muskets epitomise the gun as phallic symbol, virtually raping her as she stands, and erect to challenge the approaching highwayman. It is hard to believe that the imaginative response of the young reader would be corrupted or harmed by this illustration, but it is equally certain that the response to the poem would be formed to a significant extent by the illustration. That this is more likely for the Keeping illustration would no doubt be due to the whole poem being accompanied by a number of illustrations. The adult reader may see the work of Keeping as a more valid response to what is in the poem, but be dubious about the foregrounding of sexual desire and sacrifice. The force of the Keeping illustrations moves the whole text more towards picture book rather than illustrated poem. The illustrations themselves also raise the question of the role of artistic and aesthetic value in determining the type and extent of the reader's response, questions that I can acknowledge but do not have the time to explore in this paper.

However any of these four illustrations is 'read' each reflects a similar ideology of the imagination: it is to be stimulated but controlled. The mere presence of illustrations to a poem shapes the imaginative response to the poem: the nature of picture gives the specific and particular to the poem, gives detail and substance to what may only be suggested (or suggestive) within the text. The perceived complexity of poetry discourse is not usually found in picture books; the assumption is that these poems do not require illustrations to help the child to understand them, they are needed to direct the imaginative response so that it is appropriate, ideologically sound, and culturally approved.

I would argue that the presence of illustrations in poetry texts long after poetry ceases to be an oral shared experience has three further implications. First it suggests that poetry needs to be mediated, reinforcing the perceived 'doubleness' of poetry signification. That is, poetry is positioned as having layers of meaning, of being a discourse that has to be solved like a problem or a puzzle, and thus to understand what a poem means the reader responds to or requires a pictorial guide.

Second it valorises the poem as a result of the imagination where the only appropriate accompaniment is an elite presentation of different kind of imaginative acts. The association of famous painting with poem is found in texts for the child and for the adult. To give just two examples, the Tate Gallery (1986) in London published an anthology of poems written in response to a painting within the collection; and for children, Charles Sullivan (1989, 1996) has edited two collections which pair poems and paintings from America, *Imaginary gardens* and *Imaginary animals*. Third there is the implicit assumption that there is a correlation not only between the imagination and a 'piece of art' but also between types of creative response or acts of the imagination. Being in touch with a work of art, the product of the imagination, may stimulate the imagination of the viewer, and may even lead to the production of an artistic response by that person. Lewis wrote: 'Fiction is written basically as an imaginative act, with the unspoken message from author to reader: '"Now let's imagine..." The child [reads] not only to understand the author's message, but to reflect upon it, assess it and *move beyond it imaginatively*' (1975, p.176, my italics). The assumption is that the imagination is not necessarily limited to, or associated with, one type of creative response. Michael and Peter Benton (1990) have compiled a school anthology, using the same title as this paper, based on this principle, linking poem and painting for mutual understanding.

I began this paper by suggesting that it would be useful to highlight the process which lead to its existence. This would not only provide the structure of the paper, through a series of questions, but it would reinforce the need to examine the fundamental assumptions that are part of the theoretical and critical discourse on children's literature. The questions centered around a defining ideology and the possible functions of the concept of the imagination. While I have limited my argument to the imagination and its associations with poetry there is no suggestion that this is the only unexamined concept in children's literature. It is important for a healthy critical dialogue that no assumption remain unexamined and that an overt process of questioning be used where least expected.

To end at the beginning: this paper is titled 'Double vision', not only because of the assumptions that are made about the linking of two creative processes, that of the artist and the poet but also because 'vision' has implications for the way in which we create an understanding of 'imagination'. Together the words suggest that the illustrated poem may be a doubling process, one of compound benefits, but it may also be one which blurs, perhaps deliberately, what is really happening when something is being created, and more importantly, what happens when we, child or adult, look at or read the end product. I began by arguing that the imagination of the child is positioned as an intrinsic and important part of childhood. Here the imagination is valorised, its role in the creative act is foregrounded. But the qualities with which we have imbued the concept of the imagination means that it must be controlled and tempered. This control is most needed with the multiple possibilities of meaning offered by poetry, and the most effective means of control, one that at the same time reinforces the importance of the imagination as such is the illustration.

# References

Adams, P. (1986). *With a poet's eye.* London: Tate Gallery Publications.

Barto, A. (1979). Children's responses to illustrations of poetry. *Children's Literature in Education*, **10**, 1, 11-17.

Benton, M. and Benton, P. (1990). *Double vision.* London: Hodder & Stoughton.

Bradford, C. (1993). The picture book: Some postmodern tensions. *Papers,* **4**, 3, 10-14.

Brewer, J. (1997). *The pleasures of the imagination.* London: HarperCollins.

Coleridge, S.T. (1975). *Biographia literaria*, ed. G. Watson. London: J.M. Dent.

Hamilton, E. and Colvin, D. (1991). *Patterns and pictures.* Melbourne: Longman Cheshire.

Harrison, M. and Stuart-Clark, C. (1990). *The Oxford book of story poems.* Oxford: Oxford University Press.

Lear, E. and Kubick, D. (1996). *The owl and the pussy-cat.* London: Walker Books.

Lear, E. and Voce, L. (1991). *The owl and the pussy-cat.* London: Walker Books.

Lewis, R. (1975). Fiction and the imagination. *Children's Literature in Education,* **19**, 172-177.

Matthews, S. (1998). *The eye of the soul.* Queensland: Magpies Magazine.

Mayne, W. (1984, 1997). *The book of Hob stories.* London: Walker Books.

Nodelman, P. (1988). *Words about pictures: The narrative art of children's books.* Athens: University of Georgia Press.

Paul, L. (1989). Intimations of imitations: Mimesis, fractal geometry and children's literature. *Signal,* **59**, 128-137.

Rosenblatt, L.M. (1978). *The reader, the text, the poem.* Carbondell: Southern Illinois University Press.

Smerdon, G. (1975). Children's preferences in illustration. *Children's Literature in Education,* **20**, 17-31.

Singer, J. and Singer, D.G. (1981). Television and reading in the development of the imagination. *Children's literature.* Vol.9. New Haven: Yale University Press, pp.126-136.

Stephens J. (1989). 'I am where I think I am'; Imagination and everyday wonders in William Mayne's Hob stories. *Children's Literature in Education*, **20**, 1, 37-50.

Sullivan, C. (1989). *Imaginary gardens.* New York: Harry N. Abrams.

Sullivan, C. (1996). *Imaginary animals.* New York: Harry N. Abrams.

# Part IV

# Gendered subjects

# 8. Embodied subjectivities: Female-authored texts and female friendships

## Clare Bradford

**Abstract:** In her introduction to *Engendering the subject: Self-representation in contemporary women's fiction* (1991) Sally Robinson argues that feminist theory needs to work in two directions at once: to dismantle the patriarchal categories in which woman is man's opposite (and negative), and to explore the multiple and contradictory ways in which women experience and manifest subjectivity; that is, to negotiate between the category Woman, and the various positions from which women speak. In this paper I concentrate on some female-authored texts for young adults (including Jane Gardam's *Bilgewater*, Judith Clarke's *Friend of my heart*, Margo Lanagan's *Touching earth lightly* and Emma-Kate Croghan's film *Love and other catastrophes*) to consider their representations of female friendships; how they locate such friendships within narrative and ideological frameworks and how they construct women as gendered subjects. In particular, I argue that while representations of female friendships in these texts are built on and articulate women's embodied experience, they are far from homogeneous in their writing of the female body; and that they argue different modes of female subjectivity. Thus, in *Bilgewater*, the friendship of Marigold and Grace, is located within a conservative political and social order which constructs female friendship in relation to the masculine, whereas Lanagan's representation of the friendship of Chloe and Janey, in *Touching earth lightly*, writes a version of the female body (and female friendship) which at least in part works as a critique of masculinist discourses and their positioning of women.

Feminist literary theory during the 1990s has seen a move away from 'attempts to specify the "difference" of women's writing' (Millard, Mills and Pearce 1996, p.154) (that is, its difference from men's writing) towards a more nuanced and complex view of writing, by women and men. For a focus on the *difference* between women's writing and men's writing always involved the danger of spiralling back into the masculinist constructions of Woman against which it reacted. Thus, discussions of difference easily became 'lost in an identification with the feminine as defined by the masculine' (Robinson 1991, p.95) because the category Woman relies on 'the humanist fiction of Western Man as universal subject and of Woman as the negative term which guarantees his identity' (Robinson 1991, p.3).

It's partly for this reason that two important articles on children's literature and the feminine, Lissa Paul's 1987 'Enigma variations' and Perry Nodelman's 1988

'Children's literature as women's writing' now seem so dated.  Both, drawing on gynocriticism and (to a lesser extent) French feminisms of the 1970s and 80s, depict children's literature as manifesting a set of thematic and discursive features which make it an essentially feminine field.  It's clear, reading these articles a decade on, that they reflect a necessary and important stage in feminist theory and criticism, but that their view of children's books as 'women's writing' homogenises both children's literature and the feminine.  No-one could possibly argue with the fact that historically, women have been far more involved than men in the production of texts for children, in critical work on such texts and in the teaching of children's literature within the academy; but it doesn't follow that all women writing for children write in similar ways, or that their work is informed by a common range of ideologies.

Sally Robinson suggests that thinking of women as a 'plural and heterogeneous category' (1991, p.3) enables feminist theory to move from a narrow and limited view of sexual difference, based on 'Woman's difference from Man' (1991, p.3) to a consideration of the multiple and contradictory ways in which women experience and manifest subjectivity.  Such a move is especially useful to theoretical and critical work on children's literature, because many of the interests addressed in contemporary feminist criticism (that is, questions of subjectivity, identity, location, and the varied positions from which texts are produced and received) are also crucial to the study of children's texts.  Moreover, a view of women's writing as a category Other to men's writing always tended to subsume other forms of difference (for example, of race, class, education, ethnicity and age) whereas an emphasis on differences *within* women's writing allows for the consideration of the ways in which these various kinds of difference intersect.

A common preoccupation in Young Adult texts is that of identity formation, a key aspect of which is the development of gendered subjectivities.  In this paper I'm looking at representations of female friendships in a set of female-authored texts: Judith Clark's underrated novel *Friend of my heart* (1994), Jane Gardam's *Bilgewater* (1976), and Margo Lanagan's *Touching earth lightly* (1996).  I'm not arguing that these are representative texts, or indeed that they're necessarily feminist texts; but by focusing on them I'll try to identify some of the differences *within* women's writing, differences which have to do with 'the politics of enunciation – who speaks, to whom, from where, and to what end' (Robinson 1991, p.27).  My discussion draws in part upon Sandra Gilbert and Susan Gubar's formulation of what they call 'female affiliation complex' (in Mills 1995, p.58), 'a textual signalling to the reader that the writer or the persona is affiliating with a particular literary tradition, either a mainstream one dominated by male writers and hence displaying value-systems which foreground maleness and masculinities, or, in a much more problematic way, a female tradition' (Mills 1995, p.58).  In Sara Mills' development of this idea, there are three possibilities for women writers: to 'adopt a supposedly masculine voice and align themselves with a male tradition; or…[to] adopt a stereotypically feminine voice and align themselves with the same set of values, since they are not challenging the status quo. The third position is one where women writers, mainly feminists, signal their alignment with a female tradition, by a range of cues within the text' (Mills 1995, p.58).

All the novels I'm discussing affiliate themselves, through their choices of point of view and focalisation, with a readership composed mainly of young women. *Bilgewater* frames Marigold/Bilgewater's first-person narrative within a prologue and epilogue focalised through a young woman known in the prologue only as 'the candidate' but in the epilogue as 'Miss Terrapin'. In *Friend of my heart,* focalisation shifts with some fluidity among characters, more often female than male; but when male characters, such as William or Valentine, are focalisers, their versions of events are set against the perspectives of female characters, as though against more authoritative readings. In *Touching earth lightly*, both sections of the novel switch between focalisation through the character of Chloe, and through a narrator whose perspective is close to Chloe's own.

All three novels, then, speak to female readerships; but the 'politics of enunciation' which they display are quite different. First to *Bilgewater,* and Bilgewater's stream of consciousness as she ponders on her friend, Grace Gathering:

> Grace I saw as a figure far, far above coarseness or sloppiness − a figure of real.
>
> Romance, a creature of turrets, moats and lonely vigils, gauntlets and chargers, long fields of barley and of rye.
>
> And now I was to be associated with her…I saw Grace Gathering in a floating dress and a tall cone of a hat with a flimsy bit of net fluttering behind it, drifting down to a river and lying flat out in a boat and the boat drifting smooth, smooth, down the river into a pearly haze beneath bridges. And I heard Grace's voice singing, singing, softer, softer and stopping, and then at the last bridge Lancelot himself leaning sadly over, sadly gazing.
>
> He said, 'She had a lovely face The Lady of Shalott.'
>
> And beside him on the bridge stood I - Bilgewater. It was to me he said it…
>
> (pp.54-55)

Here Marigold is represented as invoking the law of the father by speaking as 'Bill's daughter', Bilgewater, for her view of Grace is aligned with a particular strand of masculine writing in which Woman is objectified: that is, the Romantic fantasy through which male desire constructs Woman as beautiful, passive, unreachable and (in this case at least) conveniently dead. As Bilgewater observes Grace Gathering through the eyes of Lancelot, she seems to collude with his version of the feminine; she is, after all, his confidante, standing beside him on the bridge and watching him 'leaning sadly over, sadly gazing'. But this is a too-straightforward reading of the episode, because Gardam has written into Bilgewater's narrative a self-consciousness which suggests an ironic distance between implied author and narrator. The phrase 'a tall cone of a hat' invokes popular culture versions of medievalism (a hat like this might be hired for a fancy dress party); and the shifts of register in 'a flimsy bit of net' and 'lying flat out in a boat' disrupt the poetic (pseudo-Tennysonian) style of 'floating smooth, smooth, down the river into a pearly haze beneath bridges'.

Such disruptions of register, and the way in which Bilgewater's monologue teeters on the parodic, draw attention to the language itself, and to its mimicry of a masculine style. Mimicry can play a subversive function, as it does in many feminist texts, but in this episode from *Bilgewater* mimicry is directed not so much at masculine fantasies about prone and helpless women drifting along in boats, but more at Bilgewater herself, at her inappropriate and comical alignment with the masculine. At the same time, this episode normalises masculinist values, since it constructs relations between Bilgewater and Grace as subordinate to a romantic outcome between Bilgewater and Lancelot, who's identified later in the episode as 'Jack Lancelot'; that is, Jack Rose, Bilgewater's romantic ideal at this stage of the narrative. The episode ends as follows: 'Together we walked off the bridge, together forever with Grace Gathering's great big white and gold body sloshing about under the bridge and tipping about on the tide' (p.55).

Grace's body is here made into a spectacle and so objectified. This is clearly a signal to the reader of Bilgewater's displacement of her anxieties about her own body, which she regards as vastly inferior in shape and appearance to that of Grace. Of course, Bilgewater's obsession about the inadequacies of her body is a particularly feminine one, but the fantasy she creates is aligned with the well-worked masculine tradition in which the female body is the object of an appropriating and depersonalising gaze.

The narrative shape of *Friend of my heart* is dance-like, built on a pattern of couples forming, separating and reforming. Two of these couples are pairs of female friends: the young characters Daz and Joanna; and Daz's grandmother Sheila Thredlow and her girlhood friend Bonnie Lewis, whom she calls 'the friend of my heart'. Sheila Thredlow suffers from dementia and as her memory slips backwards and forwards between her girlhood and her life in the Sunset Rest Home, she mourns the loss of Bonnie, a loss intensified by the fact that she's unable to find a prized photograph of Bonnie as a young girl. The search for the photograph, and its final recovery, constitute the central strand of the narrative, and allow for comparisons between past and present which make both strange, avoiding a false universalism which represents the past as merely a version of the present.

I noted how Bilgewater's fantasy of Grace Gathering is aligned with a masculine view of the female body; in contrast, Daz and Joanna become friends when they argue about whether or not Joanna is fat or − as her mother has told her − merely has 'Big bones'. Daz insists that 'lots of people take size sixteen' (p.100) and that the *very* thin Joanna Winter (who wears size eight) 'looks like a snake' (p.100). The girls' developing friendship is metonymised by the chant they collaboratively create:

> 'Snakes wear eights! Sticks wear six!' they sang.
> 'And, and hens, Joanna; hens wear tens!'
> In that moment, chanting joyfully together, dancing towards the
> school gates, Daz and Joanna became friends. (p.101)

The values promoted to female readers throughout this episode are aligned with feminist agendas which resist the objectification and commodification of female bodies, as the text constructs a reading position which encourages resistance to dominant social norms about the desirability of thinness in women. The narrator-focalised sentence which concludes the passage displays Joanna and Daz acting out their resistance playfully, noisily; and *by way of their bodies* as they '[dance] towards the school gates'. In this way, Daz and Joanna's dance is aligned with traditions in feminist writing which seek to resignify female bodies by naming and celebrating women's embodied experience.

The principal story of female friendship in *Friend of my heart,* that of Bonnie Lewis and Sheila Thredlow, locates such friendship within a patriarchal system in which marriage to a steady provider is all that a girl should require to be happy. As Sheila Thredlow's memory ranges back and forward in time, she revisits her marriage to such a steady provider:

> He was a good man, she said again, slowly, like a child repeating a lesson it
> has to get by heart. A good man. But the phrase brought with it such a wave
> of overwhelming desolation that she had to sit down for a minute, right down
> on the floor with her back up against the wall, as if someone had knocked the
> breath right out of her. (p.119)

The struggle between convention and experience is articulated through the switch of focalisers, between Sheila's statement of what she knows she ought to think ('He was a good man') and the narrator-focalised comparison 'like a child repeating a lesson it has to get by heart'; but in the depiction of Sheila's bodily reaction to emotion, it's the fluidity of focalisation (both within and from outside Sheila's perspective) that provides an opening for young readers to understand the emotional journey of an eighty-year-old character. Sheila's memories of her husband Ken are juxtaposed against her memories of Bonnie Lewis; and this switch from husband to friend enacts the contrast, in Sheila's mind, between marriage and friendship. Her search for Bonnie's photograph is thus also a search for the memory of a relationship characterised by a warmth and intimacy lacking in her marriage: 'she'd have given her life, her very soul, for one brief glimpse of Bonnie's face' (p.119).

*Touching earth lightly* is centrally concerned with constructions of the feminine, and particularly of the female body, frequently represented in visual terms; Janey's transmutation from Goth to blonde, for example, symbolises her attempt to remake herself following her escape from her pathological family. On one hand, it seems that, merely by changing the way she looks, Janey can change the way she's looked *at*; but the narrative undermines her groping for identity in two ways: because it's focalised always through Chloe, never through Janey; and because the friendship of Janey and Chloe is represented within a scheme of binary oppositions. The first of these factors, focalisation through Chloe, means that Janey is always interpreted, explained, described, watched. Isaac and Chloe exchange glances over Janey's head 'like parents' over a sickly child' (p.58); after her transformation from Goth into shorn blond, Chloe, Nick and Isaac examine her 'new' face and discuss it almost as though *she* weren't present. And after Janey's death, Chloe's healing is effected largely through a process of visualisation and categorisation, during which Chloe photographs and labels places and objects associated with Janey, defining and fixing her in death in a way never possible in life.

Secondly, Janey's search for agency is undermined by the way she's depicted as the opposite of Chloe: within this scheme she appears as monstrous feminine, driven by her sexuality, with Chloe as 'normal', uncomplicated, under control. Several aspects of *Touching earth lightly* are clearly aligned with feminist agendas: Janey's frank enjoyment of her body, for example; Chloe's choice of Janey over Theo (that is, female friendship over conventional romance); Janey's subversive use of her father's pornographic magazines for cutouts to create the découpage images required by her teacher: 'Cupids. Roses. Girls in bonnets' (p.117). But these feminist agendas and strategies are countered by a powerful determinism which constructs Janey as subject to corporeality, ruled by the phases of the moon and of her menstrual cycle, and this style of representation is very close to the 'mixture of horror and desire that characterizes male constructions of the female body within Western discursive traditions' (Robinson 1991, p.129).

Another problematic feature of *Touching earth lightly* concerns its intersections of sexuality and class. Just as Chloe is all niceness, so her family is, as Janey says, 'like...angels or something' (p.8) and this generalised niceness attaches to the signifiers of middle-class life: the 'smells of wood fire and roasting lamb' (p.21) the 'elegant shoebox' (p.199) of the beachhouse where Chloe stays, her mother's occupation as a university lecturer. Janey's family, on the other hand, is entirely

Other: drunkenness, violence and incest are located within a class difference identified by the speech patterns of Janey's family and by the squalor of their home. These associations of class difference with sexual pathologies assume a programmatic social structure which adds to the sense of determinism surrounding the figure of Janey. In passing, I think that, like Grace Willow, the mother in Sonya Hartnett's *Sleeping dogs,* Janey's mother demonstrates the very great difficulty, for women writers, of writing an evil maternal: faced with the problem of depicting mothers within families where physical and sexual abuse occur, both Hartnett and Lanagan represent such mothers as blank or unknowing; hence, as less culpable than *knowing* mothers would be.

I'll conclude by considering how female friendships are located within the ideologies of the three novels as they manifest in narrative closure. *Bilgewater* ends in an enigmatic and unsettling fashion: the reader's discovery, in the epilogue, that Bilgewater is Lady Boakes, the Principal of Caius, requires a rereading of the novel which retrospectively transforms it from a *bildungsroman* to a more complicated narrative, one involving loss and compromise. For Miss Terrapin sees Bilgewater as 'saddish', as a person who's 'never done anything silly in her life' (p.200) and these two descriptors resonate with Bilgewater's message to Terrapin through his daughter: 'Will you say I'm sorry. About the tower' (p.200). The tower (rickety and unsafe) represents the moment of choice when Bilgewater rejected Terrapin for the more solid and lasting qualities of Boakes, now, in the words of Terrapin's irreverent daughter, 'old Sir Edward Boakes. Architect-architectorum. Excellentissimus. Magnificissimus' (p.199). In this way, the apparent closure of the final chapter, in which Paula returns, Miss Bex is discomfited and Boakes and Bilgewater find that they've won interviews at Cambridge, is undermined, because the epilogue interrogates Bilgewater's shaping of her own story (see Krips 1990).

Grace Gathering, who, as her daughter says, 'went off' and now lives in the Earls Court Road, represents a set of values and priorities utterly different from those which have formed Bilgewater as Lady Boakes, first woman Principal of Caius. But Bilgewater's search for subjectivity isn't marked for gender, since in the world view which Gardam proposes, being female is to fit within social and ideological structures created and sustained by masculine desires. For the same reason, female friendship doesn't carry significances in itself, but only insofar as it relates to broader humanist themes, which adhere to a male universal norm.

In *Friend of my heart*, closure is subverted by its constructedness. The characters form couples as though they were players in the final scene of a Shakespearean comedy, drawing attention to the cleverness of a plot which ends with such symmetry, everyone with a partner (or the hope of a partner). But this dance-like patterning is destabilised by its promise of a new beginning to the dance, occasioning new formations and relationships. Within this ending, with its promise of dissolution, the friendship of Sheila and Bonnie is the stable point around which everything else revolves, so that female friendship is privileged over romance, and romantic outcomes are treated as mutable and temporary.

At the end of *Touching earth lightly,* Chloe discovers what readers are cued to recognise from early in the novel: that she and Isaac are 'made for each other'. Chloe's former lover Theo implicitly provides a comparison with Isaac through their contrasting views of Janey. To Theo, she constitutes a threat to his relationship with Chloe, whereas to Isaac, Chloe's loyalty to Janey and her steadfastness are her most lovable qualities. At the same time, it's because of Janey's death that a romantic closure is, in narrative terms, both possible and desirable. For the relationship between Janey and Chloe is constructed as an inherently unequal one: Janey as needy and as unwell; Chloe as healthy and as burdened by Janey's needs. Isaac is thus the corrective to all Janey's flaws, being sane, healthy and rich. When the two relationships are lined up in this way, it's clear that many of the contrasts between them derive from Janey's representation as monstrous feminine; a romantic outcome thus effects a curiously conventional closure: as safety, resolution and certainty.

Quite without meaning to, I've considered three novels featuring dead young women, and it's not too much to say that they all die because they're Woman – that is, they're defined through their difference from (and dependency on) the masculine. In Bilgewater's fantasy, Grace/the Lady of Shalott dies of longing for Lancelot; Bonnie is discovered to have died young because she joined the army as a nurse, despairing of gaining the love of Sheila's brother; Janey dies of an excess of femaleness. The novels align themselves quite differently from traditions of narrative, but the three dead girls show how durable and powerful the discursive figure of Woman is. If 'narrative is one arena in which gender and subjectivity are produced in powerful ways' (Robinson 1991, p.10), it's also an arena in which the tensions between Woman and women manifest in disruptions and contradictions.

# References

Clarke, J. (1994). *Friend of my heart.* St Lucia: University of Queensland Press.

Gardam, J. (1976). *Bilgewater.* London: Hamish Hamilton.

Krips, V. (1990). *Bilgewater:* A rose by any other name? In *Fiction for adolescents: Proceedings of Children's Literature Conference.* Melbourne: Victoria College, pp.77-89.

Lanagan, M. (1996). *Touching earth lightly.* Sydney: Allen & Unwin.

Millard, E., Mills, S. and Pearce, L. (1996). French feminisms. In *Feminist readings/Feminists reading*, eds S. Mills and L. Pearce. London: Prentice Hall, pp.153-184.

Mills, S. (1995). *Feminist stylistics.* London: Routledge.

Nodelman, P. (1988). Literary theory and children's literature. Children's literature as women's writing. *Children's Literature Association Quarterly,* **13**, 1, 31-34.

Paul, L. (1987). Enigma variations: What feminist theory knows about children's literature. *Signal,* **54**, 186-201.

Robinson, S. (1991). *Engendering the subject: Self-representation in contemporary women's fiction.* Albany: State University of New York Press.

# 9. Shaping girls in an Australian context: Constance Mackness, educator and author (1882-1973)

**Pam Macintyre**

> For history is not simply a record of 'what happened'; it involves competing recounted versions of the past. Some versions get suppressed, they do not get written, or alternatively they are neglected or discredited in favour of received versions. (Hergenhan 1988, p.xii)

**Abstract:** Books written for, and read by girls formed an important part of their culture and their perceptions of themselves as female. Women who shaped the texts, helped to shape the culture. This paper will examine the construction of gender identity through this significant form of cultural transmission, stories written for girls and young women during the early twentieth century in Australia. It is concerned with the socio-cultural context of the production and reception of these texts and constructs an analysis of them to explicate what they say, represent and what they are about – their themes, viewpoints and ideologies. Such an analysis demonstrates how cultural sites shape narrative fictions and how texts affect the culture by shaping the consciousness of young readers. The exploration of this duality is the task of this paper, specifically in relation to gender identity.

Constance Mackness's life and work will be used as an example. Her public role as a shaper of culture is twofold, as educator and writer, and the relationship between the personal and public milieu will be examined for connections, separations, tensions, contradictions. As a principal of a Church school, she is not typical of her kind, in background or position. A probing of the importance of meritocracy in her personal life, her public life as an educator of girls and its reflection in her fiction should prove revealing as will the contrast between the freedom of spirit, independence and potential public success valued in her girls, both real and fictional and the position, demeanour, roles and happiness of the women in her novels, both mothers and teachers. The passive ideology revealed in her fiction makes apparent what her personal memoirs and public writings do not; the dominant social ideology is so pervasive and strong that it persists in the face of fifty years of personal experience which appear to contradict or at least question it.

This paper seeks to investigate the construction of gender identity through one of the most significant forms of cultural transmission, stories written for girls and young women. There has been no systematic research to document the lives and milieu of the women who wrote for girls as there has been for women who wrote for adults, in Modjeska's *Exiles at home* (1981) for example. While these writers for girls and their writing were not part of the male high culture and were ignored by that culture, their lives and work formed a significant part of the popular subculture of women and children including the spheres of education and schools. Women's magazines of the 1920s, 1930s and 1940s such as *The Australian Woman's Mirror* and *Woman's World* included articles about the authors and reviews of their works. Similarly, the major reviewing journal of the period, *All About Books*, under the editorship of Nettie Palmer, incorporated reviews of books written for girls, usually in the category of 'Popular reading'. Today, contemporary histories of Australian children's literature (Wighton 1979; Saxby 1969, 1971, 1993; Niall 1979; Lees and Macintyre 1993) source these stories for girls and acknowledge their significance in the development of a national literature and the indebtedness of current writing to the heritage. Readers also saw these books as important in defining what it meant to be an Australian girl, and they were widely read. In 1933, for example, in what Angus and Robertson described as a 'bleak time for both literature and life', Amy Mack's stories, nevertheless, sold over 80,000 copies, with Mary Grant Bruce's sales exceeding 40,000 excluding the Billabong series, figures that would make most contemporary authors for young people incredulous (Dutton 1984, p.9).

Books written for, and read by, girls formed an important part of their culture and their perceptions of themselves as female. Women who shaped the texts helped to shape the culture. However, the construction of girls in Australian fiction and the lives of the women who created those images in stories for girls is still largely a void in the documentation of the culture of Australian writing and gender construction. Histories and commentaries of writing for children are rarely integrated into the discussion of mainstream literature; they are always acknowledged in their category of 'children's literature'.

For most of the nineteenth century, (since the first generally acknowledged book published in Australia for children, Charlotte Barton's *A mother's offering to her children* 1842), writing for children was dominated by the boy's adventure story, written for an overseas readership with Australia providing a rich and exotic setting for what had become a formulaic story of taming the elements and the soul. Frequently the writers of these stories had not, or only briefly, visited Australia. While the protagonists were most often young men, girls and women were not absent from the stories of frontier life. Most often, their role was as household fairy, to add gentility and refinement as they set a nice table with a crisply ironed cloth, even in the roughest of outback settings, earning the eternal admiration and respect of the bushman.

Towards the end of the nineteenth century as the states moved towards nationhood, settler stories, romances, fantasies and fairy tales, school stories and family stories, aimed at a local readership, challenged the pre-eminence of the adventure story and moved the action to the domestic setting (the most famous being Ethel Turner's *Seven little Australians* 1894). A common feature of these stories was the need to stress what it meant to be Australian often in opposition to being British: authors regarded themselves as Australian. Girls in these stories took up centre stage as often as did the boys. In the tradition established by Turner, many of these fictional girls were allowed freedom, adventurousness and a good deal of high spirits. Revolting against too-fast strictures was presented as the province of girls as well as boys, especially when it was as trivial as wearing stockings or speaking nicely. However, social distinctions were still to be kept even though they may be a source of conflict.

So, while girls had always read their brothers' books, in the early decades of the twentieth century increasingly books were published specifically for them, many by Ethel Turner's publisher Ward Lock. In the twentieth century girls' stories took over. That books were readily and acceptably labelled as 'books for boys' or 'books for girls', suggests a separation of spheres of interest, occupation and behaviour along clear gender lines. In this, the Australian context differs little from the English.

However, many writers were conscious of being 'Australian', of writing out of a place that was 'other' than England, about people who were 'other' than English, as Ethel Turner's famous opening to *Seven little Australians* epitomises:

> If you imagine you are going to read of model children, with perhaps a naughtily inclined one to point to a moral, you had better lay down the book immediately and betake yourself to Sandford and Merton, or similar juvenile works. Not one of the seven is really good, for the very excellent reason that Australian children never are. (1894, p.7)

Turner is here suggesting that she has no intention of writing the stock characters of domestic fiction, though Pearce (1997) argues ultimately that is what Turner does. *Seven little Australians* (Turner 1894) was read by Australian writers as disparate as Christina Steed, Hal Porter, Randolp Stow, Nancy Keesing, and Dorothy Hewitt who felt passionate about it (Dutton 1984, pp.50-54) and as Brenda Niall says in *Seven little Billabongs*, 'it would be hard to think of any other Australian book which is so widely known' (1982, p2).

Mary Grant Bruce's novels, with their rural, bush settings identified what being Australian meant to many of their readers: 'The only feeling of being Australian, and the only ideas about Australia came to me through the Billabong books' (Alexander 1979, p.98). Stephen Murray Smith in his response to Geoffrey Dutton's survey of childhood reading says: 'The message of the Turner/Bruce books was basically a fairly simple one: that there really was a country called Australia about which people wrote books and towards which it was not eccentric to feel a measure of affection', to which Dutton adds 'This modest message is in fact the basis of a national literary tradition' (Dutton 1984, p.62). Dutton further points out that six of the most popular writers in his survey were women.

Gender is ideologically implicit, constructed and construed in these books, and certainly Bruce and Turner presented their ideas on what it was to be an Australian girl. To suggest, however, that fiction merely reflects life, is simplistic and naive. The interaction between the social milieu influencing writers and the writers shaping the text to create their interpretation of the world at a given time is a complex one. However, texts can be examined to show what society thinks about itself and how writers attempt to construct a cohesive structure of our culture. As Modjeska says:

> When literary texts are seen as bearers of meanings and ideologies within a culture, it becomes clear that women's writing has had a great deal to offer a broader social history...Fiction can articulate not just what is imposed as a social and intellectual system, but the lived experience of it and the conflicts within it...Thus a novel can at once resonate with the values of liberal ideology and patriarchal culture and be simultaneously critical of them. (1981, p.10)

This can apply just as well to the novels of women writers who wrote for girls as it does to the writers in Modjeska's study. Ideas of femininity are worked out in the public sphere of school and professional life as well as in families. As fiction, also in the public sphere, seeks to shape the world presented to girls, it is an important site of cultural construction.

In analysing the construction of identity by women writers for girls, in Australia, and the contribution made to recording and shaping girls' culture that women writers have made, it is important to probe *why* women writers were shaping an understanding of gender identity − what were the historical, social, political, class and personal factors that made gender identity a central concern of their fiction? Also significant is an understanding of *how* they were shaping a gender identity. Many were professional women who were breaking up the nineteenth century tradition of the genteel woman writing as a hobby. They were middle class women writing from an educated, middle class viewpoint and who saw their readers as similar to themselves. How they shaped identity is both elaborated and confined by class.

In constructing fictional lives for girls within families and schools, authors were writing during a period when imperialist doctrine was still the single most defining philosophy describing what was 'womanliness' and what was 'manliness', largely in opposition to each other. No doctrine even if strongly held, is static nor is it expressed in the same fashion by every exponent. And while concepts of femininity and masculinity derived from a British imperialist society it was a society that had been redefining those concepts throughout the nineteenth century. The nineteenth century ideal of the woman as the 'Angel in the house' was being challenged by a new independence, with women seeking meaningful existence outside the domestic sphere. However, this movement for paid work in establishing women's independence and a sense of meaningful occupation must be seen in class terms. It meant little to working class women who worked for survival in occupations that enforced hardship rather than value.

While Australian women writers who wrote for adolescent girls during 1910-1950 dominated the juvenile field, there were qualifications to their achievement. In fact, White suggests that many writers were writing their domestic and romance tales for young audiences as 'the lesser option' because they lacked the support and guidance necessary to survive in the mainstream (White 1993, p.87). Certainly the life and work of Lilian Turner is evidence of that and joining the stable of Ward Lock suggested a particular audience and style, the 'flapper' novels as Niall refers to them. There is evidence that in writing about talented girls whose ambitions were frustrated by domestic repression, authors were writing out of their own experience, and like the adult writers Marjorie Barnard and Jean Devanny for example, expressing their own frustrations while attempting to protest concerning the 'woman question'. The tensions of working within the model of womanhood constructed by imperial ideology while simultaneously being critical of it are evident in the works of writers for young women.

Many of the writers were journalists often being editors of children's pages, or having published poetry, non-fiction and adult titles as well as their writing for children. Some, like Constance Mackness and Ruth Hawker, were teachers, others like Marion Downes worked as secretaries. Apart from the occasional documented contact, such as Ethel Turner's encouragement of Vera Dwyer there is little evidence of a support network. Whether most of them were encouraged to maintain their child audience while wanting to move into the adult field, like the Turners almost being children's writers by default, is yet to be revealed.

During the period after Federation, Australia, a former colony, was busy defining what it meant to be 'Australian', against what was 'British'. So for writers there was this 'double definition' of what it meant to be female and feminine, and what it meant to be an *Australian* female. Writers such as Bruce, the Turner sisters, Vera Gladys Dwyer and Norma Handford demonstrate the plurality of construction and the differing tensions in writing within the dominant orthodoxy of imperialism. While their novels reveal a consciousness of the restrictions this dominant orthodoxy placed on girls pushing against the strictures, they were aware of presenting to adolescent girls, images and roles of women that were consistent with the roles available to women and girls within the imperialist doctrine. Writing about spirited, independent girls seemed to propose few difficulties. Having these girls grow into acceptable womanhood was a problem, so severe for some, that their characters were killed off. Of course, the girls in fiction are as various as their authors and growing up never posed a problem for Mary Grant Bruce's androgynous Norah Linton.

What these writers do have in common, despite the plurality of their voices, is that the image of girls provided by British imperialism is modified by them, in the context of Australia as nation (newly fledged), in which a sense of national identity, idiom and place serve to temper the central tenets of the doctrine, and the centrality of the doctrine in the lives of Australian fictional girls. Turner's girls, most notably Judy, are headstrong, fierce and, as Niall says, 'There is not much heroic about the careers of the Woolcots...In suffering and death, in noble sentiments and actions, their record is mediocre – that is, in comparison with the standard set by their literary predecessors' (Niall 1979, p.61).

Annette (Cheyne 1941), Gem (Mackness 1914), Jennifer (Lister 1941), Poppy (O'Harris 1941), Betty (Lilian Turner 1906), Norah and Judy between them run away, act, write, paint, build a house, muster sheep, hide a bushranger, fight bushfires, expose spies while remaining clean and neat and sometimes being able to cook up a storm or at least set a nice tea table. The setting of Australia itself determines some of these actions as distinctly Australian. But that setting is also busy creating an identity in which authors are situated and out of which they write. Judy and Betty would know how to behave in an English drawing room but they'd much rather be running or galloping through a bushy paddock or telling stories in a backyard. While they may want to pursue their careers or interests after marriage and feel the pressures of the domestic, they would recognise marriage, being a wife and mother, as the true feminine vocation, and love a motivating force often able to conquer all.

> A large part of any book is written not by its author but by the world the author lives in. (Hollindale 1988, p.32)

Constance Mackness (1882-1973) was an educator and children's author and the first female dux of Fort Street Model Public School, Sydney. After graduating from the University of Sydney, she became a teacher at Presbyterian Ladies College, Croydon, then at Pymble and finally headmistress of Presbyterian Girls College, Warwick where she remained for thirty-two years until her retirement.

She wrote ten novels for girls between 1914 and 1937. The biographer of her entry in the *Australian dictionary of biography* pays tribute to her achievements:

> Her scholastic career was quite spectacular for a woman of her background and her period. As a headmistress in Queensland she was outstanding, and

her books were in most school libraries when I was a girl. They appeared often as Sunday School prizes and as family gifts, particularly in church-going families. (Bonnin 1983)

Muir (1992) lists five editions of *Gem of the Flat*, four of *Miss Pickle* and two of *The Glad School*, evidence in support of Mackness's books being widely read.

Constance Mackness is additionally interesting as, being born in Australia, from a humble rural background and state educated, she is not typical of other Church, especially Presbyterian, private school principals of the period. She is situated in the vanguard of women entering tertiary institutions. Ideas and understandings of meritocracy as the ideal system of authority and its motivation of her private and public lives shapes her milieu. She was one of the first female principals of a Presbyterian girls' school at a time when the Church's organisation was patriarchal. Her childhood, during the agricultural depression in a small rural community in the 1890s, frames her attitudes towards those country families for whom wealth was an idea not a reality. One might also place significance on her Scottish background, and the commitment to learning.

In literary terms she began writing after the fierce *Bulletin*-inspired nationalism of the 1890s, in the wake of Ethel Turner's *Seven little Australians* (1894). Her literary influences are eclectic, having read 'some Shakespeare, Goldsmith and even Dr Johnson' before commencing school. Australian literature was not studied at the University of Sydney during her undergraduate tenure though for her *The fortunes of Richard Mahoney* 'is still Australia's greatest novel' (Mackness 1972). While her books were widely read, and she was reasonably prolific, writing was secondary to her educational role. There is no evidence of involvement in literary societies or groups. Writers for young people had none of their own and she was not championed as was Ethel Turner, by A. G. Stephens and the *Bulletin*, although she apparently wrote for it. Considered an educational reformer she was a literary conservative, her books fitting well into Ward Lock's range and being deemed suitable to a genteel English audience.

Mackness was a product of a society that was asserting its nationhood yet still acknowledging England as the mother country, and basing its ideology on pervasive expressions of imperialist ideals. She was employed for nearly all her working life by a male dominated, patriarchal church body and there were tensions in her life and work that suggest her shaping of girls' identity and culture bear close analysis.

The importance of being clever and educated is central to Mackness's ethos, whether the clever person is male or female. The centrality of intelligence and academic success is understandable in an author whose life is tribute to the success and empowerment provided by an understanding of meritocracy as the best measure of authority. Constance sat for Matriculation at end of her first year at Fort Street

Model School when she was fifteen years old, but was not entered for 'one of the only three bursaries given to girls' (Mackness 1972). They had been awarded to Sydney High School girls. 'I heard that I had come top! I had to wait a year and sit again when I was sixteen'. There is little rancour in her account of this policy and perhaps the experience of being 'special' for having matriculated so young coated the slightly bitter pill as did the further confirmation of the success of meritocracy in effecting change in her life and giving her access to independent power. This experience has echoes in her fiction and may be seen as an early influence on the development of her philosophy at Presbyterian Girls' College. 'I had the pleasure of winning the top bursary again and going on to the University [at an early age and at a time when women students were in a minority]. Fort St had been a happy two years – 1897 and 1898 – for me, and first implanted in my mind the idea of a "Glad School" which I got a chance to work out in Warwick more than twenty years later' (Mackness, 1972). There is little to draw upon to connect her school experience with her later educational philosophy but the strong, clever girl allowed to work largely independently and achieve success happily and without apparent barriers suggests that the climate of learning was influential rather than any specific curriculum or pedagogy.

> At PLC Croydon the teachers & girls were all friends, and the Principal Dr Marden was honoured and loved by us all for his unfailing courtesy, kindness, brilliant brain and integrity. (Mackness 1972)

This environment of friendly relations between teacher and pupils was a major aspect of the atmosphere and philosophy of her own school. It is a maternal, caring view, fostering the ideology of women and girls' emotional strengths and positions, and a sense of democracy in the power relations between teachers and pupils. It is also a philosophy that relies on a child-centred approach to learning and teaching and a genuine liking and respect for girls. Her admiration for Dr Marden is in terms of his demonstration of those feminine and democratic attributes, as well as his intellect.

A second Presbyterian Ladies College at Pymble was being constructed and Dr Marden asked Constance Mackness to be his Headmistress there. She accepted. He was Principal of both schools.

> The Headmistress certainly had the busiest time, looking after the boarders in health & sickness, supervising the housekeeping, teaching English, French & European history to Seniors & Sub-Seniors & finding time to entertain visiting parents & V. I. P.'s. However, I had delightful girls to teach and to live with, the lovely bushland round the school was a constant joy and I had always liked work. All the same feminist ideas worried me at last. There was a general idea that when the setting was complete, Dr Marden would remain at Croydon & a VP would be made Principal at Pymble. I had tried him in the balance of my mind & found him wanting. (Mackness 1972)

Constance decided to resign and Marden told her he was negotiating the Principalship of the Warwick school. It is difficult to deduce from her remarks concerning the sudden dawning of her feminism (a dawning one senses had been resisted or at least reluctant) whether it was prompted by an objection to the individual vice-principal or, perhaps more likely considering her wording, an affront to her sense of fair play, her ideas of meritocracy which had thus far prevented her from acknowledging the patriarchal culture of the Presbyterian Church. She had evidently worked hard, long and efficiently and dissented at being overlooked in favour of someone she regarded as less than herself, apparently on the grounds of gender prejudice:

> What gave me a personal twinge of revolutionary fervour was that Dr Marden whose invariable courtesy and kindness made his female staff forgive that the male head of a girls school had to leave much of the most difficult and valuable part of moulding the girls' characters to them, but himself received almost all the reward for it. (Mackness undated)

While no parallel event is included in her school fiction, there is no doubt that the happiest school, The Glad School, is one that is run and attended exclusively by women and girls and in accordance with feminised attitudes.

Constance became Principal of the Warwick school from its opening in February 1918 till she resigned at the end of 1949.

> I was sorry to leave my Pymble girls who included two particularly brilliant ones − Marie Byers, the first woman solicitor in NSW & author of many works on Oriental religions & Maisie Grieg-Smith, who dropped the Smith when she wrote a series of popular romances. (Mackness 1972)

The use of the maternal 'my girls' sits happily beside the acknowledgment that success and fame are important to women, confirming her interest in meritocracy. Nurturing fosters achievement, freedom of experience and expression. Mackness regards equally, academic and popular writing, perhaps because her own writing was considered to be 'popular'.

Her commitment to meritocracy, interwoven with her childhood and her conception of herself as the daughter of a 'college man' was influential in the shaping of Presbyterian Girls College, Warwick.

> And have we any true conception of the tragedy intellectual starvation means to bright children? The child of uneducated parents, with little inherited taste for knowledge, feels no want of a better school than the one the lonely bush can supply, but it is otherwise with the child of a college man.
>
> (Mackness 1919)

So while she abhors overt 'snobbishness' and serves it harsh treatment in her novels, her egalitarian spirit is tempered by passive ideas of class as exhibited in this nexus between her life and her educational philosophy – she may have been brought up in impecunious material circumstances, but with a strong sense of intellectual superiority.

The inclusion of science, mathematics and Latin, as well as French, arithmetic, geography, mark her curriculum as modern, and influenced by the New Education movement and not solely fitting her students to be competent in the traditional female accomplishments.   Her curriculum was inclusive, integrating and giving equal regard to the 'housewifery' subjects of dressmaking, needlework and cookery alongside drama, music, art and original writing.   She also introduced classes in shorthand, typing and bookkeeping, which may have been a reaction to the opening of business colleges, but also a recognition that many of her students were not academically able, yet should be prepared to support themselves.  Past students have expressed their gratitude for these skills which allowed them working independence rather than a return to domestic slavery on family properties.

Constance's writing, whether her school stories based on her own teaching experiences, or her family stories was characterised by her construction of a distinct, girls' culture.  As Mitchell (1995, p.3) argues, girls' culture suggested new ways of being, new modes of behaviour, and new attitudes that were not yet acceptable for adult women.   A strong aspect of Mackness's writing was the portrayal of outspoken, lively, physically active girls who were not afraid to defy authority, and who recognised that they could be such girls for only a brief few years before they grew up to be traditional women.  Her girls were not apprentice conventional adult women: they were allowed behaviours, attitudes and activities that were to be encouraged in girls while not yet acceptable for adult women.  Her fictional girls were based on a conscious awareness of their own culture and an acknowledged, even celebrated, discord with adult expectations; they were largely androgynous, had freedom and few proscriptions.  Their independence and forthrightness seemed to have little adverse effect on their femininity or desirability as wives and mothers, once they became adults.  However Mackness was conscious that the lives of girls in her fiction must change once they were required to undergo adult metamorphosis.

While Constance's commitment to meritocracy was fundamental to her life and fiction, it had its limits; it did not challenge the separate spheres and women's role within, or outside them.   While she was keen for her pupils to do well and she emphasised class rankings, competition and prizes, the encouragement to move into the public sphere was in terms of good works.  Her books are about thirteen and fourteen-year-old girls who suit her story interests by being able to get up to all sorts of escapades which as 'juniors' they do not have to give up to the more serious side of study, or to the more important business of becoming grown up and lady-like.

This is not to suggest that she was unaware of contemporary debates, especially women's rights as concrete issues. In *Miss Pickle* (1924) she is sardonic about Maria and Eliza, 'who regard themselves as socialists' and who instigate debates on 'Should a slavey be called Miss and sit down to meals with the Boss and the Missus?' or 'the nationalisation of industries'. 'Eliza, a champion of women's rights, was a bitter enemy of man the oppressor – at least in theory. She had a lean lanky father and two leaner and lankier brothers on the far-back station at home, whom she adored, but that was a detail that did not count' (1924, p.127).

She is placed by personal circumstances in a situation which is reflected in the lives of several of her fictional teachers, that is working to support the family.

> There was a dark side to Aunt's life. Always her decisions were governed by her deep love and sense of duty to her family, religion and moral beliefs. Because of the nature of the illness of her brother Len, [he suffered from epilepsy] and her need to provide for him, she refused the opportunity of marriage to a man she loved and respected. A wealthy man, he was willing to shoulder her family responsibilities, but her sense of fair play and fierce independence would not let her accept his offer. (Letter from her niece Phyllis Wilbe (1984) confirmed by Leslie de Conlay's husband John Manning)

These family circumstances and romantic mythology find expression in her stories. The teachers in her school stories are all either supporting elderly parents or family, or teaching only as an interim before finding a suitable husband – falling in love, that is. Constance is committed to the reforming and romantic power of love and the true and satisfying vocation for women as wife and homemaker, and perhaps this is because her own family placed itself above her public life. Her success as a principal and her early promise as a scholar were ignored by her family.

> She [Constance] felt deeply that she did not have the respect and affection from her family that was so readily given her by her students and associates. She had sacrificed many of the desires and dreams of her youth to succour her family, and suffered because she felt that these sacrifices were unappreciated by those who owed her so much. (Phyllis Wilbe 1984)

This can be seen however within the terms of her own 'motherhood' of her pupils. While she readily acknowledges her commitment to the welfare of her students in her memoirs, and many of her past students recall instances of her care, it is her fiction that reveals unacknowledged tensions between her actual family circumstances and her ideals:

> 'It is a shame,' [Mrs Channing] said 'to inflict such a silly sounding name on a dear little girl. If it suited her, even! But she is the quietest, gentlest, sweetest little soul imaginable, dignified and old-fashioned enough just to suit her real name, Frances Monica Catherine.'

'Do you think so?' smiled Miss Martin. 'Those eyes spell imp, or I am much mistaken.'

'Do you think so?' repeated Mrs Channing unconsciously, and in a tone of bewildered incredulity. 'I have had her with me for a week and − well, you see what a lamb she is.'

'Has she been with other children?'

'Well, no she hasn't.'

'Then, my dear Mrs Channing, your estimate of Wuzzie will want revising for school use. Children with grown-ups, and children with other children, are very different things.'

Mrs Channing lifted her eyebrows sceptically. She did not believe that years spent in training the young entitled Miss Martin to be a quicker judge of youthful character than was she, who had brought up four stalwart sons. It was absurd enough, as it was, for such a blue-eyed, yellow-haired, doll-like creature, who claimed to be almost forty and looked just twenty, to be running a big school, and running it efficiently; but let her not presume to know more about children than those older and stouter and taller than her petite self. (1927, pp.2-3)

Later, Miss Martin (alias a prettier Mackness) is proved correct when Wuzzie climbs a perilous tree to rescue a kitten and entertains her audience by leaping over a garden chair. Mackness reveals attitudes towards motherhood and bringing up girls that are a constant theme in her work, and also the prejudice she may well have suffered from the well-to-do (who receive short shrift in her fiction). In this story she attributes it to youthful beauty (only one of which belonged to her − youth) and the putative superiority of actual rather than virtual mothering. But it may well be a metaphoric displacement of prejudice based on her social and educational background.

> ...how do you think I'll ever grow like dear little mother − sweet and good and a lady? (Mackness 1914, p.3)

Her first book *Gem of the Flat* (1914) is based on her early life 'on a smallholding in a family which lived by gold fossicking, rabbit-shooting and small crops' (Bonnin 1986, pp.318-319) and yet there are differences between life and art. Gem is an orphan and only child whereas Constance had parents and siblings. The story is set on 'Needy Flat' where the family is comprised of Gem and her grandfather. Gem's father, a law student, with a highly regarded published book, met her mother at University. 'They were both clever, both wrote poetry...' (p.4). After their marriage, her father gave up law to become editor of a country paper. When Gem was two, her father died of typhoid leaving her mother penniless. Her mother's wealthy parents, angry at her poor marriage, refused to help her. It appears she died of a broken heart. Constance's sense of the romantic paints a poignant scenario but perhaps also reveals a sense of wistful imagining of her ideal parents and of being an only child.

The supposed life Constance gives her parents reveals the ambiguity in what she values, tensions and ambiguities that run through all her fiction. There is no doubt that the independent side of her – as evidenced in the portrait of Gem and in the following excerpt from *The Glad School* (1927) (referring to the Principal, a disguised Constance) '…I guess she was some player-up when she was a youngster. That's why when she comes down, she does it with a grin of sympathy' (p.166) – admired, loved and respected her father, and her fictional reincarnation of him as Gran.

And yet, another side of her was clearly attached to the importance of formally recognised academic achievement – meritocracy had proved its authority in her life. While just as she came from fairly humble beginnings she retains sympathy for similar characters in her books, for example scholarship girls, especially if minister's daughters, and is harsh on snobbishness, she is also very pejorative of any display of 'common' behaviour. Well bred or brought up girls always display the characteristics of gentility even if they are pranksters. Freedom of spirit, admirable enough in a young girl and perhaps a man, needs to be subordinated to the proper model of a young lady.

Perhaps in removing the parents from Gem's life, Mackness was acknowledging a common pattern of the time in the fiction written for children and following that fashion. Perhaps also, it suited her narrative and ideological purposes to have Gem largely uncircumscribed by parental restrictions, to be independent, to have the freedom to roam in a rural environment. No doubt this was appealing to her British as well as Australian readers. At a narrative level it is a successful device as Mackness from the beginning sets up tension between the actual life of Gem (which is most appealingly drawn) and her ideal life which would to be a 'lady' like her mother 'cultured, capable, charming'. This operates to unsettle the desirability of ladylikeness; the reader is only given Gem's idea of what constitutes being a 'lady' and therefore it is likely to be distrusted by the reader, not because Gem is an unreliable narrator but because we wouldn't find her nearly as appealing if her activities and spirit were subdued by her idea of being ladylike. As well there is an absence of the actual lady against which the ideal might be measured.

> Gem was a willful little woman, with a love of her own way and belief in her
> own ideas. Full of ambitions and aspirations herself…She was a bookworm
> and a dreamer like her father, but with it all no child was ever more practical.
> (1927, p.11)

The book from its very opening declares what Mackness sets up to be the irony, that
the quest to be 'lady' is constantly thwarted by Gem's forthrightness, independence
and frankness.  It may appear that Mackness is intending to query the importance of
being a 'lady' but rather she seeks to portray a twelve-year-old child (an important
choice of age – still a child but on the cusp of adolescence and aware of her
imminent period of transformation) whose lively temperament is to be fostered
rather than quashed.  Gem never has to sacrifice her personality or independence,
but neither is she a true rebel.  Although she might long to wear bright pink, fussy
clothes, she is given a more demure cashmere, clothing that is symbolic of the
modification of her spirit when she becomes a 'young lady'.

Mackness, as educator and writer, is constructed by her circumstances.  Her shaping
of girls is influenced by her life, milieu, commitment to meritocracy, Christianity
and her class.  There are inherent tensions in the writings of a woman who had not
married nor had children, had a career and professional education, yet saw her
primary role as educating girls to become wives and mothers.  One of the
characteristics of her style of education was 'motherliness', and the family an
institution to which she retained a strong commitment.  The unacknowledged point
of unease between her sense of the importance of meritocracy in shaping her life,
and the lives of women, and the placing of her family above that successful public
life is not readily resolved in her life, or in her fiction.  Keeping her exuberant,
mischievous, headstrong heroines young, allows her to avoid confronting,
uncomfortable possibilities.

# Bibliography

## Novels

Barton, C. (1842). *A mother's offering to her children.*  Sydney: The Gazette.

Bruce, M. G. (1910). *A little bush maid.*  London: Ward Lock.

Cheyne, I. (1941). *Annette of River Bend.*  Sydney: Angus & Robertson.

Lister, G. (1941). *Jennifer stands by.*  Sydney: Angus & Robertson.

Mackness, C. (1924). *Miss Pickle.*  London: Oxford University Press.

Mackness, C. (1925). *Gem of the Flat.* Sydney: Cornstalk.

Mackness, C. (1927). *The Glad School.* Sydney: Cornstalk.

O'Harris, P. (1941). *Fortunes of Poppy Treloar.* Sydney: Angus & Robertson.

Turner, E. (1984). *Seven little Australians.* London: Ward Lock.

Turner, L. (1906). *Betty the scribe.* London: Ward Lock.


## Commentaries

Alexander, A. (1979). *Billabong's author: The life of Mary Grant Bruce.* Sydney: Angus & Robertson.

*Australian Woman's Mirror* (1921). Dec 14, p.10.

Bonnin, N. (1986). Constance Mackness. In *Australian dictionary of biography.* Vol.10: 1891-1939. Melbourne: Melbourne University Press, pp.318-319.

Bratton, J. S. (1981). *The impact of Victorian children's fiction.* London: Croom Helm.

Bratton, J. S. (1989). British imperialism and the reproduction of femininity in girls' fiction, 1900-1930. In *Imperialism and juvenile literature,* ed. J. Richards. Manchester: Manchester University Press. (Studies in Imperialism) pp.195-215

Dever, M. (ed.) (1994). *Wallflowers and witches*: *Women and culture in Australia 1910-1945.* St Lucia: University of Queensland Press.

Dutton, G. (1984). *Snow on the saltbush; The Australian literary experience.* Ringwood: Penguin.

Ferrier, C. (ed.) (1985). *Gender, politics and fiction: Twentieth century Australian women's novels.* St Lucia: University of Queensland Press.

Hergenhan, L. (ed.) (1988). *The Penguin new literary history of Australia.* Ringwood: Penguin.

Hollindale, P. (1977). *Signs of childness in children's books.* Stroud: Thimble Press.

Lees, S. and Macintyre, P. (1993). *The Oxford companion to Australian children's literature.* Melbourne: Oxford University Press.

Mackness, C. (1919). Letter. *The Presbyterian Outlook,* **2**, 13 July, 1

Mackness, C. (1972). Facts about my life, 1882-1972. Handwritten manuscript. Mitchell Library, State Library of New South Wales.

Mackness, C. (undated) 'Facts re my life' Handwritten manuscript Ah 15 held at Scots Presbyterian Girls College Warwick, Queensland.

Mitchell, S. (1995). *The new girl: Girls' culture in England 1880-1915.* New York: Columbia University Press.

Modjeska, D. (1981). *Exiles at home: Australian women writers 1925-1945.* Sydney: Angus & Robertson.

Niall, B. (1979). *Seven little Billabongs: The world of Ethel Turner and Mary Grant Bruce.* Melbourne: Melbourne University Press.

Niall, B. (1984). *Australia through the looking glass: Children's fiction 1830-1980.* Melbourne: Melbourne University Press.

Pearce, S. (1997). Literature, mythmaking and national identity: The case for *Seven little Australians. Papers*, **7**, 3, 10-16.

Richards, J. (ed.) (1989). *Imperialism and juvenile literature.* Manchester: Manchester University Press. (Studies in Imperialism)

Saxby, M. (1969, 1971). *A history of Australian children's literature.* Sydney: Wentworth Books. 2 vols.

Saxby, M. (1993). *The proof of the puddin': Australian children's literature 1970-1990.* Sydney: Ashton.

White, K. (1993). The real Australian girl? Some post-federation writers for girls. In *The time to write: Australian women writers 1890-1930,* ed. K. Ferres. Ringwood: Penguin.

Wighton, R. (1963). *Early Australian children's literature.* Melbourne: Lansdowne, pp.73-87.

Wilde, W. H., Hooton, J. and Andrews, B. (1994). *The Oxford companion to Australian Literature.* 2nd edn. Melbourne: Oxford University Press.

# 10. Masculinity and animal metamorphosis in children's literature

## Jo Coward

**Abstract:** This paper studies the nature of masculinity that is depicted through writers' use of animal metamorphosis in children's literature.

It examines the concept of boy/animal transformation by exploring the ideology behind the metaphor. Content and discourse analyses include the application of gender and psychoanalytic theories and include an assessment of the operation of binary oppositions.

The texts were chosen from a selection of available literature published from the 1970s to the present day and have been taken from European culture. Fairy tales are used as a reference point for comparing and contrasting development in the topic.

In these narratives the notion of masculinity and animal metamorphosis has been developed through a rites of passage motif. Male alienation is an overriding motif in the texts; it will be debated how the animal metaphor is used to illuminate this, especially within the influence of developing feminism.

Although superficially there might appear to be a difference in the treatment of animal metamorphosis over the years, there is an underlying similarity of purpose in its employment. Whether these stories reflect or construct social and ideological positions can be debated, however, they are all a comment on contemporary gender mores.

It concludes that the development in current awareness of the view that masculinity has evolved from a single patriarchal perspective to one of multiple masculinities is not always apparent in these narratives. Awareness of this shift in opinion appears to be uncommon in these fictional representations of young men who, through a traditional animal analogy, are perpetuating a mostly negative image of masculinity.

'The concept of metamorphosis is wonderfully compelling' (Babbitt 1988, p.15) and few can dispute that at times there is a strong desire to be other than what they are. This popular notion is frequently developed in children's literature. Bridging the unbridgeable gap, in this case between animals and humans, provides an arena where the issue of identity can be explored. This negotiation of the space between animals and humans has sometimes produced powerful discourses, not least of which are those concerning metamorphoses.

These transformation tales are embedded in an ancient lineage and occur cross culturally. They generally contain a common universal thread of the beast/man combination in which the duality in men's nature, 'the beast in man' is emphasised. This darker side of the duality is also marked by the alienating characteristics of predatory behaviour and murder. Incorporated within the human/animal composite are binaries and conflicts of known/unknown, masculine/feminine and culture/nature. Jill Milling comments:

> Whether he is depicted as a wereanimal (half-human, half-beast) or a changeling (human transmuted into beast, beast into animal), the combinational creature is the product of a metaphorical process that discovers relationships between contrasting human and animal characteristics; the partial transformation of these related opposites into the image of the beast-man symbolises a union of or conflict between nature and culture rooted in man's uncertainty about his own nature and his place in the universe. (Milling 1990, p.110)

The composite of the human/beast appears to acknowledge the connection between animal and human whilst recognising the fear and sometimes dread that this relationship engenders.

Metamorphosis appears to be a traumatic process and more thought provoking than might at first be supposed. Leonard Massey states: '…the characteristic issues of metamorphosis…tend to be gross and shocking [although] others are more respectable and humanistic' (Massey 1976, p.17). Whilst occurring to both boys and girls in narratives, in boys it appears to be occurring more commonly in their adolescence.

In young adult literature the young men often feel a need to escape adolescent pressures. The animal metamorphosis becomes a male rite of passage in which issues of identity can be explored and sometimes, but not always, resolved.

An individual's identity is rooted in beliefs of self worth, connectedness and gender orientation, amongst others, which comprise an idea of self-hood. The increasing awareness of feminist issues in recent years has affected how masculinity is presented, and by extension how animal metamorphosis is used. At times, as Jenny Wagner has demonstrated in her 1995 version of *The werewolf knight*, it has been helpful to have the traditional male wild image diluted. In this text Princess Fioran assumes the same status as Sir Feolf and therefore reduces his animalistic 'burden'. At other times feminism has been damaging in ways that may not have been predicted. In some cases the overt leaning towards a feminist narrative has trapped men within the same old stereotype. Nicholas, in *Scale of dragon, tooth of wolf* (Isle 1996) sustains a restrictive and single faceted representation of masculinity in the face of Amber's burgeoning self-confidence as a trainee sorceress. Thus feminism can be said to have had an alienating influence on men's notion of self and identity.

The issue of alienation is essential in any discussion of masculinity and animal metamorphoses. The actual transformation procedure involves a change of one state into another – 'the other', an alienating process in itself. In the context of the texts which will be discussed, masculinity is constructed as being defined by the other. The other, that which is unknown, is also represented by the image of the beast itself, or animal or wildness; demonstrating how the binaries are interwoven. The male is always in opposition to something, hence the need to explore how the male image is positioned within the concept and how this position can shift. As will be seen, a feeling of estrangement from society, for whatever reason, is pivotal in most of the narratives to be discussed.

The theoretical base for this paper is concerned with gender and psychoanalytical studies, and includes a discussion of the binary oppositions that operate within these narratives. The texts that I will talk about demonstrate the various ways that writers have used the device of animal metamorphosis since 1970.

Secure family and peer relationships can contribute to positive feelings of self worth and therefore help forge identity. In *Stag boy* (1972) by William Rayner and *Foxspell* (1994) by Gillian Rubinstein, much of the alienation felt by the male protagonist is situated in some degree of dysfunctional behaviour in the family.

Jim, in *Stag boy*, is living apart from his mother. His father, with whom he had a good relationship, has recently died. The other males in the text are one dimensional with unattractive characteristics of arrogance and snobbery with an inability to communicate with young adults. Jim is therefore missing a father figure in his life and this, plus an absent mother, leads to his feelings of abandonment and contributes to difficulties in his emotional life.

The emotional problems that he has are compounded by chronic physical ill health. He feels that his body, alienated by illness, is out of his control. He conceptualises his illness as an internal creature who is an enemy that has taken over his life. His alienation from his current situation is brought into prominence by his historical interest in the past. His physical and emotional isolation is highlighted in his estrangement from contemporary life.

In *Foxspell* the alienation process that Tod goes through also has its roots in the presence of absent fathers. Tod's family has moved to Adelaide from Sydney after his father has returned to England for an undetermined period of time. With his mother and two sisters Tod is staying in his maternal grandmother's house in a family dominated by females and with no close male relative or friend. Not only is he geographically isolated from his father, but also from his home environment in Sydney.

At school Tod joins forces with Adrian and Martin, the two other loners in his class. They are opposite in character: Adrian is an outgoing live-wire, Martin is clever and quiet. These oppositions are continued in the portrayal of the adult males in the text. One sister's boyfriend is a pompous and conservative policeman, the other is the leader of the local gang, the Breakers. Tod, situated as he is in the middle between two polarised images of masculinity, is not at ease with either of them. At various times he is irritated by and is uncomfortable with the limited views of each opposite. In his apartness he becomes involved with feral elements. He negotiates an uneasy alliance with the Breakers, the group of feral youth; and in his metamorphosed state becomes a fox, a feral animal that is also on the outside of human society. Thus a circle of alienation is formed.

In *Foxspell* the alienated in both nature and culture have to invade the other's space in order to survive, illustrating how the binaries of nature/culture dissolve within a symbiotic relationship. Environmentally the bush is on the edge of the suburb; but as the suburbs encroach on the bush the fox's need for food drives him over the boundary. Similarly Tod's emotional need for escape drives him into a metamorphosis that reduces life to the essentials and obviates any need to try to untangle the messy complications of relationships:

> It was only being human again that made him [Tod] doubtful and scared. His fox mind had been clear and straightforward, and linked directly to his body. A fox wouldn't have stood here now, scuffling its feet and wondering what to do. He wanted more than anything else to feel that certainty again.
>
> (Rubinstein 1994, p.123)

As Tod's metamorphosis progresses he is increasingly submerged within the fox persona. Similarly Jim in *Stag boy* gradually develops his animality through his instincts. However, for Jim, becoming the stag means controlling the animal. Unlike Tod in *Foxspell* who is happy to lose his human identity to that of the fox, Jim uses his human instincts to overrule those of the stag.

This metamorphosis for Jim is a medium in which he can exercise control through possession of the stag's body; hence the conflict between human and animal. The danger becomes apparent when in his human form Jim attempts to force himself 'animal-like', on his girlfriend – the urgent animal instincts having reasserted themselves over the suppressed human – and he has to fight to regain 'civilised' human control.

Anne Cranny-Francis states that the notion of male desire being uncontrollable is condoned because it is linked to the idea that this is common behaviour in some male animals. Therefore a lack of sexual control becomes a representation of 'natural' urges; in essence a 'patriarchal interpretation of animal behaviour becomes a "natural" explanation of human behaviour' (Cranny-Francis 1992, pp.99-100).

In adolescence, young boys are encouraged by the social mores to consider as normal an aggressive and rapacious sexuality that is unable to be tamed and be brought within the boundaries of normal behaviour. They are subject and vulnerable to a patriarchal construct of themselves at this stage of their lives as wild and untameable, which can then become self-fulfilling. In textual terms this often translates as boys being depicted as not only out of control over their own bodies and instincts, but also with various elements in society. In negotiating this minefield, boys are also negotiating self and identity. This negotiation is frequently demonstrated as a rites of passage narrative both in traditional and non-traditional literature in the form of the hero tale.

Rites of passage narratives usually demand a sacrifice from the protagonist. In *Foxspell* the sacrifice is as ambiguous as the open ending. It is very possible that Tod will remain seduced by the natural world and be lost to reality. As in *Stag boy* the pull of the fantasy world is more potent than the responsibilities of the real world. Tod can see an alternative life that beckons:

> He saw the harsh fox life, with its brevity and pain, but he saw that the pain was not like human pain. It was purely physical. It did not tear at the heart or torment the mind. And it was short, and after it came death, but the death was just a diving back into the earth, the eater became the eaten, feeding as well as being fed. (Rubinstein 1994, p.142)

For numerous reasons the boys in these two books have become separated from their home environments, families and peers. They have also become alienated from the masculine in their lives; either in the shape of their father, or a similarly loved male role model. Other male role models prove to be inadequate. In the absence of suitable male images to emulate, the boys turn to animals: stag and wolf, to provide mentorship. The process has been traumatic and dangerous. There is lingering doubt about the kind of survival that Jim will enjoy, and if Tod will survive at all.

Less traumatic animal metamorphoses can be seen in traditional stories. The fairy tale of *Beauty and the beast*, for example, depicts a rather lack-lustre image of masculinity that uses the beast/prince as a vehicle for Beauty's rite of passage, albeit within a patriarchal discourse. The beast's own development, if any, takes second place. *Beauty and the beast* illustrates clearly Cranny-Francis's thesis of the hunter and the wolf, or in this instance, of the father and the beast. The father is the attractive civilised character, the authority figure; the beast is the predatory male, the 'natural' man. Two complementary images of masculinity are presented, that are nonetheless in conflict. Both men are suspicious of the seductive qualities of the other – the civilised and the rational versus the wild and irrational. In contemporary literature this pattern is clearly demonstrated in *Foxspell*. Tod is positioned between the two extremes with his friends, and his sisters' boyfriends. Cranny-Francis believes that this competitive view of masculinity is damaging and illustrates that patriarchy is just as repressive to men as it is to women (Cranny-Francis 1992, pp.81-84).

In 1972 Jenny Wagner published *The werewolf knight*, a traditional story that has a similar depiction of masculinity to that in *Beauty and the beast*. Twenty three years later, in 1995, Wagner produced another rendering of *The werewolf knight* which contained significant differences from her first version.

In the earlier version (1972) the narrative begins with a declaration supposedly about universal male behaviour: 'It is not generally known that a man who is in other ways quite polite and gentle may leave his bed at night and run wild in the forest as a ravening beast' (Wagner 1972, unpaginated).

The use of the terms 'wild' and 'ravening beast' emphasise the animality of the piece and enforces the opposition contained in 'polite' and 'gentle' men. In the 1995 version this transformation trait is singled out for just the one man in an unemotional statement: 'Feolf was a knight and a good friend of the king, but at other times he was a werewolf' (Wagner 1995, unpaginated).

Both versions describe a similar scene: whenever the moon rose over the tree tops Feolf would hide his clothes, changing into a wolf before spending the night 'running' (a metaphor for his sexual exploits) in the forest. At dawn he would change into a man again 'And no-one was any the wiser' (unpaginated). There is an implication here that sexuality and being a man are mutually exclusive, and that the former is the dark side of the masculine that is best concealed. However in this later adaptation there is a major difference in that Feolf is allowed to take pleasure in his nightly wanderings: 'enjoying his dark and wolfish things' (unpaginated). This enjoyment takes the place of the compulsion that Feolf feels in the 1972 version to go into the forest. The forest is representative, in Jungian terms, of the unconscious, its passions and instincts concentrated in the animal image of the wolf.

Princess Fioran is to marry Feolf and it is stressed in both accounts that she is unsuspecting about his nightly transformations. When Feolf reveals his secret to her she enlists the help of the court magician. In the 1995 version this magician has an ulterior motive in that he also wants to marry Fioran; the illustrations bear witness to his duplicity with the shadows that are depicted in his room where a skull and raven/crow are also present. These shadows extend from his room to the outside forest, in opposition to the well lit court scenes in the palace, emphasising the binary of the warmth and safety of family 'inside' to the darkness and danger of being on your own 'outside'. Thus the two eligible men in Fioran's life are on their own except for the presence of shadows: her father, the 'safe' man ventures out to hunt in the forest with his friends, but he returns to the family scene.

Feolf is 'exiled' outside for autumn and winter until he is unwittingly saved by the king on a hunting expedition. He and Fioran marry but again the ending differs in the versions. The earlier 1972 interpretation tells:

> Feolf and Fioran led the dance that night, and when the moon rose, Feolf did not go to the forest, but stayed with his bride and forsook his wolfish ways. For he had taken his fill of running under the cold stars, and from now on he was content with his horse, and his falcon, and Fioran.
>
> (Wagner 1972, unpaginated)

The implication is clear that his bachelor days are over and that marriage will now satisfy all his needs. However it is a different story in the 1995 interpretation:

> That night when the moon rose Feolf did not go to the forest, but was content to stay with his bride.
>
> But sometimes in the years that followed, on evenings when the air was full of change and the moon particularly bright, Feolf slipped away.
>
> And this time Fioran went with him. (Wagner 1995, unpaginated)

There is now space for the external and the internal in both Feolf and Fioran's lives. The wildness has been incorporated and welcomed into both the masculine and the feminine and in so doing the stigma of an exclusive rapacious male sexuality has been lifted.

Not so in *Scale of dragon, tooth of wolf* (1996) by Sue Isle, where the female stereotype is overturned, but not the male. Amber is a rebellious fourteen year old trainee sorceress living in a quasi medieval world. In a dream she shape-changes into a wren that is attacked by a falcon described in dominant sexual tones: 'This bird was three times my size, with a wicked beak and gleaming predatory eyes. Sharp claws were outstretched to grip my tender body' (Isle 1996, p.65).

On subsequent nights the dream recurs with different animals in the same scenario. In the last transformation dream she becomes a she-wolf and finds a male wolf following behind her. The previous animals had been described as 'it', but the wolf is 'he'. They run together. He is then revealed as a man, Nicholas: '...a pale, weak, nearly hairless thing. The most harmless form of all, and the most terrible' (p.78).

Thus in human form Nicholas has been disempowered and the traditional ferocious animal transformations are still needed to demonstrate his masculinity and their sexuality, her imposed late twentieth century femininity already being amply illustrated in her forthright nature and mystical powers.

Feminism appears to reverse the traditional patriarchal code in Isle's *Scale of dragon, tooth of wolf* by having a demanding and dominant heroine. However this heroine falls for a cardboard cutout figure of a male who is introduced to both her and the readers within the most universal of connotive animal discourse. In her dreams she is constantly being harried by predatory creatures as a sexual initiation. Their aggressive behaviour might seem to indicate their maleness and yet the ungendered 'it' is used to describe them. It is only when both Amber and Nicholas are the same animal, a wolf, that Nicholas's maleness is made literally apparent. To make a distinction about 'it' and 'he' appears unnecessarily fine in the light of what seems to be a glib, and not necessarily true, account of associating sex with brutal and forceful animality. The overt sexual allusions point to an undeveloped and damaging idea of masculinity which by association gives no credit, either, to the feminist cause.

On the first reading of some of the books in the popular Animorph series by K. A. Applegate, little difference is apparent in the treatment of the three boys and two girls in regard to their metamorphosis. The range of animals that they change into, in the earlier books at least, is quite extensive and shows no gender specificity. However a difference can be noted in their reactions to specific animal changes.

At different times both Tobias and Rachel change into a cat. Rachel describes her feelings at the time as '...I was just so totally, totally in control and graceful...that cat confidence' (Applegate 1996b, p.48). Earlier in the series Tobias remembers his cat transformation as '...so strong...all this coiled power' (1996a, p.51). The feeling of strength and potency is expressed more firmly from Tobias's description, than from Rachel, marking a more gendered male/female divide.

Discursive 'slip-ups' as demonstrated here reveal how deeply cultural ideologies of gender can be embedded. The Animorph series is not an obviously biased feminist narrative and on the surface it appears to present a balanced gender picture of the teenagers and their metamorphoses. However a traditional patriarchal binary endures which privileges strength and power over grace, although the inclusion of Rachel's feeling of control would indicate a slippage of the traditional male/female dualism.

In this series there is another example of using metamorphosis as an escape. Tobias comes from an unhappy family background. The ability to transform into another state is wonderful for him. When he overruns his time limit and is destined to remain as a hawk there is doubt whether it was an accident or intentioned. For the foreseeable future he is, quite happily, trapped in an animal form. Tobias's metamorphosis is again an escape from the intense alienation provoked by the complexities of reality.

Alienation is the overriding motif in two of the most powerful narratives, *Stag boy* and *Foxspell*, which help trace the development in the notion of beast, or nature, in contemporary realistic settings. Traditionally the protagonist returns to his human shape with some degree of wildness retained within him. It has been in some part an educative experience in which the human being remains paramount. However in *Stag boy* the human and animal wrestle for supremacy, the human barely winning; in *Foxspell* it may well be that the animal has won. Marina Warner writes about this turnaround in the motif, which she has noticed in video games but which is equally applicable in this context:

> ...metamorphoses are running counter to the traditional current of western myth and folklore, in which the human absorbs the animal, by taming it and mastering it. Even more fundamentally, it contradicts the underlying value...that the human hero remains superior however deep his reliance on his beastly ally, however urgent his attachment. The new myth of the wild calls into question the privilege of being a human at all.
> (Warner 1994, pp.58-59)

It could be conjectured that the alienation felt by these young men is so overwhelming that to become an animal other, while already feeling isolated within their society, is but a small step. It is a step that would grant immediate power and control, but the price of losing the human state seems high. Ursula Le Guin (1979) considers that there are benefits to trusting in animal instincts. However these instincts should only be relied upon to a certain point, after which they must be put aside. The human should then reassert itself, and be stronger because of the animal experience (Le Guin 1979, p.67). To remain voluntarily trapped within an animal form suggests an inability to face reality and taken in a broader context could have devastating ramifications for fictional perceptions of masculinity.

When adolescent boys are being positioned within an animal metaphor in order to solve problems of identity it reflects a preference in coping with the human by involving the defining other. As the two are set in opposition then each is creating the other. The animal represents the power and certainty which the boy feels is lacking in his normal life. Masculinity is traditionally characterised in this society as fundamentally patriarchal, the masculine being situated as the focus of power. If he does not feel that he is measuring up successfully against this ideal then the insecurity might lead to a boy's lack of self-worth, and a confusion of sexual identity.

An inherent conflict therefore exists between what Cranny-Francis calls the conflict between the patriarchal benevolence of 'social man' and the wolfish rapacity of 'natural man' (Cranny-Francis 1992, p.87). This is illustrated by the uneasy relationships depicted between man and animal. In *Foxspell* Tod is illustrative of being trapped between the polarities of masculinity in his 'normal' world (the safe and the unsafe), and having no affinity with either. So his only recourse is the animal world in which he feels safe, although it can plainly be seen that this is a dubious safety.

It can be debated whether these stories reflect or construct social and ideological positions. Nonetheless these narratives are being read by adolescents at or before a particular borderline point in their development when social demands are made of them. It is also a time when physiological and psychological pressures can be great, leading to a sense of disempowerment.

Power is not necessarily negative. Male identity can be assertive and empowering, whilst acknowledging vulnerability within a discourse which is equal with women. This has been demonstrated in *The werewolf knight* (1995). Jenny Wagner has adapted her work successfully by admitting that the wild side, that of male sexuality, can be and should be a legitimate attractive element not only for men, but also for women. Fioran's wild side is also acknowledged by her empowerment to run wild as well as Feolf. This illustrates how feminism can benefit the male image by depicting a more balanced view of masculinity – one that is multi dimensional.

David Buchbinder has commented on current ideas of plural masculinity that include heterosexual, homosexual and various individualities. Unfortunately the existence of these does not seem to exclude the traditional idea of a single patriarchal masculinity prevailing in some areas of society (Buchbinder 1994, p.22).

A single identity is presented in the metamorphosed animal in these texts. In most of those that have been discussed it is a serious comment on the issue of masculinity, that of innate and instinctive power: stag, fox, beast and wolf. It is a negative view that indicates an unsocial male with little humane qualities. This negativity is continued when the narrative is examined for the reasons surrounding this usually traumatic transformation. The impetus for the metamorphosis stems from immense stress; it does not arise out of a happy situation. The impulse is the result of a desperate choice or a compulsion to change the circumstances in the maturation process. It does not occur as a natural development in the human psyche, neither do the young men ultimately appear happy or stable (outside fairy tales) in those narratives of which the outcome is known.

If as Buchbinder already states, '...behaviour characterised as masculine or feminine, in the first place is *learned*' (p.2) then there is little positive feedback available from the reading of these narratives which include the metamorphosis process. The literary discourse is one way to receive ideas about attitudes and behaviours appropriate to gender identity. Unfortunately the motif of metamorphosing boys into animals appears ambiguous and problematical.

## Primary references

Applegate, K. A. (1996a). *The invasion.* New York: Scholastic Inc.

Applegate, K. A. (1996b). *The message.* New York: Scholastic Inc.

Brett, J. (1990). *Beauty and the beast.* Herts: Simon & Schuster.

Isle, S. (1996). *Scale of dragon, tooth of wolf.* Rydalmere: Hodder Headline Australia.

Rayner, W. (1972). *Stag boy.* London: Collins Lions.

Rubinstein, G. (1994). *Foxspell.* South Melbourne: Hyland House.

Wagner, J. (1972). *The werewolf knight,* illus. K. Homes. South Melbourne: MacMillan.

Wagner, J. (1995). *The werewolf knight,* illus. R. Roennfeldt. Sydney: Random House.

## Secondary references

Babbitt, N. (1988). Metamorphosis. *Magpies,* **5**, 13-16.

Buchbinder, D. (1994). *Masculinities and identities.* Carlton: Melbourne University Press.

Cranny-Francis A. (1992). *Engendered fictions.* Kensington: New South Wales University Press.

Le Guin, U. (1979). The child and the shadow. In *The language of the night,* ed. S. Wood. New York: Putnam, pp.59-71.

Massey, I. (1976). *The gaping pig: Literature and metamorphosis.* Berkeley: University of California Press.

Milling, J. (1990). The ambiguous animal: Evolution of the beast-man in scientific creation myths. In *The shape of the fantastic. Selected essays from the Seventh International Conference on the Fantastic in the Arts,* ed. O. H. Sacuk. New York: Greenwood Press, pp.103-118.

Warner, M. (1994). *Managing monsters. Six myths of our time. The Reith Lectures 1994.* London: Vintage.

# Part V

# Rich diversity

# 11. Narrativity in factual writing

## Jill Holt

His special talent was for dramatising inquiry, for casting a strong narrative spell even when he was being strictly analytical. (Roth 1998)

**Abstract:** This paper examines the use and literary effect of narrativity in creating 'reality' or information writing for children. It posits that narrative, employed for meaning, bears an aesthetic harvest.

Attributing fictional status to natural history places the writer in the position of awarding the factual world symbolic dimensions. Domesticity, explicated ideas, complete social structures in the animal world have a clear symbolic value. Examples of this approach are Dick King Smith's *Godhanger* (1966) and, of course, *Watership Down*.

Some recent writers employ narrativity disassociated from representations of human society. Though they are creating symbolic order in the natural world, they are not using it to comment metaphorically on human society. It would seem that in choosing to use a narrative structure as an aid to meaning, some authors create an aesthetic rather than a hermeneutic dimension. It is thus through narrative that some of these informative texts become literature. This paper is informed by Barbara Foley's (1996) discussion of the narrative as history in the adult documentary novel and Susan S. Langer's idea of public and private narratives.

This is a brief investigation into the role of narrative in two recent information publications for children. I examine the use and literary effect of some narrativity in creating 'reality' when writing information for children. I suggest that narrative bears an intellectual harvest through the employment of aesthetic elements.

I am aware of the immense scholarship in diverse directions on theories of narrative from Bakhtin and Gennette to Australian John Stephens, and I do not pretend to a contribution in this area. However I note Barbara Foley's (1996) idea that investigating 'the truth-telling claims of the documentary novel…illuminate[s] the assertive capacities of fiction…' The writers I am discussing, who are reporting and explaining facts, have employed narrative elements in a manner which suggests they, too, recognise the assertive capacities of fiction. They find elements of fiction a powerful mode for their didactic purpose. Foley notes that documentary novels 'replicate features of actuality' alongside novelistic conventions, requiring the reader to accept the real world in the novel's frame. The reader is invited to read fiction but to accept some elements of the real world as being part of the fictive characters' lives. We see this actualised in an early 1990s film, *Forest Gump*, where the hero shakes hands with President John Kennedy, who died in 1965. Anything is possible.

The children's writers I am looking at begin from an opposed tangent of placing the reader in a world of assumed actuality, a realm of accumulating fact, but they use fictional devices in order to more powerfully present the 'truth' about this factual world.

I begin with one image from a non-fiction book about animals. *The robot zoo* (Kelly, Whitford and Obin 1994) is based on a single, powerful, metaphorical transformation that signals a foray into narrative. Every diagram transforms an animal into a machine. In this comparison between the factual and the fictive there is an implied assumption that machines are more real (to a child's imagination) than animals, and through machines (imaginary ones) we learn about real animals. A further implication here is that animals belong to the realm of the imagination and that they are made believable through mechanical explanation. This Cartesian metaphor, presenting animals as machines, shows its assertive capacities in these drawings.

The first book I note is Jane Goodwin's (1997) *Dreaming of Antarctica*. The sketches by Terry Denton are superimposed on photographs. Goodwin and Denton use a single visualised motif to present an embodied narrator. This narrator, a child of indeterminate gender, whom I shall call she, has a dual role. She comments on the photographs in simple didactic prose, and simultaneously projects a strong personal presence. In a register poised between explanatory spoken English and the exclamation mode of a seven year old, she 'explains' Antarctica before a backdrop of stunning full colour photographs. That is, the educational purpose is achieved through fictional devices against a factual background.

## Fictional devices

The child is sketched in front of the photographs, usually looking slightly to one side so that the reader has a companion: narrator and reader are viewing the Antarctic together. This mix of a fictional personal narrator with photographs breaks from the conventions for non-fiction in that it is a poetic representation of reality. The reader is expected to view the photographs imaginatively, to read in an affective, not exclusively analytical way.

On page one the child is enmeshed in the physical ice and the warm nest of her bed simultaneously. The reader accepts this whimsical device, as long as it is maintained as an imaginary one. This juxtaposition of the real (ice), and unreal (child in bed), creates a gap, providing thinking time for the reader.

For the most part this narrator is truly convincing, because we accept the narrator's voice. The child in a lying position, head in hands, ankles crossed, as if on a lawn on a summer's day, surveys the icefloes. She explains, it is 'the coldest, driest, windiest, cleanest, loneliest place on earth.' This literary piling up of adjectives ending in *loneliest,* with its affective quality, ties the reader to the personal narrator. On the final page, she is floating in pyjamas on the ice looking out at the reader. How is this aura of intimacy maintained without condescension? It is a mixture of the young narrator's physical image and her voice.

There are two major stylistic devices, one being the visible imagined narrator embedded in the photographs, and one to do with text which indicate a blending of two genres leading to the book's particular conviction. Large chunks of the text are in straightforward expository prose and these passages mostly consist of timeless generic or habitual statements expressed in the simple present tense – as is usual for this genre. Here are two examples:

> Icebergs float in the ocean for many years, slowly breaking up and melting. In the winter when the sea freezes, it locks the icebergs in. They have to wait for the springtime when the sea-ice melts again and lets them go.

> The mother emperor lays her egg, then she walks, or sometimes slides on her tummy, a long way to the sea to feed on fish and squid. The father stays on the ice, looking after the egg by balancing it on the top of his feet, where some very warm feathers hang over.

However, interspersed with the above text in the simple present are personal comments from the child. Her physical appearance, looking out to the reader, strengthens this personal text. She describes her feelings and future plans in progressive verb forms typical of conversational speech but not of expository prose: 'I keep imagining those icebergs.' She uses the present continuous to express the future: 'I'm going to Antarctica', and elaborates, 'I don't mean tomorrow, or in the summer holidays, but one day I'll go there.' This is a close immediate address to the reader attained by using elements of speech genre. In addition to the progressive verbs, these include contractions, use of first person, and direct address to the reader: 'Isn't it beautiful?' This speech genre confirms the 'reality' of the young narrator, and provides a pattern for the reader to wonder, to think beyond the written text. It also serves the function of making the reader hesitate, to include an affective imagining element which facilitates the making of inferences.

Thus both the illustrations and the text, used directly, reveal the blending of the two. Together the motif of the sketched actualised child and the elements of spoken narrative in the text enable children to interpret photographs and text with some complexity.

*Dyptoe, the yellow-eyed penguin,* by Mary Taylor (1997) is a factual text using some narrative elements and symbolic, yet realistically detailed paintings.  Allusion, symbols, and images in the verbal text together with the informative paintings and a clear but never explicated theme create the richness of a narrative.

John Stephens (1992) drew up a table enumerating elements of narrative, as opposed to story.  I am interested in that part of narrative he referred to as 'symbols, allusions, intertext', as Taylor has constructed an artful, allusive, symbolic text told by an unpersonified narrator.  In this text, the theme that there is a deeper reality than the surface of things is resolved through a referential quality centred not only on a pictures/text nexus but on a relentless use of deliberately literary features in a factual context.  It must be iterated that there is no personification in this book.  The penguins are animals.

I am not suggesting that we find here the depth of conflict, human emotion, and the social constructions we expect in novels.  There is no Aristotelian plot (Miller 1995).  What we do see contributing to a narrative is a life cycle used to create a symbolic pattern and elaborate a theme, the repetition of phrases and motifs, and the syncopation of real and fictional conventions.  In keeping with a narrative mode, contrasts between light and dark, life and death, long ago and the present, the sea and the land are used to create an artistic tension and depth.

Taylor uses the literary device of alliteration, alternates the real and the fictive, constructs sentences of a literary style, and uses a tense more commonly employed in media.  In the same way as Goodwin, her text leads the reader from the particular story to general information and from factual to symbolic understanding.  The narrative elements of a factual text and the detailed paintings which are simultaneously symbolic and factual both demand more extended thought from readers.

## Literary constructions

The sentence construction is often literary, and the literary elements push the reader into elliptical thinking about wider implications. 'Far out at sea, where the albatross glides, swims Dyptoe.' The vivid quality of 'swims' and 'glides', is given weight by the sentence construction emphasising the sea (where the albatross glides) and Dyptoe is *small* in the endless sea. The inversion of the noun and the verb provide solemnity and a finish, 'This is the way of the yellow-eyed penguin.' Not only is this used twice, it introduces a timeless grandeur, suggesting generations before and after have lived this way.

'Gasping, spinning, spiralling, Marina feels the bands close around her throat, her bill, her chest and her yellow crown. Then the darkness comes over her eyes.' These are literary constructions: the accumulated action in gasping, spinning, spiralling, as much as the use of the verb 'feels', draw the reader into an active imagining. 'On the surface of the sea, there's a fishing boat. The winch grinds, the drum turns, the net rises...' There is an inexorable heaviness in the repetition. The fish captured are so plentiful that they break the frame at all points. The sea 'harvest' includes, 'the body of one yellow-eyed penguin.' The irony of a pictured harvest is deliberate. Dragnet fishing is not mentioned: the visual/text narrative allows a distance and a space for the reader to make their own deductions.

## Real and fictive alternate

The first example of this is the syncopation of the richly decorative framing of the pictures with the correct full name of the penguin and the careful listing of the long ago animals, both of which indicate fact. The framing invites comparison with illuminated scripts and Taylor herself has said, 'They denote value'. The foregrounding of the enemy sea lion (now extinct) prevents the reader from imagining the past was idyllic.

After Marina's death there is insufficient food to feed both penguin chicks. The reader is informed both factually and metaphorically. The first factual statement is: 'Dyptoe struggles to pull away and turns toward Underbelle who pecks at his cheeks. Dyptoe feeds her, but there isn't enough'. This is a factual warning that Dyptoe is not seeking double quantities of food for the two chicks. Then we have a 'poetic' sentence: 'That night the stars and moon are cloaked by cloud and it is very dark'. The darkness, of itself a metaphor for death, echoes Marina's death. Underbelle's final death knell is pealed on a factual not a poetic note, 'Dyptoe hunts at sea in the mornings. He passes the afternoons on the preening rocks.' That is, he is not fishing long enough to feed two chicks. Underbelle starves to death.

## Simple present tense

Not only does Taylor use narrative in the service of exposition, she emphasises the narrative immediacy of the text by using a specific marked tense form, the 'historic present' throughout the book. The simple present tense is normally used to express generic situations, 'Plants grow'. It also occurs in oral step-by-step presentations, for instance cooking demonstrations on television. The unmarked (or normal) form for relating narrative events is the simple past tense ('He dived for the fish.'). Typically the historic present occurs at dramatic moments in a story, usually an oral narrative: 'Then she grabs the books and flings them...' Taylor, in using the historic present is making every moment immediate. She tells Dyptoe's story as if the events were unfolding before the reader's eyes.

> Dyptoe the yellow-eyed penguin dives. His flippers are as wings and he steers with his feet...Dyptoe the lone hunter skims the ocean floor...Next day, Marina leaves and feeds well at sea...She works all day and...

The simple present brings a vividness to the text, it's immediate. Even as Marina dies it is continued: 'Then the darkness comes over her eyes'.

Most information about penguins is slipped into the narrative of the individual penguins:

> Now Marina and Dyptoe work together as true partners. One goes to sea while one keeps the eggs warm. Each night they rest together, one on the nest and one close beside...On the forty-third day of incubation when Dyptoe's on the nest and the sun is overhead, a star-shaped fracture appears on one egg.

The same register is maintained, but the alert reader extrapolates from individual penguins to yellow-eyed penguins in general. Despite the focalisation on Dyptoe, the reader is led to an understanding of the total environment and ecology that govern the lives of yellow-eyed penguins. The narrative strength rests on the book's in-built comfort with referential thinking, with allusion, with image, with symbol.

## Paintings

Taylor's paintings are not solely factual. Symbolic icons abound. The picture on page twenty-five when Underbelle has died, is of a single screeching penguin bursting out of the frame: Taylor says she was thinking of the expressionist painting, *The scream* by Eduard Munch. The moulting episode, with jagged broken circles in the picture, reiterates the darkness, blowflies, and suffering of the two female penguins, 'He bleeds and the blowflies arrive.' Taylor has said that in this picture she is using the phoenix motif of rebirth through fire. In the last painting the circle, and the cycle of life, are complete. The icons of the land and of the sea betokening food and protection, surround Dyptoe, with his sleek back to the viewer, looking to the bright sea, and a future. Again complex understandings are available because the life cycle continuation is a symbolic and a narrative resolution suggesting a stronger reality and eternal truths. This is a factual warning that Dyptoe is not seeking double quantities of food for the two chicks. Then we have a 'poetic' sentence: 'That night the stars and moon are cloaked by cloud and it is very dark'. The darkness, of itself a metaphor for death, echoes Marina's death. Underbelle's final death knell is pealed on a factual not a poetic note, 'Dyptoe hunts at sea in the mornings. He passes the afternoons on the preening rocks'. That is, he is not fishing long enough to feed two chicks. Underbelle starves to death.

Writers of information books for children are sometimes torn between a didactic framework and the allure of artist, writer, creator. Employing narrative techniques in information books may allow richer meaning and multi-layered thinking. Narrative rather than purely expository prose invokes an affective as well as analytical response to the text.

Whereas the novel employs narrative to create the illusion of reality, Taylor recognises narrative in the physical world and in her artistic, allusive use of it, invites the reader beyond information about the yellow-eyed penguin toward reflection about the environment – and contemplation about life. The reiteration of Dyptoe's diving 'for joy' is the final sign that the book is not just about yellow-eyed penguins.

## Endnotes

1.     I would like to thank Robyn Hooper for her valued help with tense and sense.

2.     When presented, this paper was illustrated by coloured transparencies.

## References

Fleischman, S. (1990). *Tense and narrativity: From medieval performance to modern fiction.* Austin: University of Texas Press.

Foley, B. (1996). The documentary novel and the problem of borders. In *Essentials of the theory of fiction*, eds M. J. Hoffman and P. D. Furphy. London: Leicester University Press.

Goodwin, J. and Denton, T. (1997). *Dreaming of Antarctica.* Melbourne: Puffin.

Kelly, J. Whitfield, P. and Obin, P. (1994). *The robot zoo.* Bathurst: Crawford House Press.

Miller, H. J. (1995). Narrative. In *Critical terms for literary study*, eds F. Lentricchia and T. McLaughlin. Chicago: University of Chicago Press.

Roth, P. (1998). *New Yorker*, August 3.

Stephens, J. (1995). *Language and ideology in children's fiction.* London: Longman.

Taylor, M. (1997). *Dyptoe the yellow-eyed penguin.* Auckland: Scholastic.

# 12. Treading a fine line: Morris Gleitzman's provocative fiction

## Jeri Kroll

**Abstract:** Morris Gleitzman published his twelfth book, *Water wings,* in late 1996. This novel in many respects is like the earlier controversial, *Two weeks with the Queen.* Can these two be called literary, simply because they confront more sensitive issues, or are there significant stylistic differences that set them apart from his other novels? Certainly the *Wicked!* series of six (all published in 1997), co-authored with Paul Jennings, read much more like popular fiction. This paper, then, considers how we understand popular as opposed to literary.

Using Gleitzman's two most challenging works, *Water wings* and *Two weeks with the Queen*, as benchmarks, I investigate this issue, looking particularly at how he balances humour and pathos in his treatment of sensitive material. I incorporate, from interviews I conducted in 1992 and 1997, Gleitzman's extensive comments on his work. His perception of himself as both a writer and a parent, his understanding of market forces and his ability to manipulate different narrative points of view all contribute to the complexity of his most successful fiction.

## Introduction: Popular yet provocative

Morris Gleitzman is a writer who balances humour with a perceptive treatment of the psychic and social difficulties children face on the brink of adolescence. He demonstrates the fine line between what is funny and what is painful. Gleitzman has performed this balancing act since 1989; in 1998 he published his twelfth novel, *Bumface*, which deals with contraception and arranged child marriages. Mentioning those words would probably raise a flurry of stage gasps in many a primary school staffroom in the nation.

Provocative as he is, Gleitzman is nevertheless popular, one of Australia's bestselling authors for 'middle-aged children' (Foster, et al. 1995, p.178) to use the American term. *Misery guts* (1991) received adult recognition when it was chosen as a Children's Book Council of Australia Honour Book for Younger Readers in 1992. The recognition he has received from his target audience, however, is far more noteworthy. Gleitzman's novels average sales of 100,000 copies each (Gleitzman 1997); most of his books have won children's choice awards or been short-listed. This popularity has perhaps encouraged critics to regard him with suspicion. Certainly someone who is one of the boldest authors for this age group in Australia has received scant attention to date.

This paper contends that Morris Gleitzman produces accessible yet challenging novels by deliberate narrative strategies that vary with the sensitivity of the material. It canvasses a number of works, demonstrating how he exploits point of view to tackle his favourite subjects: the child's struggle to fit into a family structure; need to be valued; acceptance of parental irresponsibility; realisation that he/she will survive no matter what the crisis. More specifically, in his most disturbing fictions, *Two weeks with the Queen* (1992) *Water wings* (1996*)* and *Bumface* (1998) Gleitzman develops meanings implicit in previous novels by choosing a limited third-person point of view, which sets up tensions between child and adult perceptions of the world, inviting readers to make their own moral meanings in the spaces between.

## The first person tells the tale

> The author makes his readers. If he makes them badly – that is, if he simply waits, in all purity, for the occasional reader whose perceptions and norms happen to match his own, then his conception must be lofty indeed if we are to forgive him for his bad craftsmanship. But if he makes them well – that is, makes them see what they have never seen before, moves them into a new order of perception and experience altogether – he finds his reward in the peers he has created. (Booth 1961, p.398)

Gleitzman attempts to make his readers 'see' (as Wayne Booth suggests all writers do) a moral universe – in this case one where children have to confront not only the unsettling experiences of preteens, but the fallibility of the adults who should support them. By investigating Gleitzman's exploitation of narrative point of view, we can discern how it alters with the increasing sensitivity of the subject matter. His development of first-person narrators will be discussed first, because both the way in which Gleitzman came to use them and the type of plot in which he employs them distinguish his work from other popular fiction. Generally, first-person narrators ease young readers into the text, encouraging identification with its values, which often implicitly support the dominant culture (Coppell 1998, p.9). Morris Gleitzman, however, came to the first-person by a different route. In fact, he started out employing a third-person narrative voice and this choice came directly out of his previous career – as a filmwriter and scriptwriter (five years on the *Norman Gunston* show) (Kroll 1992, p.11).

Gleitzman remarked that screenwriters go through 'a normal process of grief' (Kroll 1992, p.11) whenever they see their work tampered with by all those involved in the production process. By writing fiction, however, he felt he had a 'chance to tell the story to posterity, where I was the producer, director, actors, and make-up people' (Kroll 1992, pp.11-12). He became, in effect, the God-Author, in total control: 'I found it so exciting to be able to go inside the characters' heads' (Kroll 1992, p.12). This choice also allowed him to reject '*the intimacy*' of screenwriting: 'Screenwriting is in many ways much closer to the first-person, because you are putting so much weight on the dialogue. So part of the joy for me of writing books was discovering that my voice could be a part of the story...I never wanted my voice to be too intrusive, so I found a way of making my author's voice very close to the voice of the actual character' (Kroll 1992, p.12).

Gleitzman describes here a process that Gérard Genette analyses in *Narrative discourse*; every writer must decide on a fiction's appropriate 'narrative postures...to have the story told by one of its "characters", or to have it told by a narrator outside of the story' (Genette 1980, p.244). Gleitzman begins his career aiming to blend these two approaches and at this point his solution is the limited third-person point of view.

Eventually, however, Gleitzman wanted to experiment with the first person and then found a character who demanded that approach: Rowena Batts in *Blabber mouth* (1992) 'With Ro, it seemed to me that this is very much a story that is coming from her head' (Kroll 1992, p.12). Gleitzman's central character is 'vocally disadvantaged'; she cannot speak because she is 'missing bits in her throat,' as she explains, 'but she's a very good communicator, be it in writing letters, using sign language, or stuffing frogs in errant kids' mouths' (Kroll 1992, p.12). *Blabber mouth* is a novel about 'imperfect communications' (Kroll 1992, p.12) that is rich in 'ironic contradictions' (Kroll 1992, p.12). It eventuates that Rowena 'is unable to communicate something very important to the most important person in her life (her father) but the communication problem is not the result of the fact that she can't speak' (Kroll 1992, p.12). The novel revolves around her efforts to make her father and her new friend Amanda understand what she feels: embarrassment at his behaviour and disappointment at Amanda's (who treats Rowena as a charity project). But Gleitzman also pushes his protagonist to the point where she perceives that her own evaluations of others (especially her father) need revising.

The sequel, *Sticky beak* (1993) too, presents Rowena speaking to the reader 'from her head', developing the lack of communication theme, but the focus here is Rowena's inability to decipher her own behaviour. It turns out to be motivated by unacknowledged jealousy of her father's new wife and her fear that she will lose his affections. Gleitzman allows her to experience this epiphany, however, in her own consciousness.  No omniscient narrator intrudes to convey her deliberations second-hand.  In *Sticky beak*, Gleitzman subtly portrays not only Rowena's jealousy in this way, which readers gradually come to realise just as she does, but her genuine fear that a step-sibling might suffer from her own 'vocal disadvantage'. This fear only becomes evident at the conclusion, when Rowena visits her father and Ms Dunning (his new wife) in hospital after the birth.  This is her response as soon as she sees the baby:

> Come on, I said inside, come on.
>
> 'This is your sister,' said Dad in a wobbly voice.
>
> 'Her name's Erin.'
>
> Even when I heard that I didn't stop holding my breath, not until Erin opened her mouth and gave a howl that rattled the windows.
>
> Then I realised I was bawling my eyes out, but it didn't matter because Dad and Ms Dunning were too. (*Sticky beak* 1993, pp.115-116)

Her relief allows emotional catharsis for all concerned; obviously here she does see her 'vocal disadvantage' as something that she does not wish her sister to share. Yet Gleitzman moves her back to the earlier positions of both *Sticky beak* and *Blabber mouth* where being unable to speak is only an inconvenience, not an insuperable handicap.  Rowena has the same human frailties and strengths as her peers.  She proclaims this at the novel's conclusion:

> 'Look,' said the kid to a nurse, 'the girl that's got something wrong with her, she's picked up that baby.'
>
> I turned and spoke to her.
>
> I knew she was too young to understand hand movements, but I wanted to say it.
>
> 'This is my sister,' I said, 'and there's nothing wrong with either of us.'
> (*Sticky beak* 1993, p.116)

Gleitzman's only other first-person narrator (apart from Dawn in the co-written *Wicked!* series[1]) is Mitch in *Belly flop* (1996) a novel that treats the subject of imperfect communications, but in a spiritual, rather than a domestic context.  Mitch has a guardian angel, Doug, whom he addresses throughout, but Doug never answers.  So a monologue takes place in Mitch's head whenever he is in doubt, despair or danger – which is often, what with being a bank officer's son in an outback town in the middle of a drought.  In *Belly flop* Gleitzman maintains he did not want to focus on the religious impulse in human beings *per se*; rather, he was 'interested in the relationship between a kid and a protector. The really important thing for me is that it be on a basis of faith. Mitch never sees or hears his guardian angel so he believes he has seen the result of Doug's work when certain things have happened at certain times' (Gleitzman 1997).

A first-person narrative point of view is an effective way of conveying this will to believe and the accompanying doubts. By providing a commentary on his life, Mitch at once questions that belief and yet tries to prove to Doug that he is a worthy candidate for help. No external narrator remarks on the stability of Mitch's mental state; readers only observe the internal tug-of-war he experiences. Gleitzman exploits the unreliable narrator in a traditional way here; readers draw their own conclusions, both laughing at and sympathising with Mitch.

In this and subsequent first-person fictions, then, Gleitzman has 'focalised' (Genette and Culler 1980, p.10) the action so that everything that happens 'is focused *through* the consciousness' (Genette and Culler 1980, p.10) of his characters. The adult world view appears only by implication. Rowena herself evaluates her behaviour and the effect it has on others. The reader's ability to judge is coloured continually by her descriptive powers and her mental state. Although we sympathise with Gleitzman's unreliable narrators, we also discern the ironies of their situations. We shall see now how Gleitzman's manipulation of the limited third-person point of view allows him to achieve his most complex characterisation in novels that tackle provocative subjects for preteens. In *Water wings* and *Bumface*, in fact, he pushes the boundaries of black comedy and moves closer to a tragic perception of the world. It is only the inherent optimism and toughness of his characters that prevent these novels from becoming tragic.

## Irony and voice: Use of the limited third person

> There is continually an interior life and an interior kind of dialogue with the self going on for all of my characters through the books in a way that's totally absent from much popular fiction for young people. (Gleitzman 1997)

Gleitzman's most controversial works, *Two weeks with the Queen; Water wings* and *Bumface*, employ a third-person point of view, demarcating the boundaries between the adult's and child's understanding of society. Readers are given a vivid sense of the internal lives of his preteen characters, who do not comprehend the complexity of the issues facing them, but the narrative itself is filtered through an objective consciousness that can utilise irony at crucial moments. By judicious and often painfully funny comments, the narrator reveals the inadequacy of adults and the heroic efforts of the young to cope. The centre of consciousness is clearly the child's, though the framework is more knowing.  This consistent ironic strategy, which is also inherent in the plots and in the titles themselves, enables  Gleitzman to tread a fine line between acceptability and outrage.

*Two weeks with the Queen* concerns Colin, who is shipped off for the rest of his summer holidays to his relatives in the United Kingdom when his parents learn that his younger brother Luke is dying of incurable cancer.  Naive but also willingly self-deceptive, Colin decides that he will be the family's saviour by contacting the Queen's own doctor, who surely will be able to save his brother.  Colin's adventures in London lead him to a friendship with a gay man whose partner is dying of AIDS.

Gleitzman makes acerbic points about adult misconceptions of childhood innocence by having his hero oblivious of his English relatives' desire to avoid mentioning the 'C' word, when all he wants to talk about is finding a way to cure his brother.  Not exactly engrossed in 'the biggest Do-It-Yourself Hardware Centre in Greater London' (*Two weeks* 1992, p.48) the ultimate sightseeing experience according to Uncle Bob, Colin naively tells them the truth:

> 'Do you mind if we go now?' said Colin.  'I'm finding it a bit hard to concentrate on hardware while Luke's got cancer.'
>
> The silence that followed lasted long enough for Alistair to cut his finger on a wallpaper scraper. (*Two weeks* 1992, p.49)

Readers are already aware that Alistair's parents are rabidly overprotective. Ironically, Colin's mention of the word they have been passionate to keep from being said (a social calamity) leads directly to a physical one (in the parents' eyes).

It all comes down to a sense of proportion, which Colin begins to develop in London and his relatives patently do not possess.  Uncle Bob and Aunt Iris remain ignorant of the maturation Colin undergoes, just as they remain committed to euphemisms throughout the novel: 'The important thing is, relax and take your mind off, you know, things' (1992, p.52).  These tedious remarks have a painful edge while humorous in the context, reminding readers of John Cleese's refrain in *Fawlty Towers* – 'Don't mention the War.'  In comparison, it is the willingness of Ted, the gay man, to treat Colin honestly that gives him credibility: 'I'm sorry.  Has your brother got cancer?' At last.  An adult who wasn't a doctor had actually said the word' (p.81).  Finally, Colin does not want to be protected from the world; by the conclusion he proves himself tolerant and emotionally tough.  It is the adults who have been childish.  This reversal is a continuing source of irony in the novel.

The limited third-person also allows Gleitzman to keep readers in touch with Colin's developing consciousness of how he feels about his brother's impending death, as well as to temper the sensitivity of the material. For example, although Colin is of course naive in believing that he can find a doctor to cure Luke when his parents cannot (the Queen's doctor has obviously got to be better than any Australian) Gleitzman does suggest that there are subliminal reasons for Colin's zany belief. When the novel opens he is indulging in a fit of jealous pique when Luke receives a plane (his choice) and Colin new school shoes for Christmas. Ordinary sibling rivalry is exacerbated soon after by Luke's collapse. Finding a cure, Colin reasons, will make his parents grateful and he will be a hero in his family. As the local doctor remarks:

> 'Bit of a pain, eh, having your kid brother in hospital. Bloke gets a bit ignored when his kid brother's in hospital.'
>
> Colin didn't say anything. He wondered if the doctor would agree to swap brains with Dad. The first double brain transplant in Australia. Probably not. *(Two weeks* 1992, p.18)

Gleitzman mixes dialogue and the limited third-person here to convey in a child-centred way – brain swapping – Colin's wish to engineer a change in his father's perception. Readers are reminded of his jealousy but also of the fact that the person he is jealous of is ill.

Colin's fantastic plans allow him to avoid facing that his brother, as annoying as he can be, is dying. When the air ambulance takes Luke away, before he is diagnosed with terminal cancer, Colin has a premonition, but immediately represses it:

> 'See ya, Luke,' said Colin and suddenly it was swirlier inside his chest than it was out on the airstrip.
>
> A horrible thought snuck up on him. What if it's something worse than gastric? Something really crook like glandular fever or hepatitis?
>
> Just for a second Colin's guts went cold, like when he remembered he hadn't done his homework, only worse. Then he did what he usually did with homework.
>
> He stopped thinking about it. *(Two weeks* 1992, p.29)

Gleitzman's strategy is to withdraw from these menacing thoughts, distracting the reader as well as Colin by taking refuge in the third-person. The focus shifts to Luke being loaded onto the air ambulance and to Colin's father, who instructs him to 'Look after Mum for me, old mate' *(Two weeks* 1992, p.29).

Once in London, Gleitzman has Colin come to a gradual awareness of what being terminally ill involves. Watching Ted and his partner Griff, as well as others in the cancer hospital, Colin discerns that sick people need their loved ones around them, that he can make a difference to his brother. Later at Aunt Iris', when Ted breaks down over tea, Colin finds himself doing the same. We simultaneously understand his feelings and yet can observe him undergo this catharsis:

> Colin felt his own body shudder and his own face crumple and his own tears spill out of his eyes.
>
> Not anger this time, but grief.
>
> And as he wept, grief and sadness running out of him in bucketfuls, and as he watched Ted doing the same, it wasn't Mum and Dad he was thinking of, or himself.
>
> It was Luke. (*Two weeks* 1992, p.122)

Readers understand that with this simple naming of his brother, Colin has begun to face the thoughts he has repressed. By returning home, where he will do what he can for his brother, he acknowledges that Luke is dying, and also begins the grieving process.

Even more than with *Two weeks with the Queen*, Gleitzman knew that he was travelling precariously with the content of *Water wings*. He describes it and *Belly flop* as 'probably two of my three most difficult books in terms of subject matter' (Gleitzman 1997). Gleitzman admits, 'I can well imagine that some of those parents who see that they have allowed me [or my books] to become important in their kids' lives' (Gleitzman 1997) might be taken aback. Euthanasia is a contentious subject for adults, let alone young people. He insists that he would be 'happy to sit down with any parent in Australia and justify both that book and what the kid does, but it could be totally abhorrent in terms of that family's beliefs and attitudes about death and dying...' (Gleitzman 1997).

*Water wings* reveals just how much Gleitzman allows his protagonists to challenge authority, unlike those in most fiction for middle-aged children. Pearl is the strong-willed girl who asks questions of her mother, her mother's boyfriend and society. Why do animals have to die? Why do people? Should they be allowed to suffer if there is no hope? By not conforming, Pearl is able to accept the complexity of human relationships. By choosing to use a limited third-person narrative, Gleitzman at once communicates Pearl's confusion and society's hypocrisy. He sets up an ironic counterpoint between her grapplings with her adopted Gran's suffering and stock adult responses to it.

With its audacity and offbeat humour, *Water wings* compares admirably with *Two weeks with the Queen*. It is not so much a sequel to *Belly flop* as a fraternal twin, for the genesis of both books was the same. 'I started out to write a book that then turned into two books' Gleitzman (1997) explains. Realising that he was trying to do too much, he saved the euthanasia issue for the sequel. Mitch, Doug the guardian angel and Gran all reappear in *Water wings*. Readers also learn that Gran, who coughed her way through *Belly flop*, is dying of lung cancer. The fact that Gran comes from Pearl's hometown turns out to be more than fortuitous; it relies on the tobacco industry and hence Gleitzman creates multiple ironies.

One of the thematic connections between the two novels is related to Gleitzman's juxtaposing of adult and child world views. He explains that 'in two different ways I'd had ideas that were to do with having an emotional dream kind of come true, but then having to let go' (Gleitzman 1997). In *Belly flop* Mitch begins to feel pressure to give up belief in his guardian angel. In *Water wings*, Pearl desires a grandmother to fill the void in her emotional life; she is from a single-parent family and her mother, the manager of the local tobacco cooperative, never has time for her. She believes in a conservative feminine grandmother, but then she must settle for Gran, who, as well as being rough and gruff, is only on loan. She is the mother of Howard the vet, Pearl's mother's boyfriend.

In the course of *Water wings*, both children have to face the truth about their fantasies. Mitch learns that Doug is the name of Gran's drowned boyfriend; she had made him into a guardian angel years before to allay his fears. Pearl not only swiftly realises that grandmothers do not come in just one model, but soon after she learns to love Gran, she is forced to give her up. This clash between fantasy and reality is reinforced by the alternate closeup and distancing of the limited third-person point of view.

This variation of perspective works most effectively in Gleitzman's manipulation of Pearl's pet Winston, 'the kindest bravest guinea pig in the whole world' (*Water wings* 1996, p.1). Her intense relationship with him is at once funny and sad, emphasising her emotional starvation. Winston serves a similar function to Doug, the guardian angel in *Belly flop*. Pearl discusses everything with him; he is her alter ego, sibling, parent, who listens, understands and totally accepts. Readers learn, too, that 'Dad gave him to me for my birthday, just before he left' (*Water wings* 1996, p.21). So Winston is a replacement for her absent father.

Gleitzman is able to maintain distance while creating an impression of a first-person narration through the frequent conversations that Pearl holds with Winston (he squeaks and wiggles his nose at appropriate points). When he falls ill at the advanced guinea pig age of six and must be put to sleep – killed, as Pearl knows – she nevertheless cannot give up the connection. Unable to bear the thought of burying him, even in her mother's herb pot, she decides to keep her confidante close: 'Then she carried Winston into the kitchen, opened the freezer, and laid him carefully at the back under the peas and sweet corn he loved so much' (*Water wings* 1996, p.31). Pearl's retrieval of Winston from the freezer at critical moments supplies much of the black humour of the novel, since inevitably he becomes brittle and, alas, others do not quite understand the necessity for a dead, frozen guinea pig.

In addition to highlighting the differences between adult and child perceptions, Winston allows Gleitzman to connect Pearl and Gran on an emotional level, leavening their interactions with humour. Gran understands Pearl's desperate need for someone to care about her. She first offers the grandmotherly wisdom that Winston will preserve better laid between two slices of bread in a plastic container. Eventually Pearl trusts Gran, who shares her way of remaining in contact with her late husband. Pearl realises that one's memories of the dead are more important than their earthly remains.

When she decides to have a funeral for Winston, she proves that she has matured, explaining to him that 'he'd find being inside her head much nicer than being inside a freezer' (*Water wings* 1996, p.92). Winston's funeral sets the stage for Gran's send-off at the novel's end. Winston functions, therefore, as a comic foil for Gran, since both are important to Pearl, both suffer and both need to find peace. Luckily, both do not spend eternity in the freezer. Winston enjoys a Viking funeral, which is Gran's idea, and Gran, aided by Pearl and Mitch, floats out to the centre of the lake, where she dies before sinking beneath the water.

The conclusion of *Water wings* proves that Gleitzman's fiction pushes the boundaries of what might be acceptable in preteen literature, but demonstrates how the third-person narrative allows him to avoid tastelessness or sentimentality. Gleitzman gave the ending much thought, realising the implications of his various options, both for sales and for his reputation (Gleitzman 1997). Originally, he planned for the children to be more active in aiding Gran to die, but changed his mind, perceiving how complex the implications would be if the children had acted instead of Gran. He felt that he would have needed another book to deal with them (Gleitzman 1997). Although Pearl does make her a lethal drink and brings it to the hospital, finally Gran herself takes control, realising what the children offer: '"I don't need you to help me cark it," she said, "but I could use a hand with the travel arrangements"' (*Water wings* 1996, p.137).

The third-person point of view allows Gleitzman to shift the focus to Gran and to let her choose at the crucial moment in the hospital. This flexibility of perspective is most powerful on the last page of the novel. When Gran, Mitch and Pearl are all in the water, the effect is of a camera panning back, allowing readers to watch the children as Gran vanishes into the lake:

Slowly, arms spreading in welcome, Gran slipped from sight.

Then Pearl remembered Mitch couldn't swim.

She looked anxiously over at him.

He wasn't thrashing around in distress.

He was on his back, gazing at the sky with an amazed, tear-streaked face.

Floating.

Pearl rolled over and floated next to him. (*Water wings* 1996, p.139)

Readers recall that, throughout the novel, Mitch has been a failure at floating, let alone swimming. But they now share a moment of peace, together in the water, which is described in a restrained way, without being complicated by Pearl's thoughts.

In *Two weeks with the Queen* and *Water wings*, Gleitzman allows his characters an imaginative freedom that sets them apart from adults – they think and act for themselves. But he emphasises this conflict in perception by using a limited third-person point of view. His characters are not segregated as are the children of Enid Blyton, where readers hardly see adults, or the children in fantasy who move beyond our world to function as free agents. Gleitzman's young people have to cope with an imperfect society and fallible grown ups, so they challenge the dominant culture when it does not seem fair or good. If euthanasia is right for Winston, Pearl wants to know why it is wrong for Gran. She does not shy away from asking the hard questions. Similarly, once Colin realises that no one can save his brother, he will not be kept from him, despite the supposed wisdom of adults. He accepts being human, which means that he accepts the necessity for pain. Perhaps one reason for Gleitzman's popularity is that children admire how his characters will not be deterred by their youth or the relative powerlessness that comes with it. Both Pearl and Colin's behaviour as well as their free-thinking, therefore, mark them out as gutsy 'popular' heroes in fomenting 'rebellion and opposition to the prevailing social order' (Strinati 1995, p.4).

## Gleitzman's children as reluctant heroes

I'm starting off with optimistic kids who are thrown up against the potentially depressing, bleak, overpowering aspects of either their personal lives or indeed the world, for whom potentially there is a kind of death in their experience, and that is the death of the child inside themselves.

(Kroll 1992, p.12)

The above quotation might make Morris Gleitzman sound like the preteen's John Marsden, focusing on circumstances that threaten to move children all too swiftly from innocence to jaded experience.  But note that Gleitzman says 'potentially,' because his characters manage to maintain their ebullience and their faith, if not in adults, then finally in themselves.  As his gutsy characters learn their lessons about the world, however, they entertain readers.  Laugher and tears are often intertwined in these novels, just as they are in life: 'It's no coincidence that I express conflict through humour because I think humour is the most powerful and life-affirming energy we have' (Kroll 1992, p.13).

In *Two weeks with the Queen* and *Water wings*, the ironies proliferate, including those that involve the titles, underlining the difference between adult and child perceptions, but Gleitzman never pretends that children can really solve mysteries or can save the day without adult interference.  The English Queen turns out to be a useless figurehead; the queen who has the power to open Colin's eyes to the meaning of love in only two weeks, even if he cannot work miracles, is Ted, who is beaten up by local hoods, to Colin's bewilderment, simply for 'being in love with another bloke' (*Two weeks* 1992, p.103).  In *Water wings*, Pearl has the novel idea of substituting Gran in the parade in place of the injured Tobacco Queen, unaware that Gran is dying of lung cancer.  Yet her scheme gives Gran pleasure and allows her to make peace with her past.

The water wings themselves, a distressing reminder of the swimming lesson that caused the death of Gran's boyfriend, pique Pearl's curiosity so that she learns the truth about Gran's past, reinforcing her love and teaching her that individuals need emotional privacy.  Transformed through witnessing Gran's death, Mitch no longer needs water wings, finally finding that he can float.  In both cases, emotional pain matures the children and cements their belief in the value of human relationships.

Both these conclusions embody Gleitzman's philosophy of fiction, which he differentiates from gritty social realism: 'I personally think that bleak and hopeless endings are a bit easy...As a storyteller I feel that I have a more complex and useful function; and that is to say that the world is full of depressing, negative, scary and sometimes overwhelming things, but I think we have...great resources as individuals' (Gleitzman 1997).  This belief also explains Gleitzman's choice in his challenging novels of the limited third-person, which enables him to reveal the perplexing and negative side of human relationships without sacrificing the positive.  Naive and knowing world views co-exist, ensuring his characters' emotional development and yet, at the same time, protecting them.

# Conclusion: 'To boldly go where no one has gone before'

*Bumface,* Morris Gleitzman's newest novel, is the most audacious yet, and, following his strategy with contentious subject matter, is narrated in the third person. The plot mixes multiple marriages, a self-absorbed actor mother and an arranged child marriage. The hero, a reliable boy named Angus, becomes obsessed with contraception, not for himself, but for his mother. He survives by virtue of a loving personality that cherishes his half-brother and half-sister even as he is exhausted by caring for them, forced into surrogate parenthood by irresponsible adults. Struggling for balance in the shifting foundations of his family, Angus still has energy to attempt to save Rindi, a friend whose parents plan to send her to India to be married. Like Angus, she is only twelve. This comedy of failed marriages and bewildered children in the face of parental incompetence or blindness is perhaps the most caustic. Readers might feel uncomfortable because, satiric creations or not, the grown ups cause so much pain to the good-natured Angus, who, of all Gleitzman's characters, seems to discern adult egotism most clearly.

This twelfth novel confirms that Gleitzman is a popular author who 'boldly goes where no one has gone before'. Children from large families have probably thought about what will happen when the next child arrives, but no one has yet written a book investigating their apprehensions. But, by its nature, imagination is not conservative. It seeks to probe and Gleitzman does this, not by inventing new subjects, but by looking at issues from the child's perspective. What does this mean for the child in the family, rather than for the adult? By placing Angus' thoughts in the framework of a third-person narrative, Gleitzman can transform this highly sensitive material for a young audience. This is his unique contribution to the depiction of late twentieth-century family life, always tempered by his belief in the redemptive power of laughter and in the resilience of the young:

> Angus tucked the kids into bed and told them a Bumface story. It was the one where Bumface kidnapped a whole bunch of parents and took them to his secret pirate submarine base on a remote island and kept them there until they promised to spend more time with their families. (*Bumface* 1998, p.28)

## Endnote

1. Gleitzman created Dawn, a first-person narrator, for the series of six novels (published at intervals in 1997) collectively titled *Wicked!* which he co-wrote with Paul Jennings. Since she is the product of a collaboration, I have not considered her here.

# References

Booth, W. (1961). *The rhetoric of fiction.* Chicago: University of Chicago Press.

Coppell, V. (1998). The 'Goosebumps' in Goosebumps: Impositions and R. L. Stine. *Papers,* **8**, 2, 5-15.

Foster, J., Finnis, E. and Nimon, M. (1995). *Australian children's literature: An exploration of genre and theme.* Wagga Wagga: LIS Press (Literature and literacy for young people: An Australian series).

Genette, G. (1980). *Narrative discourse*, trans. J. E. Lewin, intro. J. Culler. Oxford: Basil Blackwell.

Gleitzman, M. (1992). *Blabber mouth.* Sydney: Pan Macmillan Australia.

Gleitzman, M. (1992). *Two weeks with the Queen.* Sydney: Piper (Pan Macmillan).

Gleitzman, M. (1993). *Sticky beak.* Sydney: Pan Macmillan Australia.

Gleitzman, M. (1996). *Water wings.* Sydney: Pan Macmillan.

Gleitzman, M. (1996). *Belly flop.* Sydney: Pan Macmillan Australia.

Gleitzman, M. (1997). Interview with Jeri Kroll. (Adelaide 23 March).

Gleitzman, M. (1998). *Bumface.* Ringwood: Puffin Books (Penguin).

Kroll, J. (1993). Two weeks with Morris Gleitzman. *Lowdown: Youth Performing Arts in Australia*, **15**, 1, 11-13 (interview/article).

Strinati, D. (1995). *An introduction to theories of popular culture.* London: Routledge.

# 13. Elective mutes in four contemporary books for children

**Margaret Mahy *The other side of silence***
**John Marsden *So much to tell you***
**Bernard Ashley *The trouble with Donovan Croft***
**Duncan Ball *Selby supersnoop***

## Carlisle Sheridan

**Abstract:** The four children's books I have selected are Bernard Ashley's *The trouble with Donovan Croft*, Duncan Ball's *Selby supersnoop*, Margaret Mahy's *The other side of silence* and John Marsden's *So much to tell you*. All these books have main characters who are elective mutes, that is they are able to speak but they choose not to. This lack of speech limits the opportunity for the writers to use dialogue as a means of establishing character traits. The writers of these books use other devices, such as a diary or interior monologue, to allow the reader to know the children concerned. Duncan Ball's *Selby supersnoop* is different because the main protagonist is a talking dog, and the book is humorous. However, this book offers interesting insights into the nature of the condition and its social impact.

In this paper I intend to discuss the different ways in which the children are presented in the books, and the implication of these. In Bernard Ashley's *The trouble with Donovan Croft,* Donovan's lack of speech is seen to be a problem which motivates much of the action in the book. The impact of this condition on the foster parents, welfare workers and the children and teachers at the school is the focus of the action and the reader does not learn much about Donovan's motivation at all. Donovan is missing for much of the book, and is seen to have lost control of any part of his life. In contrast, in John Marsden's *So much to tell you* we learn a lot about the main character through her diary. The book focuses on her recovery from the elective mute condition which is seen to be part of a larger problem of identity. However, in both the Ashley and Marsden novels, the elective mute condition seems to be a problem which needs to be addressed and cured. In contrast, in Duncan Ball's *Selby supersnoop* the main protagonist, Selby, who is a dog who can talk, delights in keeping his special talents secret as a way to empower him in his family. In a similar way, Hero, the heroine in Margaret Mahy's *The other side of silence* is seen to be empowered through her elective mute behaviour. At the end of the book

Hero understands her reasons for being an elective mute. Like the girl in the Marsden book, Hero writes her story, but unlike her she chooses to burn it at the end. Hero, like Selby, is seen to delight in her condition. She uses it to both social and personal advantage, but by the end of the book, she chooses to reject her condition and to speak.

This alliance of elective mutism and book burning raises issues to do with censorship, the role of language in society, and in particular the responsibility held by speakers and writers and particularly critics. All the books raise complex ideas about the role of language, literature and literary criticism. This paper will explore some of these issues through a discussion of the role of elective mutism in the books selected.

The books selected for discussion have main characters who are elective mutes, that is they able to speak but choose not to. Reber in *The Penguin dictionary of psychology* defines elective mutism, also called selective mutism, as follows:

> Quite literally, selecting not to speak. Classified as a childhood disorder, it is characterised by a failure to speak in specific social situations where speech is expected, such as school. The condition typically lasts only a few months. (Reber 1995, p.699)

The condition can persist and become habitual, or it can develop as a result of trauma in the later childhood or teenage years, so that children older than seven years, including teenagers, may be elective mutes. It is a reasonably rare condition that has no other associated mental or physical disorder. Although some children can exhibit severe personality problems most children who are elective mutes live in happy and supportive families, operate successfully socially and academically and are not significantly different from other children in the classroom.

There are a growing number of books for children and teenagers that include elective mute characters. Some of these are, Duncan Ball's *Selby supersnoop* (1995) Margaret Mahy's *The other side of silence* (1995) John Marsden's *So much to tell you* (1987) Bernard Ashley's *The trouble with Donovan Croft* (1977) and Katherine Paterson's *Flip flop girl* (1994). Morris Gleitzman's *Blabber mouth* (1992) shares many of the characteristics of these books, but his heroine is not an elective mute, she has a physical disability that prevents her from using her voice. The elective mute characters are both boys and girls, and range in age from five year old Mason in *Flip flop girl* to the teenage Marina in *So much to tell you*.

Books about children with special needs provide role models for the children who read them and provide a focus for undergraduate teaching students, most of whom are teenagers, in their learning about these children. As elective mutism is not a very common condition and as children's literature offers teachers some of the best portraits of children and their environments, books which will enrich the knowledge of teachers about the nature of the condition of elective mutism and its social impact are useful. Many of the teaching students' initial responses to elective mutism are negative because they are coloured by their reading of John Marsden's *So much to tell you* in High School English classes. They find the book powerful and memorable but bleak, and they are anxious about their ability to cope in their classes with a child like Marina who has so many serious problems. Many current books for teenagers present children in a bleak environment. Heather Scutter writes, 'Childhood is represented as a state of trusting innocence...but adolescence is represented as beset with overwhelming pain, loneliness, difficulty in communication, lack of love' (Scutter 1996, pp.7-8). There is clearly validity in books that present the world as a bleak place. However, the specific need in this situation is for books which will allow the child readers with special disabilities to see themselves in positive models, and which allow teachers to understand the positive side of children coping with problems as a contrast to their negative view about elective mutes already developed from their reading. The best books for this purpose reflect the situation in most classrooms where the children concerned have normal intelligence, are found in mainstream classrooms, but have language-related disabilities. While detailed research is needed to confirm that readers' attitudes are affected by the presentation of characters in books as strong and capable heroes and heroines, strong characters appear to be important for building readers with optimistic attitudes.

Novels that have elective mutes as heroes and heroines need to overcome the technical problems of presenting effective characterisation when speech cannot be used. This difficulty is solved in different ways in the books selected for discussion in this paper. There is not a lot of space in a paper of this length to develop a discussion in depth on the solution of the technical problems and the emerging issues raised about language and its role in the community in general. However, brief comments will be made about the presentation of elective mutism in the four books, the ways the technical problems are overcome, and some issues that are raised about the role of language.

Marina, in Marsden's *So much to tell you,* tells her story through a school journal. This has the potential to be a very pedestrian vehicle for a novel, but the reader is kept intrigued through inferring the nature and cause of Marina's situation. For example, we are led to guess about the dysfunctional nature of Marina's family life through her descriptions of her experiences with functional families such as the Lindell and Prehill families, which she describes with some wonder as being nice to each other. The book presents Marina without a name until the last page, so that all the major features of her identity, her face, her name and her speech, are missing. The book focuses on the slow development of her recovery from the elective mute condition, which is seen to be part of a larger problem of identity. This book presents adolescents in situations Scutter describes as being of 'overwhelming pain, loneliness, difficulty in communication, lack of love' (p.7-8). Donovan, the elective mute character in Ashley's *The trouble with Donovan Croft*, is a disturbed West Indian primary school boy, and his situation is similarly painful and lacking in effective communication and he feels that he is not loved. He is placed in a white foster family, away from his familiar school and neighbourhood. The family is caring, but in the school and community he is subjected to racist attitudes. The story is told in the third person, mainly from his foster brother, Keith's, point of view. The fact that Donovan chooses not to talk creates many problems for his teachers, peers and family, and these problems initiate the drama in the book. Donovan is seen to have little control of his life, he is a victim of circumstances, and this lack of control is reflected in his lack of speech and also in our lack of knowledge of his personality. In this respect Donovan, like Marina, epitomises the victim character which Scutter describes as 'one of the lamb(s) thrown to the slaughter' by the 'cruel and calculating adult world' (Scutter 1996, p.8). In *The trouble with Donovan Croft* although adults and other children attempt to solve Donovan's problems, he appears to be helpless most of the time. In fact, it is a book where all the individuals mean well, even the racist neighbours, but they are all trapped in situations beyond their control, and the events conspire to come together against the weakest person, who is Donovan.

Neither of these books present children with language problems as strong and capable heroes and heroines. The elective mute condition is seen to disempower both Marina and Donovan, despite Marina's claim that not speaking provides an opportunity for self discovery and discovery of the social environment (pp.91 and 69). She equates silence with the opportunity to learn. 'When your mouth's open, you're not learning anything. I don't say a lot (well, I don't say anything) but I notice plenty' (p.69).

This silent learning does not appear to empower her significantly in the environments of school and the host families, although it does help to lead her towards meeting her father when she speaks for the only time in the book. The outcome of the book, as in *The trouble with Donovan Croft,* is that the elective mute condition is cured. As noted in Foster et al. (1995), the emphasis in *So much to tell you* 'is on the protagonist's recovery, which proceeds at a speed similar to that at which the reader discovers from what it is that she is recovering' (p.132). The reasons for Marina's and Donovan's mutism appear to be centred in extreme conditions relating to their apparent abandonment by significant family members, resulting in the loss of trust and identity. While these books include valuable insights into many aspects of childhood and teenage life and work well as children's novels, using different devices to present a character who does not talk, they do not present a positive or balanced approach to the causes and effects of elective mutism. As books read by teenagers colour their attitudes to the issues presented in them, it appears to be important to present them with balanced social models through their literary experiences.

Ball's *Selby supersnoop* and Mahy's *The other side of silence* present main protagonists, Selby and Hero, who are empowered through their elective mute behaviour. Both characters use their silence to good effect for their own personal gain, but also for the good of the wider community. They are far from the 'victim' figures of Marina and Donovan. They live in loving families and choose to speak sometimes in specially selected situations, and can be described as 'selective' mutes. This eases the technical difficulty of the problem of creating a character without dialogue. Selby plays the part of a family pet as well as that of a highly intelligent and articulate person. His motivation for hiding his ability to talk is selfish; he takes pride in his achievements (p.iv) and the power they bring him, but he wants to retain the happy domestic setting where he is loved and accepted as a family pet. He chooses to speak as needed when he feels that he won't be found out. This often means using a device like a telephone conversation or a disguise, and most importantly, writing messages and letters. The stories are told in the third person, mainly from Selby's point of view, but there is occasionally pseudo-dialogue, for example

> Selby was about to say, in plain English, 'Ahem, excuse me, but I'd like to
> tell my version of events: I was just lying there innocently reading when this
> great galumph mistook me for a cushion,' but he thought better of it. (p.43)

This sort of speech presents the character as a slightly pompous, self righteous, dignified dog which contrasts with his facility for role-playing other characters as the circumstances require. The ongoing interest in the stories comes from the dilemmas Selby is placed in keeping his speech secret while still using his gift of speech to good effect. The humour comes from seeing how close he gets to having his ability to speak discovered. Although Selby is not a typical elective mute because no one expects dogs to speak, his lighthearted approach to keeping his speech secret is instructive and his ongoing dilemmas reflect the experiences of successful elective mute children.

*The other side of silence* is presented through Hero's point of view from two perspectives. The first is her view of the happenings in the family which she describes as 'real life' which includes vivid conversations and descriptions, and the second is her interior life which she describes as 'true life' in which the happenings of the 'real life' are transformed. The 'true life' becomes a book that she chooses to burn once she has proved to herself, and to her family, that she can write. Hero is part of a large, articulate and talented family. She enjoys explaining the experiences the family and the school has had dealing with the condition, detailing the devices they use to try to entice or trap her into speaking. She reads all her school and psychologists' reports (p.104) and the treatment strategies. Whatever the treatment, she says, 'I wouldn't speak, not to kind teachers, not to peers, only occasionally, secretly, to Athol' (p.106). Hero has a clear understanding of her condition which she uses to both social and personal advantage, but, like Donovan and Marina and unlike Selby, she finally chooses to reject the condition when she is convinced through a series of dramatic events that speech has an important part to play in her life. There are many acute problems presented in the book, but Hero is seen to have the power to make effective changes for the better.

The elective mute condition opens up issues such as the role of speech and writing in the community, with the associated issues to do with responsibilities of language usage, the right to be able to speak and issues of censorship and criticism. The reasons given in the books for the children's elective mutism are significant in this context. Selby is a dog, and therefore is not expected to speak, so his situation is different and not completely relevant. Donovan and Marina have both suffered significant personal trauma, and this is seen in the books as a reason for their mute condition. In their books the explanation is that they have been so hurt by the world that they are trying to punish the world by not talking (*The trouble with Donovan Croft* p.108 and *So much to tell you* pp.13, 25). However, Hero's situation is more complex, and the book, *The other side of silence*, presents a richer context for her condition than that in any of the other books discussed. For that reason, the rest of this paper will focus on *The other side of silence*.

Hero is proud of her quietness (p.69). She finds that being herself 'meant being silent' (p.106) and this is the way she makes herself special and 'powerful in a family in which everyone struggled to find their own power' (p.164). Her silence gives her the opportunity to be special, to be puzzling, and therefore of special interest to her parents, family, psychologists and teachers. Her brother, Athol, recognises the manipulative quality of Hero's silence (p.39). Hero's mother, Annie, is an academic who made her fame through writing a book about helping children develop their potential, called *Average – Wonderful*, in which she uses her own children as examples. Her book is followed up with conference presentations, television interviews and the development of video materials that include her own children. In their very lively and competitive household everyone listens to everyone else and in different ways uses the material they hear. Annie uses the information she hears in her academic studies, Athol uses it in his television scripts and Hero writes it in her book. In this book, speech is paralleled with written language in the form of conference papers, academic publications, a thesis, an interior monologue, and soap opera scripts – all of which take information from the immediate surroundings, transform it in some way, and present it again in an edited form. Hero writes that 'famous people become famous by somehow stealing energy from those around them' (p.178). She uses strong images to describe this use of language, for example describing Athol's collection of information for his research thesis in violent terms, 'I came to imagine the poor fact lying there, panting and helpless, and Athol ruthlessly fixing it into his notebook, not so much with the point of his pen as with a skewer of words' (p.27). She sees the negative aspects of the use of language where individuals are exploited.

However, Annie's exploitation of her children in the pursuit of academic research and its dissemination is not all negative. Her children are given every opportunity to develop their talents and interests, and all of them, including Hero, are very articulate and express themselves effectively to make their own way in the lives they have chosen. In contrast, the other speechless child in the book, Rinda, a closet child whom Hero finds in the tower room in Miss Credence's house, is stunted because her mother, Miss Credence, imprisoned her since her birth and did not provide her with the opportunity to develop language, or any knowledge of the world. Hero recognises that there is a large difference between her silence and Rinda's silence. She writes, 'I had chosen mine. Rinda had never been able to choose' (p.148). Whatever Hero's feelings about the ethics of her mother's use of her children for her research, she recognises that, unlike Miss Credence, Annie has always maintained her children's right to choose. Hero's self imposed silence and Rinda's silence as a result of abuse are contrasted yet again with Miss Credence's silence when she is in hospital after she shoots herself. In this situation Miss Credence's brain damage is such that she is completely dehumanised and has no elements of communication or choices at all.

The issue of the uses and abuses of language is explored further when Annie wants her family to foster Rinda. She is quite explicit that this is not so much to provide a loving environment for her but so that she can control the research about Rinda's language and social development (p.174). While Annie recognises that some good can come out of a tragic situation if useful research and publication can be done, this clashes with the family concern for respect for individuals. Hero's chosen silence is seen to be a response to the public recognition of family successes through her mother's publication of research based on her own children, and Annie's consequent fame, and pride in her fame. Hero's decision not to publish her own book contrasts with this when she finishes her own writing and burns the hard copy and deletes it from the computer. This allies her with other famous book burners such as Mephistopheles and Prospero where burning a book appears to be a means to limit their pride. However, the image of book burning also suggests a limitation of freedom in situations such as China's Cultural Revolution, for example.

Mahy's book suggests that individuals should have the right to express opinions, and to choose to share ideas, observations and truths through language. It raises the question about the ethics of using material from family life to further a creative or academic career, especially when children or handicapped adults like Rinda are involved who have no control over the consequent 'fame' associated with this. Yet, the book also suggests that without the use of these creative and academic pursuits the progress of knowledge is limited. As Hero writes, 'But of course, things aren't fair. They never have been' (p.180). Ethical considerations are seen to be weighed against economic necessities, where hurt to individuals in a family, for example, needs to be balanced against the good that the income from the books written about the family can generate. Language is seen to be simultaneously a tool and a weapon.

In the books discussed, not speaking may be a personal decision by the children concerned, but it creates a ripple effect in their social environment. The issues raised by their reluctance to speak suggest broader issues about the uses and abuses of language in the wider community. Some of the books present elective mutes who are strong and resourceful characters while others present their characters as victims of society. Children and teenagers develop their ideas about unusual conditions like elective mutism from reading literature, and it appears to be important that the books they are helped to select reflect a balanced account of both the positive and negative effects of elective mutism.

# References

Ashley, B. (1977). *The trouble with Donovan Croft.* Harmondsworth: Puffin.

Ball, D. (1995). *Selby supersnoop.* Pymble: Angus & Robertson.

Gleitzman, M. (1992). *Blabber mouth.* Sydney: Piper.

Foster, J. Finnis, E. and Nimon, M. (1995). *Australian children's literature: An exploration of genre and theme.* Wagga Wagga: LIS Press.

Mahy, M. (1995). *The other side of silence.* London: Hamish Hamilton.

# 14. Traditional literature in a contemporary text and context

## John Tingay

**Abstract:** Traditional stories are, by their very nature, always being re-told; firstly orally, then in print, and more recently in media and electronic formats. Variations in their re-telling are mostly to accommodate a specific audience. Although the themes remain, the bards or minstrels have been replaced by film producers and the authors of computer texts, and changes in the teller, audience and culture of a given society mean that the values inherent in these new textual variants may also change. Texts may be sanitised, expanded and undergo a process of metamorphosis not merely to accommodate specific audiences, but also to reflect a particular set of socio-cultural values.

This paper examines one traditional text and a contemporary version in another medium which is available to children in Australia. It also considers traditional stories which have spawned apocryphal off-shoots. The paper will also review the appeal to children of the contemporary versions as well as the 'original' version. It examines the values behind the adapting of a traditional text which story tellers and re-tellers make to suit their audience. In the twentieth century, approaches to texts have also changed so that what was once to most people a fairly simple matter has now become more complex. The late twentieth century re-tellers of traditional tales have recourse to a plethora of visual special effects which, although to some extent in keeping with the fantasy elements of the supernatural in traditional literature, may be said to leave less to the imagination than the original oral retellings.

'Of course, Disney got it all wrong: there are nine Muses, not five.' At least, so said the sales person who sold me the video of *Hercules*. He was concerned about 'getting it right', with fidelity to the original sources and accuracy in re-telling the original story. However the creators of traditional literature, the bards, minstrels, poets and storytellers are more concerned with truths than truthfulness. What would be of greater concern to tellers of traditional stories is that Disney changed the function of the Muses from that of inspirers of various arts to that of a Broadway chorus line. To know that there are nine Muses exhibits a mathematical accuracy; to know that each Muse was worshipped as a goddess who encouraged different arts – such as Calliope (epic poetry), Euterpe (flute playing), and Melpomene (tragedy) is to recognise a 'truth'. In addition to being good tales, myths, legends, and other examples of traditional literature explain the important values of the society that created them. These are the truths of traditional stories – they dramatise and interpret aspects of the human condition and explain central beliefs for the societies which created them. To ask 'Did it really happen?' is an irrelevance. The truth of myths and legends lies at this poetic, interpretative level, and the contrasting of myth with reality is a product of a nineteenth-century western viewpoint.

When literate societies began to write down stories contained in the myths and legends of different peoples, the stories then tended to become relatively fixed. It seems probable that until that point they changed over time to reflect several different matters, such as regional variations within the cult of a god or goddess. In some cultures there are different versions of the same traditional story which seems to indicate that at least two parallel yet distinct versions co-existed at the time when the story was first written down. It seems to me pointless to argue over which is the 'authentic' version; such variations only underline the nature of the oral literature tradition. Even the same story tellers would produce different versions because they told the stories to different audiences and for different purposes.

It was quite common in many societies for a re-telling to emphasise a link between the audience, patron or chief on the one hand, and the hero of the story on the other. Some of the records of Greek myths, for example, come from the choral songs of Pindar, in which he eulogised a member of a distinguished family who had won a victory at one of the Greek games. He would set the victory in a context of allusion to gods or heroes which reflected glory back to the victor, his family or the district from which he came. In such a context stories could be 'slightly adapted' to fit the occasion. And, of course, established links to the heroes could be extended. One of the most important attributes that any hero could have was a wide range of descendants. This meant that there were stories about that person in which many progeny (from both sides of the blanket) came into being. This may explain the visit of Heracles to King Thespius who had fifty daughters, no sons and no grandchildren. Heracles was there for the purpose of dealing with a lion, which was ravaging the livestock of the region. King Thespius promised Heracles (who was known for his sexual strengths as well as his physical ones) a companion for his bed on each night of his stay. Each night for seven weeks Heracles accepted the king's hospitable gesture and although one daughter refused, he provided King Thespius with fifty-one grandsons – the first daughter, Procris, and last daughter both had twins (Graves 1981, pp.148-149). Once this episode in Heracles' life existed in the mythology, very many people indeed could claim Heracles as an ancestor, and usually only his desirable qualities were genetically passed on to succeeding generations.

Re-telling to children traditional stories, such as those about Heracles, is well established in the tradition of oral literature. Charles Kingsley, Andrew Lang and Nathaniel Hawthorn were part of a strong nineteenth century movement, which regarded the re-telling in a written published form of myths and legends as a valid form of children's literature. With relatively small publishers' lists, they began to adapt these tales for a child audience. They avoided that which was regarded as unseemly for the sensitivities of children and re-told those episodes and actions which were suitable for a young audience. The stories often had minimal elaboration and were written in accordance with the prevailing values and morality of the times. The stories, which they re-told, were filled with heroism and fantasy and presented a world in which the values that society espoused were underlined and re-inforced. Kirk (1975) commenting on *Tanglewood tales* (Nathaniel Hawthorne's retelling of Greek myths) describes them as 'spare, simple, slightly emotional and intended for children'. 'Unfortunately,' he adds, 'they can only satisfy children or the childlike'. This apparent criticism should be regarded as part of the strength of myths and legends. Many of the written versions available today consist of the bare bones of the story. They are simple and usually unadorned; elaboration is left for the contemporary storyteller to add as is appropriate for the audience and purpose, just as the poet, minstrel and storyteller of the oral tradition had done (Tingay 1993). In Australia today members of the Story Tellers Guild will take the skeleton of a story and add the flesh of credible detail just as did the bard and poet of old. Story tellers, including contemporary film producers, will work on these bare bones and 'flesh them out' giving what W. S. Gilbert (1885) describes as 'artistic verisimilitude to an otherwise bald and unconvincing narrative'.

This paper will consider the recently Disney film *Hercules* and typical re-tellings in English of the stories written about the Greek hero Heracles (to give him his Greek rather than his Roman name). I shall use the name 'Heracles' to refer to the original and 'Hercules' to refer to Disney's protagonist. Firstly, a brief summary of the plot of the film *Hercules*.

*Hercules* is a musical film which uses five Muses as occasional narrators, and tells the story of a young man's rites of passage, growing up and proving himself as a man and hero before reaching the goal set for him by his father, the god Zeus. He has obstacles put in his way by Hades, the god of the underworld, who is the 'baddie' here trying to overthrow Zeus and assume power on Mount Olympus. The film contains many characters from the traditional stories about Heracles, but often these have their roles changed; other (new) invented characters appear in the film.

The film opens with a happy and smiling Zeus obviously in harmony with his wife Hera presenting his son Hercules to the rest of the gods and goddesses on Mount Olympus. The occasion, a celebration of birth, and is reminiscent of the opening scene in Disney's *Sleeping beauty*. Hades, an unwelcome guest at these proceedings, causes the infant Hercules to be abandoned where Amphitryon and Alcmeme find him. They adopt him and bring him up in a Greek village. Hercules grows up to be a strong boy, shunned by his fellow villagers because of his strength. He is depicted as a simple soul who cannot see what all the fuss is about. Hercules leaves the village and his adopted parents and sets out to find his own way in the world.

Meanwhile, trouble is brewing in the form of Hades and his two incompetent offsiders, Pain and Panic. Hades wishes to usurp Zeus and consults the Fates who advise him that he may be able to do this by removing Hercules; there are several unsuccessful attempts to do this until he coerces Meg (Megara) into assisting him. Hercules has now found a personal trainer, Philoctetes ('call me "Phil"') who, aided by a flying horse (Pegasus) begins to prepare Hercules for the trials of life (i.e. the 'games'). After successfully completing harrowing tasks, Hercules is beginning to feel successful when Hades tempts him with Meg and tricks him so that the attack Hades has been planning on Zeus and Mount Olympus can begin. Fortunately, Hercules recovers in time and saves the day. He is welcomed into Olympus as a worthy god and is re-united with Zeus and Hera, as well as keeping Meg who has realised the error of her ways.

The plot of *Hercules* does not come from Greek mythology. It has been constructed by Disney. It does have a few points in common with the Heracles stories: there is a fight with the Hydra which corresponds to the second of the labours, but the solution which Disney offers is very different from the traditional tale in which Heracles cuts off the heads of the Hydra and cauterizes the wound so that no more can grow. The three Fates in Greek mythology are depicted as spinners, measurers and cutters of the thread of life. They signify that when your life-span, allotted by an external and 'divine' order, has reached its end, you die. These are incorporated more or less accurately in the role they play, although the consultation by Hades is most probably apocryphal. The Fates are portrayed by Disney as bearing some substantial resemblance to the three witches in *Macbeth*.

That more or less concludes the direct links between the Heracles stories and *Hercules*. Zeus and Hera were not the parents of Heracles. They were constantly at war with each other and the tribulations of Heracles were the direct result of Hera's vindictiveness because of Zeus' infidelity. Megara was certainly Heracles' first wife, but she was killed in a fit of madness which Hera inflicted on Heracles. There are many other incidents and characters in *Hercules* which have only a remote relationship with the stories of Heracles.

Three examples of a twentieth century interpolation are worthy of mention. Firstly, two incompetent assistants to Hades, Pain and Panic, appear with the prime purpose of doing Hades' dirty work for him. The are sent to kill the infant Hercules, but fail. Their inept amateurish bumblings contribute little to the plot but provide humour as a foil to Hades and the other characters. Secondly, in an intertextual link to the Western genre, Hades points his fingers at two recalcitrants in the River Styx, fires at them, and then blows on his fingers like a cowboy blows on his gun after firing a shot. A third intrusion is the use of a pastiche of the American Express card as a reward for Hercules for killing the Lernean Hydra.

Eagleton (1983) has pointed out that structuralism has revolutionised the study of narrative, such as the narrative of myths. The considerable influence of Claude Levi-Strauss was seminal. Levi-Strauss (1966) maintained that there were constant basic structures beneath the varied myths that exist in different societies. These structures could be broken into smaller units which he called 'mythemes' where the meaning comes from their combination or 'a set of relations beneath the surface of the narrative which constitute a myth's true meaning' (Eagleton, 1983). Levi-Strauss suggested that in studying a myth, we are less concerned with the narrative content and more concerned with how the human mind classifies and organises reality through the elements of the myth. Within any re-telling of a myth such as the Disney version of *Hercules,* we are seeing the structural organising of the re-teller such as Disney. Gennette (1972) distinguishes between *récit, histoire* and *narration. Récit* is the actual occurrence of events in the text, *histoire* the original events as far as we can tell, and *narration* the action of the telling or re-telling as opposed to *narrative* which is what you actually tell. Genette list five categories of narrative analysis one of which, 'mood', includes 'perspective' which is more often described as 'point of view'. Genette also considers a fifth category, 'voice' which concerns the narration itself.

Undoubtedly, Genette's perspective, or the value systems of Disney lie in the White Anglo Saxon Protestant (WASP) tradition, with an emphasis on good morals, industriousness, male superiority, and decency of behaviour but also sometimes with a scant acknowledgment of the demands of current political correctness. *Hercules* exhibits the triumph of good over evil, despite the setbacks caused by the deceitfulness of the 'baddies'. The film proclaims the value of integrity and perseverance, yet acknowledges the merit of materialism as for example, in the presentation to Hercules of a 'Grecian Express' credit card as a reward for destroying the Lernean Hydra. When Hercules is faced with a choice between on the one hand listening to Meg who tells him to accede to Hades' request, and doing what he knows to be right, he fails the test, and yet triumphs in the end. Somehow one wonders whether Disney still feels that the temptation always emanates from the female, and that the Garden of Eden exists still - even in classical Greece. It is a standard stereotype image that still pervades the WASP mentality of current Disney films. The oral tradition of re-telling enables all story tellers, Disney included, to re-tell the skeleton of the story with contemporary values and ideals. Disney failed to create credible female roles, which, since he was not using many incidents from Greek mythology, would have reflected values in contemporary society.

There is of course an emphasis on physical fitness as Phil tries to prepare Hercules for the challenges of life, which Phil sees as success in the sporting arena at the various games such as those at Olympus or Pythia. The good, pure and uplifting lifestyle is one that Disney portrays as a characteristic of the desirable human being. The healthy body produces a sound mind (*Mens sana in corpore sano*).

A major criticism of Disney has always been that texts are sanitised to maintain the values of the WASP tradition. Critics have always pointed to the omissions that have been seen as an indication of censorship. The sexual exploits and prowess of Heracles are omitted – indeed, in *Hercules* the hero at times seems to have delusions of chastity until he finally falls in love with Meg and manages a chaste kiss on her cheek. There are references to the physical strength of the hero, but the violent nature of Heracles is played down. Traditionally the stories depict him as an impulsive, hot-tempered individual. In his youth he killed his music teacher for reprimanding him about the way to play his instrument (the lyre). Just as the first Olympic athletes (all male) performed without clothing, to a male audience, Heracles was depicted in Greek art as wearing at the most, only a lion skin. Hercules as well as the other characters in the film are dressed with simple decorum. In particular the major claim to fame of Heracles in performing the twelve labours is hardly mentioned. Heracles performed the labours at the direction of the cowardly King Eurystheus as a penance for killing his wife and children in fit of madness inflicted on him by the jealous Hera, wife and sister of Zeus. Is the concept of a penance an alien one to Disney – is it more Catholic than Protestant? This practice of sanitising for the audience, however, is not new, nor is it to be deprecated. On one occasion I was asked by a year six boy about the origins of the Minotaur. Should I have told him what the myths say happened? (Minos, King of Crete had been given a fine white bull by Poseidon, god of the seas. Poseidon had instructed Minos to sacrifice the bull to him, but Minos decided to retain the bull for stud purposes, and refused to carry out the ritual sacrifice. Poseidon was angry and caused Minos' wife, Queen Pasiphäe, to violently in love with the bull. Her passion for the animal would only be satisfied by copulation, and she arranged for the court inventor, Daedalus, to construct an artificial cow in which she hid in a position to complete the satisfaction her passion. After the beautiful white bull had obliged her, she immediately lost all interest in the animal, but gave birth to the Minotaur, which Minos concealed in a labyrinth constructed by Daedalus.) What did I do? I sanitised the story! I used a technique that I had always criticised Disney for using. I omitted details which I felt were unsuitable for my audience – or more particularly which I felt my audience's parents might regard as unsuitable. I justified this action in terms of the principle of re-telling a story in a manner that was appropriate to the audience, and to the purpose of the occasion, whether for children or any group of adults. This process, evident in *Hercules*, I have called 'Disneyfication'.

Re-tellers of traditional stories have always done this. The bard or minstrel boy would regale the warriors of the clan on the night before a battle with tales of their ancestors' bravery and of exploits which would bolster the morale of the audience.

They would omit tales of ignominious defeat and death. His stories included only the virtues and values of the clan. In this way the minstrel was a self-censoring teller of tales. Stories told to and for children follow this pattern. Tales of individuals' bravery in battle persist in twentieth century writing such as *Biggles* by W. E. Johns after the First World War, and Ivan Southall's Wing Commander Simon Black after World War Two.

Disney is a re-teller of stories in the tradition of the poets, bards and story-tellers of traditional oral texts. His versions of *Aladdin, The little mermaid* and *Sleeping beauty* are typical of the re-telling nature of his films. (*The lion king* with an original rather than a re-written script is an exception.)

It may be that this process of sanitising, this Disneyfication, has its roots in earlier films like *Dumbo* whose birth is via a large napkin carried by a stork. Some would argue that if we are constantly avoiding what we perceive as unpleasant, we are failing to provide children with experiences which will equip them for life. Should we not make the most of children's literature, which faces up to the less pleasant aspects of life such as sickness and death?

But Disney's selective re-telling may be too much; he may be investing his films with WASPish androcentric values which though not extreme in viewpoint, are at least verging towards the edge of contemporary society's values. He may also be giving an inaccurate impression of some of our traditional stories from the world of myths and legends. Sensitive teachers in upper primary and secondary classrooms can make good use of *Hercules* to introduce stories about the Greek hero Heracles, and the consideration of more balanced values.

# References

Eagleton, T. (1983). *Literary theory: An introduction*. Oxford: Blackwell.

Genette, G. (1972). *Narrative discourse*. Oxford: Oxford University Press.

Graves, R. (1981). *Greek myths*. London: Penguin.

Kirk, G. S. (1975). *The gods of the Greeks*. New York: Mentor

Levi-Strauss, C. (1966). *The savage mind*. London: Weidenfeld & Nicholson.

Tingay, J. (1993). *Quest for wonders*. Sydney: PETA.

Walt Disney Studios (1997). *Hercules*.

Marsden, J. (1987). *So much to tell you.* Montville: Walter McVitty Books.

Paterson, K. (1994). *Flip flop girl.* Dutton: New York.

Reber, A.S. (1995). *The Penguin dictionary of psychology.* 2nd edn. Harmondsworth: Penguin.

Scutter, H. (1996). Representing the child: Postmodern versions of Peter Pan. In *Writing the Australian child*, ed. C. Bradford. Nedlands, WA.: University of Western Australia Press, pp.1-16.

# Notes on the contributors

**Clare Bradford** is an Associate Professor at Deakin University's Burwood Campus, where she teaches literary studies and children's literature. She has published many articles on children's literature and four books, the most recent of which is *Writing the Australian child: Texts and contexts in fictions for children.* She has a particular interest in picture books and colonial and postcolonial literatures and is the editor of the refereed journal *Papers: Explorations into Children's Literature.*

**Jo Coward** completed an Arts degree as a mature age student in 1993 majoring in children's literature and history. The following year she did a Post Graduate Diploma in Library and Information Management. For the past two and a half years she has been teaching children's literature at the University of South Australia where she completed her Honours degree. The basis of this paper is taken from her Honours thesis.

**Alison Halliday** is working on her doctorate program at Macquarie University in Sydney. She is carrying out research into the ideology of poetry anthologies for children.

**Jill Holt** is a senior lecturer at Auckland College of Education in the Language and Reading Department where she teaches drama and children's literature and language programs. She has taught at many levels, from seven year olds to tertiary students, mostly in the large Polynesian part of Auckland. She is currently completing a PhD in the English Department at University of Auckland, on children's published writing.

**Monica Jarman** is employed part-time in a children's bookshop in Sydney. Her interests in Australian children's literature include theoretical approaches, young adult fiction, the presentation of Aborigines and Aboriginality, historical narrative, and criticism of critical histories of Australian children's literature.

**Jeri Kroll** has published critical articles on poetry, fiction and children's literature as well as fifteen books, including four collections of poems and one of short stories. Her publications for young people include six picture books. *Swamp soup* was a Children's Book Council Notable Book (1996). *A coat of cats,* illustrated by Ann James, has recently been released. Her first young adult novel, *Better than blue* was published in 1997 and a sequel, *Beyond blue,* in 1998 along with two middle-secondary novels, *Bruise* and *Goliath.* She is an Associate Professor in English at Flinders University, and convenes the creative writing program.

**Pam Macintyre** teaches children's and young adult literature in the Department of Language, Literacy and Arts Education at the University of Melbourne. Together with Stella Lees, she wrote *The Oxford companion to Australian children's literature*. She is the Chair of the Youth Literature Programming committee of the Melbourne Writers' Festival, editor of *Viewpoint: On Books for Young Adults* and reviews for *Australian Book Review* and the Melbourne *Age* newspaper. Her work on Constance Mackness is part of her PhD studies at the University of Melbourne.

**Kerry Mallan** is a Senior Lecturer in the School of Language and Literacy Education at Queensland University of Technology. Her research interests are mainly in critical discourse analysis, children's literature, and storytelling. She has written two books, *Children as storytellers* (PETA 1991) and *Laugh lines: Exploring humour in children's literature* (PETA 1993). She is currently completing her third book *In the picture: Perspectives on picture book art and artists* which is to be published by the Centre for Information Studies, Charles Sturt University.

**Robin Morrow** pioneered specialist children's bookselling in New South Wales, opening The Children's Bookshop in 1971 and running it for 25 years. Robin has a Diploma in Children's Literature (Macquarie University) and an MA in Literacy and Children's Literature (University of Technology Sydney). She has taught courses at Macquarie University, University of Technology Sydney, Australian Catholic University, and in continuing education at the University of Sydney. She is reviewer of children's books for *The Weekend Australian*. Robin has been a children's publisher and is now a freelance editor and consultant. In 1996 she received the ABPA Pixie Award for Service to the Development and Reputation of Australian Children's Books; and in 1998 the John Hirst Award for Services to School Libraries.

**Robin Pope** is a lecturer in the School of Literary and Communication Studies at Deakin University, lecturing in general and children's literature. Her research interests are in nineteenth century Australian children's reading. She is assistant editor of *Papers: Explorations into Children's Literature*.

**Robyn Sheahan-Bright** has worked as publisher, arts administrator, editor, lecturer, researcher, librarian, reviewer, critic and writer. She was founding Executive Director of the Queensland Writers Centre (1991-7), Director of Jam Roll Press (1987-94), Children's Services Librarian, Toowoomba City Council (1981-8), President, Children's Book Council of Australia (Q) (1991-3), curator of three exhibitions of cover art and *The bunyip and the night* (which is currently touring), and editor/compiler of *Nightmares in paradise* (UQP, 1994), *Original sin* (UQP, 1996), *Paradise to paranoia* (with Nigel Krauth, UQP, 1995) and *School's out* (with Colin Symes, QUT, 1998).

**Carlisle Sheridan** is a member of the School of Language Education in the Faculty of Education at Edith Cowan University. She was appointed to the Reading Education Department at Claremont Teachers College 1977 after teaching English Literature at Victoria University of Wellington, New Zealand and La Trobe University, Victoria and teaching primary school children in New Zealand. In 1994 she completed her PhD on Margaret Mahy's books for children through the English Department at the University of Western Australia. Her main research interests are in the area of children's literature, both the study of the books themselves and the effective presentation of literature to children.

**John Stephens** is Associate Professor in English at Macquarie University where his main teaching commitment is children's literature, but he also teaches and supervises postgraduate research in medieval studies, postcolonial literature, and discourse analysis. He is the author of *Language and ideology in children's fiction; Retelling stories, framing culture;* and *Metanarratives in children's literature* (with Robyn McCallum); two books about discourse analysis; and around sixty articles about children's (and other) literature. His primary research focus is on the relationships of texts produced for children (especially literature and film) with cultural formations and practices. He is the current president of the International Research Society for Children's Literature.

**John Tingay** lectures in the School of Education at Edith Cowan University in Western Australia and is involved in the Primary Education program. He has taught in schools in the United Kingdom as well as teacher training institutions both in England and Australia. His special interest is in children and their interaction with traditional literature. He has published *Quest for wonders: Myths and legends in the classroom.*

# The Adolescent Novel: Australian Perspectives

### by Maureen Nimon and John Foster

Australian authors of adolescent literature have been part of an international trend in English speaking countries to change the focus, style and content of adolescent literature. From the earlier view that adolescents should be moulded along conservative lines through what they read, there is now an emphasis on presenting adolescents with problems to solve, and confronting them with social issues.

This book is a pioneering study of the modern Australian novel. In Part 1, it sets out to define the genre, to trace its development and explain some of its principal features. There is a discussion of the characteristics of adolescent novels written in the past three decades and an exploration of the ways in which Australian adolescent novels may be seen to be unique, to offer something different from works published elsewhere, to be specifically 'Australian'.

In Part 2, there are essays on fifteen authors all of whom are indisputably important in the development of the Australian adolescent novel. These essays are offered as introductions to the work of the people selected and will be of most interest to those who have read at least some of the titles discussed in them. This book will be of interest to teacher librarians, tertiary students, teachers and senior students in high schools, children's/youth librarians, parents and all those who are interested in contemporary writing for young Australians.

Centre for Information Studies, Charles Sturt University, 1997. 250pp. soft cover
ISBN 0-949060-41-0 A$30.00 plus $5.00 post and packing (o/seas orders add $20)

## Australian Children's Literature:
# An Exploration of Genre and Theme

### by John Foster, Ern Finnis and Maureen Nimon

Australian children's literature today is a vibrant and exciting field. This book has been prepared as an introduction to the area for a general audience because interest in children's literature is spread across many sectors of the community. People of all ages will find browsing through this book enjoyable and informative, and it will stimulate them to read some of the many new titles regularly appearing on the market, as well as old favourites and perhaps some 'undiscovered' gems. *Australian Children's Literature* is also intended for use by teachers and students in both universities and schools. The structure and content are designed to provide an overview of the development and features of Australian children's literature, which will provide a springboard to deeper study of the area. The authors are all experienced teachers of children's literature and work at the University of South Australia in Adelaide.

Centre for Information Studies, Charles Sturt University, 1995. 250pp. soft cover
ISBN 0-949060-32-1 A$35.00 plus $5.00 post and packing (o/seas orders add $20)

Send Orders to: Centre for Information Studies, Charles Sturt University,
Locked Bag 660, Wagga Wagga   NSW   2678  Australia
Fax  (02) 6933 2733      Ph (02) 6933 2325   E-mail  cis@csu.edu.au
URL: http://www.csu.edu.au/faculty/sciagr/sis/CIS/cis.html

# Literature Circles: Reading in Action

## Darelyn Dawson and Lee Fitzgerald

Literature Circles are small, temporary discussion groups comprised of students who have chosen to read the same story, poem, article or book. Based on the information skills process, Literature Circles form around the choice of a text, and take participants through the process of group reading, discussion, transformation and presentation on that text. It is the group interaction which is the secret of the resounding success of Literature Circles.

This book takes you through the theory and practice of establishing and maintaining a Literature Circles program in your school. It is intended for teachers, primary and secondary, and teacher librarians. Readers are free to take what they want from the book - from adapting the full program to taking suggestions from here and there, for example, novels that have worked with students. Central to the book are the literature circles themselves: examples are provided and are arranged around themes and genres, using titles which have been successful with students, with ideas and presentations included. You can use them as they are, or adapt them to your needs.

Centre for Information Studies, Charles Sturt University, 1999. 90pp. soft cover
ISBN 0-949060-92-5 A$30.00 plus $5.00 post and packing (o/seas orders add $15)

# In the Picture:
# Perspectives on Picture Book Art and Artists

## Kerry Mallan

Picture books are in the fortunate position of being part of the literary landscape, which is accessible to all age groups. Children, teenagers and adults read picture books – such is the appeal and diversity of the genre. One of the major attractions to picture books is their illustrations. Whilst the words and images share a special relationship, it is largely the impact of the illustrations which will initially attract readers and lure them into reading beyond the cover. *In the picture: Perspectives on picture book art and artists* provides insights into the special properties of illustration and the artistic process through its detailed examination of the influences – historical, aesthetic, artistic, and cultural – which have shaped, and continue to shape, the construction and reception of picture books.

In the picture discusses wide-ranging topics and theoretical approaches to picture book art and artistry including: historical overview of picture book development, aesthetics, role of the illustrator, properties of picture book art, art movements and styles, approaches to interpretation, and researching artistic practice. It also provides case studies of picture book artists, suggestions for further research, and practical approaches to exploring illustration and picture books with students.

In the picture is an accessible and valuable introduction to picture books and will be of interest to students studying children's literature or art, teachers, librarians and general readers.

Centre for Information Studies, Charles Sturt University, 1999. 200pp. soft cover
ISBN 0-949060-93-3 A$40.00 plus $5.00 post and packing (o/seas orders add $15)
Send Orders to:  Centre for Information Studies, Charles Sturt University, Locked
Bag 660, Wagga Wagga  NSW  2678 Australia
Fax (02) 6933 2733      Ph (02) 6933 2325   E-mail cis@csu.edu.au
URL: http://www.csu.edu.au/faculty/sciagr/sis/CIS/cis.html

# NOTES: